PRAISE FOR
THE ACCLAIMED NOVELS OF
OCTAVIA E. BUTLER

"An internationally acclaimed science fiction writer whose evocative, often troubling, novels explore far-reaching issues of race, sex, power, and, ultimately, what it means to be human." —*New York Times*

"In the ongoing contest over which dystopian classic is most applicable to our time, Octavia Butler's 'Parable' books may be unmatched." —*New Yorker* (on *Parable of the Sower*)

"Brilliant, endlessly rich...pairs well with *1984* or *The Handmaid's Tale*." —John Green, *New York Times* (on *Parable of the Sower*)

"If we're talking must-read authors like Maya Angelou, James Baldwin, and Toni Morrison, the one-and-only Octavia Butler needs to be a part of the conversation. The groundbreaking sci-fi and speculative fiction author was a master of spinning imaginative tales that introduced you to both the possibilities—and dangers—of the human race, all while offering lessons on tribalism, race, gender, and sexuality." —*O, The Oprah Magazine*

"A revolutionary voice in her lifetime, Butler has only become more popular and influential." —Associated Press

"Butler is one of the finest voices in fiction—period...A master storyteller with a voice that cradles and captivates, Butler casts an unflinching eye on racism, sexism, poverty, and ignorance, and lets the reader see the terror and beauty of human nature." —*Washington Post Book World*

"More than any novel I've ever read, Octavia Butler's *Wild Seed* examines power, what it means to wield it responsibly, and what it means to resist it when it is wielded capriciously." —Rion Amilcar Scott, PEN/Robert W. Bingham Prize–winning author of *Insurrections*

"*Parable of the Sower* [is] even more impressive than it was when first published...It's not surprising that Octavia Butler became the first science fiction writer ever to receive a MacArthur 'Genius' Award, or that she inspired millions of readers who had never seen themselves in science fiction or future fantasy before...or that she now has been translated and read in countries around the world."
—Gloria Steinem

"I read the first page [of *Wild Seed*] and my eyes nearly popped out...I bought that book and read the hell out of it and my mind was blown."
—Nnedi Okorafor, international award-winning author of *Binti* and *Who Fears Death*

"Butler felt to me like a lighthouse blinking from an island of understanding way out at sea. I had no idea how to get there, but I knew she had found something life-saving. She had found a form of resistance. Butler and other writers like Ursula Le Guin, Toni Morrison, and Margaret Atwood...used the tenets of genre to reveal the injustices of the present and imagine our evolution."
—Brit Marling, *New York Times*

"Prescient...Butler does not appear to have intended the *Parable* novels to be a guidebook—and yet they are. That's true for all of the most powerful science fiction novels: they offer not only accurate visions of the future, but also suggestions for coping with the resulting changes...Brilliant."
—N. K. Jemisin, Hugo Award–winning author of the Broken Earth trilogy

"*Wild Seed* is a book that shifted my life...It is as epic, as game-changing, as moving and brilliant as any science fiction novel ever written...Octavia Butler was a visionary."   —Viola Davis

BOOKS BY OCTAVIA E. BUTLER

Lilith's Brood or Xenogenesis Series
Dawn
Adulthood Rites
Imago
Lilith's Brood (omnibus edition)

Earthseed Books
Parable of the Sower
Parable of the Talents

Patternist Series
Wild Seed
Mind of My Mind
Clay's Ark
Survivor
Patternmaster
Seed to Harvest (omnibus edition excluding *Survivor*)

Standalone Novels
Kindred
Fledgling

Short Story Collections
Bloodchild and Other Stories
Unexpected Stories

OCTAVIA E. BUTLER

DAWN

GRAND CENTRAL
PUBLISHING
NEW YORK   BOSTON

Grand Central Publishing
Hachette Book Group
1290 Avenue of the Americas, New York, NY 10104
grandcentralpublishing.com
twitter.com/grandcentralpub

Originally published in hardcover in 1987
First trade paperback edition: April 2021

Grand Central Publishing is a division of Hachette Book Group, Inc. The Grand Central Publishing name and logo is a trademark of Hachette Book Group, Inc.

The publisher is not responsible for websites (or their content) that are not owned by the publisher.

ISBN: 978-1-5387-5371-2 (trade paperback reissue)

Printed in the United States of America

LSC-C

Printing 3, 2022

In memory of Mike Hodel who, through his READ/SF campaign for literacy, sought to share with everyone the pleasure and usefulness of the written word.

DAWN

PART I

Womb

1

Alive!
Still alive.
Alive...again.

Awakening was hard, as always. The ultimate disappointment. It was a struggle to take in enough air to drive off nightmare sensations of asphyxiation. Lilith Iyapo lay gasping, shaking with the force of her effort. Her heart beat too fast, too loud. She curled around it, fetal, helpless. Circulation began to return to her arms and legs in flurries of minute, exquisite pains.

When her body calmed and became reconciled to reanimation, she looked around. The room seemed dimly lit, though she had never Awakened to dimness before. She corrected her thinking. The room did not only seem dim, it *was* dim. At an earlier Awakening, she had decided that reality was whatever happened, whatever she perceived. It had occurred to her—how many times?—that she might be insane or drugged, physically ill or injured. None of that mattered. It could not matter while she was confined this way, kept helpless, alone, and ignorant.

She sat up, swayed dizzily, then turned to look at the rest of the room.

The walls were light-colored—white or gray, perhaps. The bed was what it had always been: a solid platform that gave slightly to the touch and that seemed to grow from the floor. There was, across the room, a doorway that probably led to a bathroom. She was usually given a bathroom. Twice she had not been, and in her windowless, doorless cubicle, she had been forced simply to choose a corner.

She went to the doorway, peered through the uniform dimness, and satisfied herself that she did, indeed, have a bathroom. This one had not only a toilet and a sink, but a shower. Luxury.

What else did she have?

Very little. There was another platform perhaps a foot higher than the bed. It could have been used as a table, though there was no chair. And there were things on it. She saw the food first. It was the usual lumpy cereal or stew, of no recognizable flavor, contained in an edible bowl that would disintegrate if she emptied it and did not eat it.

And there was something beside the bowl. Unable to see it clearly, she touched it.

Cloth! A folded mound of clothing. She snatched it up, dropped it in her eagerness, picked it up again and began putting it on. A light-colored, thigh-length jacket and a pair of long, loose pants both made of some cool, exquisitely soft material that made her think of silk, though for no reason she could have stated, she did not think this was silk. The jacket adhered to itself and stayed closed when she closed it, but opened readily enough when she pulled the two front panels apart. The way they came apart reminded her of Velcro, though there was none to be seen. The pants closed in the same way. She had not been allowed clothing from her first Awakening until now. She had pleaded for it, but her captors had ignored her. Dressed now, she felt more secure than she had at any other time in her captivity. It was a false security she knew, but she had learned to savor any pleasure, any supplement to her self-esteem that she could glean.

Opening and closing her jacket, her hand touched the long scar across her abdomen. She had acquired it somehow between her second and third Awakenings, had examined it fearfully, wondering what had been done to her. What had she lost or gained, and why? And what else might be done? She did not own herself any longer. Even her flesh could be cut and stitched without her consent or knowledge.

It enraged her during later Awakenings that there had been moments when she actually felt grateful to her mutilators for letting her sleep through whatever they had done to her—and for doing it well enough to spare her pain or disability later.

She rubbed the scar, tracing its outline. Finally she sat on the bed and ate her bland meal, finishing the bowl as well, more for a change of texture than to satisfy any residual hunger. Then she began the oldest and most futile of her activities: a search for some crack, some sound of hollowness, some indication of a way out of her prison.

She had done this at every Awakening. At her first Awakening, she had called out during her search. Receiving no answer, she had shouted, then cried, then cursed until her voice was gone. She had pounded the walls until her hands bled and became grotesquely swollen.

There had not been a whisper of response. Her captors spoke when they were ready and not before. They did not show themselves at all. She remained sealed in her cubicle and their voices came to her from above like the light. There were no visible speakers of any kind, just as there was no single spot from which light originated. The entire ceiling seemed to be a speaker and a light—and perhaps a ventilator since the air remained fresh. She imagined herself to be in a large box, like a rat in a cage. Perhaps people stood above her looking down through one-way glass or through some video arrangement.

Why?

There was no answer. She had asked her captors when they began, finally, to talk to her. They had refused to tell her. They had asked her questions. Simple ones at first.

How old was she?

Twenty-six, she thought silently. Was she still only twenty-six? How long had they held her captive? They would not say.

Had she been married?

Yes, but he was gone, long gone, beyond their reach, beyond their prison.

Had she had children?

Oh god. One child, long gone with his father. One son. Gone. If there were an afterworld, what a crowded place it must be now.

Had she had siblings? That was the word they used. *Siblings.*

Two brothers and a sister, probably dead along with the rest of her family. A mother, long dead, a father, probably dead, various aunts, uncles, cousins, nieces, and nephews...probably dead.

What work had she done?

None. Her son and her husband had been her work for a few brief years. After the auto accident that killed them, she had gone back to college, there to decide what else she might do with her life.

Did she remember the war?

Insane question. Could anyone who had lived through the war forget it? A handful of people tried to commit humanicide. They had nearly succeeded. She had, through sheer luck, managed to survive—only to be captured by heaven knew who and imprisoned. She had offered to answer their questions if they let her out of her cubicle. They refused.

She offered to trade her answers for theirs: Who were they? Why did they hold her? Where was she? Answer for answer. Again, they refused.

So she refused them, gave them no answers, ignored the tests, physical and mental, that they tried to put her through. She did not know what they would do to her. She was terrified that she would be hurt, punished. But she felt she had to risk bargaining, try to gain *something*, and her only currency was cooperation.

They neither punished her nor bargained. They simply ceased to talk to her.

Food continued to appear mysteriously when she napped. Water still flowed from the bathroom faucets. The light still shone. But beyond that, there was nothing, no one, no sound unless she made it, no object with which to amuse herself. There were only her bed and table platforms. These would not come up from the floor, no matter how she abused them. Stains quickly faded and vanished from their surfaces. She spent hours vainly trying to solve the problem of how she might destroy them. This was one of the activities that helped keep her relatively sane. Another was trying to reach the ceiling. Nothing she could stand on put her within leaping distance of it. Experimentally, she threw a bowl of food—her best available weapon—at it. The food spattered against it, telling her it was solid, not some kind of projection or mirror trick. But it might not be as thick as the walls. It might even be glass or thin plastic.

She never found out.

She worked out a whole series of physical exercises and would have done them daily if she had had any way of distinguishing one day from the next or day from night. As it was, she did them after each of her longer naps.

She slept a lot and was grateful to her body for responding to her alternating moods of fear and boredom by dozing frequently. The small, painless awakenings from these naps eventually began to disappoint her as much as had the greater Awakening.

The greater Awakening from what? Drugged sleep? What else could it be? She had not been injured in the war; had not requested or needed medical care. Yet here she was.

She sang songs and remembered books she had read, movies and television shows she had seen, family stories she had heard, bits of her own life that had seemed so ordinary while she was free to live it. She made up stories and argued both sides of questions she had once been passionate about, *anything*!

More time passed. She held out, did not speak directly to her captors except to curse them. She offered no cooperation. There were moments when she did not know why she resisted. What would she be giving up if she answered her captors' questions? What did she have to lose beyond misery, isolation, and silence? Yet she held out.

There came a time when she could not stop talking to herself, when it seemed that every thought that occurred to her must be spoken aloud. She would make desperate efforts to be quiet but somehow the words began to spill from her again. She thought she would lose her sanity; had already begun to lose it. She began to cry.

Eventually, as she sat on the floor rocking, thinking about losing her mind, and perhaps talking about it too, something was introduced into the room—some gas, perhaps. She fell backward and drifted into what she had come to think of as her second long sleep.

At her next Awakening, whether it came hours, days, or years later, her captors began talking to her again, asking her the same questions as though they had not asked them before. This time she answered. She lied when she wanted to but she always responded. There had been healing in the long sleep. She Awoke with no particular inclination to speak her thoughts aloud or cry or sit on the floor and rock backward and forward, but her memory was unimpaired. She remembered all too well the long period of silence and isolation. Even an unseen inquisitor was preferable.

The questions became more complex, actually became conversations during later Awakenings. Once, they put a child in with her—a small boy with long, straight black hair and smoky-brown skin, paler than her own. He did not speak English and he was terrified of her. He was only about five years old—a little older than Ayre, her own son. Awakening beside her in this strange place was probably the most frightening thing the little boy had ever experienced.

He spent many of his first hours with her either hiding in the bathroom or pressed into the corner farthest from her. It took her a long time to convince him that she was not dangerous. Then she began teaching him English—and he began teaching her whatever language he spoke. Sharad was his name. She sang songs to him and he learned them instantly. He sang them back to her in almost accentless English. He did not understand why she did not do the same when he sang her his songs.

She did eventually learn the songs. She enjoyed the exercise. Anything new was treasure.

Sharad was a blessing even when he wet the bed they shared or became impatient because she failed to understand him quickly enough. He was not much like Ayre in appearance or temperament, but she could touch him. She could not remember when she had last touched someone. She had not realized how much she had missed it. She worried about him and wondered how to protect him. Who knew what their captors had done to him—or what they would do? But she had no more power than he did. At her next Awakening, he was gone. Experiment completed.

She begged them to let him come back, but they refused. They said he was with his mother. She did not believe them. She imagined Sharad locked alone in his own small cubicle, his sharp, retentive mind dulling as time passed.

Unconcerned, her captors began a complex new series of questions and exercises.

2

What would they do this time? Ask more questions? Give her another companion? She barely cared.

She sat on the bed, dressed, waiting, tired in a deep, emptied way that had nothing to do with physical weariness. Sooner or later, someone would speak to her.

She had a long wait. She had lain down and was almost asleep when a voice spoke her name.

"Lilith?" The usual, quiet, androgynous voice.

She drew a deep, weary breath. "What?" she asked. But as she spoke, she realized the voice had not come from above as it always had before. She sat up quickly and looked around. In one corner she found the shadowy figure of a man, thin and long-haired.

Was he the reason for the clothing, then? He seemed to be wearing a similar outfit. Something to take off when the two of them got to know each other better? Good god.

"I think," she said softly, "that you might be the last straw."

"I'm not here to hurt you," he said.

"No. Of course you're not."

"I'm here to take you outside."

Now she stood up, staring hard at him, wishing for more light. Was he making a joke? Laughing at her?

"Outside to what?"

"Education. Work. The beginning of a new life."

She took a step closer to him, then stopped. He scared her somehow. She could not make herself approach him. "Something is wrong," she said. "Who are you?"

He moved slightly. "And what am I?"

She jumped because that was what she had almost said.

"I'm not a man," he said. "I'm not a human being."

She moved back against the bed, but did not sit down. "Tell me what you are."

"I'm here to tell you…and show you. Will you look at me now?"

Since she was looking at him—it—she frowned. "The light—"

"It will change when you're ready."

"You're…what? From some other world?"

"From a number of other worlds. You're one of the few English speakers who never considered that she might be in the hands of extraterrestrials."

"I did consider it," Lilith whispered. "Along with the possibility that I might be in prison, in an insane asylum, in the hands of the FBI, the CIA, or the KGB. The other possibilities seemed marginally less ridiculous."

The creature said nothing. It stood utterly still in its corner, and she knew from her many Awakenings that it would not speak to her again until she did what it wished—until she said she was ready to look at it, then, in brighter light, took the obligatory look. These things, whatever they were, were incredibly good at waiting. She made this one wait for several minutes, and not only was it silent, it never moved a muscle. Discipline or physiology?

She was not afraid. She had gotten over being frightened by "ugly" faces long before her capture. The unknown frightened her. The cage she was in frightened her. She preferred becoming accustomed to any number of ugly faces to remaining in her cage.

"All right," she said. "Show me."

The lights brightened as she had supposed they would, and what had seemed to be a tall, slender man was still humanoid, but it had no nose—no bulge, no nostrils—just flat, gray skin. It was gray all over—pale gray skin, darker gray hair on its head. The hair grew down around its eyes and ears and at its throat. There was so much hair across the eyes that she wondered how the creature could see. The long, profuse ear hair seemed to grow out of the ears as well as around them. Above, it joined the eye hair, and below and behind, it joined the head hair. The island of throat hair seemed to move slightly, and it occurred to her that that might be where the creature breathed—a kind of natural tracheostomy.

Lilith glanced at the humanoid body, wondering how human-like it really was. "I don't mean any offense," she said, "but are you male or female?"

"It's wrong to assume that I must be a sex you're familiar with," it said, "but as it happens, I'm male."

Good. "It" could become "he" again. Less awkward.

"You should notice," he said, "that what you probably see as hair isn't hair at all. I have no hair. The reality seems to bother humans."

"What?"

"Come closer and look."

She did not want to be any closer to him. She had not known what held her back before. Now she was certain it was his ali-enness, his difference, his literal unearthliness. She found herself still unable to take even one more step toward him.

"Oh god," she whispered. And the hair—the whatever-it-was—moved. Some of it seemed to blow toward her as though in a wind—though there was no stirring of air in the room.

She frowned, strained to see, to understand. Then, abruptly, she did understand. She backed away, scrambled around the bed and to the far wall. When she could go no farther, she stood against the wall, staring at him.

Medusa.

Some of the "hair" writhed independently, a nest of snakes startled, driven in all directions.

Revolted, she turned her face to the wall.

"They're not separate animals," he said. "They're sensory organs. They're no more dangerous than your nose or eyes. It's natural for them to move in response to my wishes or emotions or to outside stimuli. We have them on our bodies as well. We need them in the same way you need your ears, nose, and eyes."

"But..." She faced him again, disbelieving. Why should he need such things—tentacles—to supplement his senses?

"When you can," he said, "come closer and look at me. I've had humans believe they saw human sensory organs on my head—and then get angry with me when they realized they were wrong."

"I can't," she whispered, though now she wanted to. Could she have been so wrong, so deceived by her own eyes?

"You will," he said. "My sensory organs aren't dangerous to you. You'll have to get used to them."

"No!"

The tentacles were elastic. At her shout, some of them lengthened, stretching toward her. She imagined big, slowly writhing, dying night crawlers stretched along the sidewalk after a rain. She imagined small, tentacled sea slugs—nudibranchs—grown impossibly to human size and shape, and, obscenely, sounding more like a human being than some humans. Yet she needed to hear him speak. Silent, he was utterly alien.

She swallowed. "Listen, don't go quiet on me. Talk!"

"Yes?"

"Why do you speak English so well, anyway? You should at least have an unusual accent."

"People like you taught me. I speak several human languages. I began learning very young."

"How many other humans do you have here? And where's here?"

"This is my home. You could call it a ship—a vast one compared to the ones your people have built. What it truly is doesn't translate. You'll be understood if you call it a ship. It's in orbit around your Earth, somewhat beyond the orbit of Earth's moon. As for how many humans are here: all of you who survived your war. We collected as many as we could. The ones we didn't find in time died of injury, disease, hunger, radiation, cold...We found them later."

She believed him. Humanity in its attempt to destroy itself had made the world unlivable. She had been certain she would die even though she had survived the bombing without a scratch. She had considered her survival a misfortune—a promise of a more lingering death. And now...?

"Is there anything left on Earth?" she whispered. "Anything alive, I mean."

"Oh, yes. Time and our efforts have been restoring it."

That stopped her. She managed to look at him for a moment without being distracted by the slowly writhing tentacles. "Restoring it? Why?"

"For use. You'll go back there eventually."

"You'll send me back? And the other humans?"

"Yes."

"Why?"

"That you will come to understand little by little."

She frowned. "All right. I'll start now. Tell me."

His head tentacles wavered. Individually, they did look more like big worms than small snakes. Long and slender or short and thick as...As what? As his mood changed? As his attention shifted? She looked away.

"No!" he said sharply. "I'll only talk to you, Lilith, if you look at me."

She made a fist of one hand and deliberately dug her nails into her palm until they all but broke the skin. With the pain of that to distract her, she faced him. "What's your name?" she asked.

"Kaaltediinjdahya lel Kahguyaht aj Dinso."

She stared at him, then sighed, and shook her head.

"Jdahya," he said. "That part is me. The rest is my family and other things."

She repeated the shorter name, trying to pronounce it exactly as he had, to get the unfamiliar ghost *j* sound just right. "Jdahya," she said, "I want to know the price of your people's help. What do you want of us?"

"Not more than you can give—but more than you can understand here, now. More than words will be able to help you understand at first. There are things you must see and hear outside."

"Tell me *something* now, whether I understand it or not."

His tentacles rippled. "I can only say that your people have something we value. You may begin to know how much we value it when I tell you that by your way of measuring time, it has been several million years since we dared to interfere in another people's act of self-destruction. Many of us disputed the wisdom of doing it this time. We thought...that there had been a consensus among you, that you had agreed to die."

"No species would do that!"

"Yes. Some have. And a few of those who have have taken whole ships of our people with them. We've learned. Mass suicide is one of the few things we usually let alone."

"Do you understand now what happened to us?"

"I'm aware of what happened. It's...alien to me. Frighteningly alien."

"Yes. I sort of feel that way myself, even though they're my people. It was...beyond insanity."

"Some of the people we picked up had been hiding deep underground. They had created much of the destruction."

"And they're still alive?"

"Some of them are."

"And you plan to send *them* back to Earth?"

"No."

"What?"

"The ones still alive are very old now. We've used them slowly, learned biology, language, culture from them. We Awakened them a few at a time and let them live their lives here in different parts of the ship while you slept."

"Slept...Jdahya, how long have I slept?"

He walked across the room to the table platform, put one many-fingered hand on it, and boosted himself up. Legs drawn against his body, he walked easily on his hands to the center of the platform. The whole series of movements was so fluid and natural, yet so alien that it fascinated her.

Abruptly she realized he was several feet closer to her. She leaped away. Then, feeling utterly foolish, she tried to come back. He had folded himself compactly into an uncomfortable-looking seated position. He ignored her sudden move—except for his head tentacles which all swept toward her as though in a wind. He seemed to watch as she inched back to the bed. Could a being with sensory tentacles instead of eyes watch?

When she had come as close to him as she could, she stopped and sat on the floor. It was all she could do to stay where she was. She drew her knees up against her chest and hugged them to her tightly.

"I don't understand why I'm so...afraid of you," she whispered. "Of the way you look, I mean. You're not that different. There are—or were—life forms on Earth that looked a little like you."

He said nothing.

She looked at him sharply, fearing he had fallen into one of his long silences. "Is it something you're doing?" she demanded, "something I don't know about?"

"I'm here to teach you to be comfortable with us," he said. "You're doing very well."

She did not feel she was doing well at all. "What have others done?"

"Several have tried to kill me."

She swallowed. It amazed her that they had been able to bring themselves to touch him. "What did you do to them?"

"For trying to kill me?"

"No, before—to incite them."

"No more than I'm doing to you now."

"I don't understand." She made herself stare at him. "Can you really see?"

"Very well."

"Colors? Depth?"

"Yes."

Yet it was true that he had no eyes. She could see now that there were only dark patches where tentacles grew thickly. The same with the sides of his head where ears should have been. And there were openings at his throat. And the tentacles around them didn't look as dark as the others. Murkily translucent, pale gray worms.

"In fact," he said, "you should be aware that I can see wherever I have tentacles—and I can see whether I seem to notice or not. I can't not see."

That sounded like a horrible existence—not to be able to close one's eyes, sink into the private darkness behind one's own eyelids. "Don't you sleep?"

"Yes. But not the way you do."

She shifted suddenly from the subject of his sleeping to her own. "You never told me how long you kept me asleep."

"About . . . two hundred and fifty of your years."

This was more than she could assimilate at once. She said nothing for so long that he broke the silence.

"Something went wrong when you were first Awakened. I heard about it from several people. Someone handled you badly—underestimated you. You are like us in some ways, but you were thought to be like your military people hidden underground. They refused to talk to us too. At first. You were left asleep for about fifty years after that first mistake."

She crept to the bed, worms or no worms, and leaned against the end of it. "I'd always thought my Awakenings might be years apart, but I didn't really believe it."

"You were like your world. You needed time to heal. And we needed time to learn more about your kind." He paused. "We didn't know what to think when some of your people killed themselves. Some of us believed it was because they had been left out of the mass suicide—that they simply wanted to finish the dying. Others said it was because we kept them isolated. We began putting two or more together, and many injured or killed one another. Isolation cost fewer lives."

These last words touched a memory in her. "Jdahya?" she said.

The tentacles down the sides of his face wavered, looked for a moment like dark, muttonchop whiskers.

"At one point a little boy was put in with me. His name was Sharad. What happened to him?"

He said nothing for a moment, then all his tentacles stretched themselves upward. Someone spoke to him from above in the usual way and in a voice much like his own, but this time in a foreign language, choppy and fast.

"My relative will find out," he told her. "Sharad is almost certainly well, though he may not be a child any longer."

"You've let children grow up and grow old?"

"A few, yes. But they've lived among us. We haven't isolated them."

"You shouldn't have isolated any of us unless your purpose was to drive us insane. You almost succeeded with me more than once. Humans need one another."

His tentacles writhed repulsively. "We know. I wouldn't have cared to endure as much solitude as you have. But we had no skill at grouping humans in ways that suited them."

"But Sharad and I—"

"He may have had parents, Lilith."

Someone spoke from above, in English this time. "The boy has parents and a sister. He's asleep with them, and he's still very young." There was a pause. "Lilith, what language did he speak?"

"I don't know," Lilith said. "Either he was too young to tell me or he tried and I didn't understand. I think he must have been East Indian, though—if that means anything to you."

"Others know. I was only curious."

"You're sure he's all right?"

"He's well."

She felt assured at that and immediately questioned the emotion. Why should one more anonymous voice telling her everything was fine reassure her?

"Can I see him?" she asked.

"Jdahya?" the voice said.

Jdahya turned toward her. "You'll be able to see him when you can walk among us without panic. This is your last isolation room. When you're ready, I'll take you outside."

3

Jdahya would not leave her. As much as she had hated her solitary confinement, she longed to be rid of him. He fell silent for a while and she wondered whether he might be sleeping—to the degree that he did sleep. She lay down herself, wondering whether she could relax enough to sleep with him there. It would be like going to sleep knowing there was a rattlesnake in the room, knowing she could wake up and find it in her bed.

She could not fall asleep facing him. Yet she could not keep her back to him long. Each time she dozed, she would jolt awake and look to see if he had come closer. This exhausted her, but she could not stop doing it. Worse, each time she moved, his tentacles moved, straightening lazily in her direction as though he were sleeping with his eyes open—as he no doubt was.

Painfully tired, head aching, stomach queasy, she climbed down from her bed and lay alongside it on the floor. She could not see him now, no matter how she turned. She could see only the platform beside her and the walls. He was no longer part of her world.

"No, Lilith," he said as she closed her eyes.

She pretended not to hear him.

"Lie on the bed," he said, "or on the floor over here. Not over there."

She lay rigid, silent.

"If you stay where you are, I'll take the bed."

That would put him just above her—too close, looming over her, Medusa leering down.

She got up and all but fell across the bed, damning him, and, to her humiliation, crying a little. Eventually she slept. Her body had simply had enough.

She awoke abruptly, twisting around to look at him. He was still on the platform, his position hardly altered. When his head tentacles swept in her direction she got up and ran into the bathroom. He let her hide there for a while, let her wash and be alone and wallow in self-pity and self-contempt. She could not remember ever having been so continually afraid, so out of control of her emotions. Jdahya had done nothing, yet she cowered.

When he called her, she took a deep breath and stepped out of the bathroom. "This isn't working," she said miserably. "Just put me down on Earth with other humans. I can't do this."

He ignored her.

After a time she spoke again on a different subject. "I have a scar," she said, touching her abdomen. "I didn't have it when I was on Earth. What did your people do to me?"

"You had a growth," he said. "A cancer. We got rid of it. Otherwise, it would have killed you."

She went cold. Her mother had died of cancer. Two of her aunts had had it and her grandmother had been operated on three times for it. They were all dead now, killed by someone else's insanity. But the family "tradition" was apparently continuing.

"What did I lose along with the cancer?" she asked softly.

"Nothing."

"Not a few feet of intestine? My ovaries? My uterus?"

"Nothing. My relative tended you. You lost nothing you would want to keep."

"Your relative is the one who . . . performed surgery on me?"

"Yes. With interest and care. There was a human physician with us, but by then she was old, dying. She only watched and commented on what my relative did."

"How would he know enough to do anything for me? Human anatomy must be totally different from yours."

"My relative is not male—or female. The name for its sex is ooloi. It understood your body because it is ooloi. On your world there were vast numbers of dead and dying humans to study. Our ooloi came to understand what could be normal or abnormal, possible or impossible for the human body. The ooloi who went to the planet taught those who stayed here. My relative has studied your people for much of its life."

"How do ooloi study?" She imagined dying humans caged and every groan and contortion closely observed. She imagined dissections of living subjects as well as dead ones. She imagined treatable diseases being allowed to run their grisly courses in order for ooloi to learn.

"They observe. They have special organs for their kind of observation. My relative examined you, observed a few of your normal body cells, compared them with what it had learned from other humans most like you, and said you had not only a cancer, but a talent for cancer."

"I wouldn't call it a talent. A curse, maybe. But how could your relative know about that from just . . . observing."

"Maybe *perceiving* would be a better word," he said. "There's much more involved than sight. It knows everything that can be learned about you from your genes. And by now, it knows your medical history and a great deal about the way you think. It has taken part in testing you."

"Has it? I may not be able to forgive it for that. But listen, I don't understand how it could cut out a cancer without…well, without doing damage to whichever organ it was growing on."

"My relative didn't cut out your cancer. It wouldn't have cut you at all, but it wanted to examine the cancer directly with all its senses. It had never personally examined one before. When it had finished, it induced your body to reabsorb the cancer."

"It…induced my body to reabsorb…cancer?"

"Yes. My relative gave your body a kind of chemical command."

"Is that how you cure cancer among yourselves?"

"We don't get them."

Lilith sighed. "I wish we didn't. They've created enough hell in my family."

"They won't be harming you anymore. My relative says they're beautiful, but simple to prevent."

"Beautiful?"

"It perceives things differently sometimes. Here's food, Lilith. Are you hungry?"

She stepped toward him, reaching out to take the bowl, then realized what she was doing. She froze, but managed not to scramble backward. After a few seconds, she inched toward him. She could not do it quickly—snatch and run. She could hardly do it at all. She forced herself forward slowly, slowly.

Teeth clenched, she managed to take the bowl. Her hand shook so badly that she spilled half the stew. She withdrew to the bed. After a while she was able to eat what was left, then finish the bowl. It was not enough. She was still hungry, but she did not complain. She was not up to taking another bowl from his hand. Daisy hand. Palm in the center, many fingers all the way around. The fingers had bones in them, at least; they weren't tentacles. And there were only two hands, two feet. He could have been so much uglier than he was, so much less…human. Why couldn't she just accept him? All he seemed to be asking was that she not panic at the sight of him or others like him. Why couldn't she do that?

She tried to imagine herself surrounded by beings like him and was almost overwhelmed by panic. As though she had suddenly developed a phobia—something she had never before experienced. But what she felt was like what she had heard others describe. A true xenophobia—and apparently she was not alone in it.

She sighed, realized she was still tired as well as still hungry. She rubbed a hand over her face. If this were what a phobia was like, it was something to be gotten rid of as quickly as possible. She looked at Jdahya. "What do your people call themselves?" she asked. "Tell me about them."

"We are Oankali."

"Oankali. Sounds like a word in some Earth language."

"It may be, but with different meaning."

"What does it mean in your language?"

"Several things. Traders for one."

"You are traders?"

"Yes."

"What do you trade?"

"Ourselves."

"You mean...each other? Slaves?"

"No. We've never done that."

"What, then?"

"Ourselves."

"I don't understand."

He said nothing, seemed to wrap silence around himself and settle into it. She knew he would not answer.

She sighed. "You seem too human sometimes. If I weren't looking at you, I'd assume you were a man."

"You have assumed that. My family gave me to the human doctor so that I could learn to do this work. She came to us too old to bear children of her own, but she could teach."

"I thought you said she was dying."

"She did die eventually. She was a hundred and thirteen years old and had been awake among us off and on for fifty years. She was like a fourth parent to my siblings and me. It was hard to watch her age and die. Your people contain incredible potential, but they die without using much of it."

"I've heard humans say that." She frowned. "Couldn't your ooloi have helped her live longer—if she wanted to live longer than a hundred and thirteen years, that is."

"They did help her. They gave her forty years she would not have had, and when they could no longer help her heal, they took away her pain. If she had been younger when we found her, we could have given her much more time."

Lilith followed that thought to its obvious conclusion. "I'm twenty-six," she said.

"Older," he told her. "You've aged whenever we've kept you awake. About two years altogether."

She had no sense of being two years older, of being, suddenly, twenty-eight because he said she was. Two years of solitary confinement. What could they possibly give her in return for that? She stared at him.

His tentacles seemed to solidify into a second skin—dark patches on his face and neck, a dark, smooth-looking mass on his head. "Barring accident," he said, "you'll live much longer than a hundred and thirteen years. And for most of your life, you'll be biologically quite young. Your children will live longer still."

He looked remarkably human now. Was it only the tentacles that gave him that sea-slug appearance? His coloring hadn't changed. The fact that he had no eyes, nose, or ears still disturbed her, but not as much.

"Jdahya, stay that way," she told him. "Let me come close and look at you...if I can."

The tentacles moved like weirdly rippling skin, then resolidified. "Come," he said.

She was able to approach him hesitantly. Even viewed from only a couple of feet away, the tentacles looked like a smooth second skin. "Do you mind if..." She stopped and began again. "I mean...may I touch you?"

"Yes."

It was easier to do than she had expected. His skin was cool and almost too smooth to be real flesh—smooth the way her fingernails were and perhaps as tough as a fingernail.

"Is it hard for you to stay like this?" she asked.

"Not hard. Unnatural. A muffling of the senses."

"Why did you do it—before I asked you to, I mean."

"It's an expression of pleasure or amusement."

"You were pleased a minute ago?"

"With you. You wanted your time back—the time we've taken from you. You didn't want to die."

She stared at him, shocked that he had read her so clearly. And he must have known of humans who did want to die even after hearing promises of long life, health, and lasting youth. Why? Maybe they'd heard the part she hadn't been told about yet; the reason for all this. The price.

"So far," she said, "only boredom and isolation have driven me to want to die."

"Those are past. And you've never tried to kill yourself, even then."

"...no."

"Your desire to live is stronger than you realize."

She sighed. "You're going to test that, aren't you? That's why you haven't told me yet what your people want of us."

"Yes," he admitted, alarming her.

"Tell me!"

Silence.

"If you knew anything at all about the human imagination, you'd know you were doing exactly the wrong thing," she said.

"Once you're able to leave this room with me, I'll answer your questions," he told her.

She stared at him for several seconds. "Let's work on that,

then," she said grimly. "Relax from your unnatural position and let's see what happens."

He hesitated, then let his tentacles flow free. The grotesque sea-slug appearance resumed and she could not stop herself from stumbling away from him in panic and revulsion. She caught herself before she had gone far.

"God, I'm so tired of this," she muttered. "Why can't I stop it?"

"When the doctor first came to our household," he said, "some of my family found her so disturbing that they left home for a while. That's unheard-of behavior among us."

"Did you leave?"

He went smooth briefly. "I had not yet been born. By the time I was born, all my relatives had come home. And I think their fear was stronger than yours is now. They had never before seen so much life and so much death in one being. It hurt some of them to touch her."

"You mean . . . because she was sick?"

"Even when she was well. It was her genetic structure that disturbed them. I can't explain that to you. You'll never sense it as we do." He stepped toward her and reached for her hand. She gave it to him almost reflexively with only an instant's hesitation when his tentacles all flowed forward toward her. She looked away and stood stiffly where she was, her hand held loosely in his many fingers.

"Good," he said, releasing her. "This room will be nothing more than a memory for you soon."

4

Eleven meals later he took her outside.

She had no idea how long she was in wanting, then consuming, those eleven meals. Jdahya would not tell her, and he would not be hurried. He showed no impatience or annoyance when she urged him to take her out. He simply fell silent. He seemed almost to turn himself off when she made demands or asked questions he did not intend to answer. Her family had called her stubborn during her life before the war, but he was beyond stubborn.

Eventually he began to move around the room. He had been still for so long—had seemed almost part of the furniture—that she was startled when he suddenly got up and went into the bathroom. She stayed where she was on the bed, wondering whether he used a bathroom for the same purposes she did. She made no effort to find out. Sometime later when he came back into the room, she found herself much less disturbed by him. He brought her something that so surprised and delighted her that she took it from his hand without thought or hesitation: A banana, fully ripe, large, yellow, firm, very sweet.

She ate it slowly, wanting to gulp it, not daring to. It was literally the best food she had tasted in two hundred and fifty years. Who knew when there would be another—if there would be another. She ate even the white, inner skin.

He would not tell her where it had come from or how he had gotten it. He would not get her another. He did evict her from the bed for a while. He stretched out flat on it and lay utterly still, looked dead. She did a series of exercises on the floor, deliberately tired herself as much as she could, then took his place on the platform until he got up and let her have the bed.

When she awoke, he took his jacket off and let her see the tufts of sensory tentacles scattered over his body. To her surprise, she got used to these quickly. They were merely ugly. And they made him look even more like a misplaced sea creature.

"Can you breathe underwater?" she asked him.

"Yes."

"I thought your throat orifices looked as though they could double as gills. Are you more comfortable underwater?"

"I enjoy it, but no more than I enjoy air."

"Air ... oxygen?"

"I need oxygen, yes, though not as much of it as you do."

Her mind drifted back to his tentacles and another possible similarity to some sea slugs. "Can you sting with any of your tentacles?"

"With all of them."

She drew back, though she was not close to him. "Why didn't you tell me?"

"I wouldn't have stung you."

Unless she had attacked him. "So that's what happened to the humans who tried to kill you."

"No, Lilith. I'm not interested in killing your people. I've been trained all my life to keep them alive."

"What did you do to them, then?"

"Stopped them. I'm stronger than you probably think."

"But . . . if you had stung them?"

"They would have died. Only the ooloi can sting without killing. One group of my ancestors subdued prey by stinging it. Their sting began the digestive process even before they began to eat. And they stung enemies who tried to eat them. Not a comfortable existence."

"It doesn't sound that bad."

"They didn't live long, those ancestors. Some things were immune to their poison."

"Maybe humans are."

He answered her softly. "No, Lilith, you're not."

Sometime later he brought her an orange. Out of curiosity, she broke the fruit and offered to share it with him. He accepted a piece of it from her hand and sat down beside her to eat it. When they were both finished, he turned to face her—a courtesy, she realized, since he had so little face—and seemed to examine her closely. Some of his tentacles actually touched her. When they did, she jumped. Then she realized she was not being hurt and kept still. She did not like his nearness, but it no longer terrified her. After . . . however many days it had been, she felt none of the old panic; only relief at somehow having finally shed it.

"We'll go out now," he said. "My family will be relieved to see us. And you—you have a great deal to learn."

5

She made him wait until she had washed the orange juice from her hands. Then he walked over to one of the walls and touched it with some of his longer head tentacles.

A dark spot appeared on the wall where he made contact. It became a deepening, widening indentation, then a hole through which Lilith could see color and light—green, red, orange, yellow...

There had been little color in her world since her capture. Her own skin, her blood—within the pale walls of her prison, that was all. Everything else was some shade of white or gray. Even her food had been colorless until the banana. Now, here was color and what appeared to be sunlight. There was space. Vast space.

The hole in the wall widened as though it were flesh rippling aside, slowly writhing. She was both fascinated and repelled.

"Is it alive?" she asked.

"Yes," he said.

She had beaten it, kicked it, clawed it, tried to bite it. It had been smooth, tough, impenetrable, but slightly giving like the bed and table. It had felt like plastic, cool beneath her hands.

"What is it?" she asked.

"Flesh. More like mine than like yours. Different from mine, too, though. It's...the ship."

"You're kidding. Your ship is alive?"

"Yes. Come out." The hole in the wall had grown large enough for them to step through. He ducked his head and took the necessary step. She started to follow him, then stopped. There was so much space out there. The colors she had seen were thin, hairlike leaves and round, coconut-sized fruit, apparently in different stages of development. All hung from great branches that overshadowed the new exit. Beyond them was a broad, open field with scattered trees—impossibly huge trees—distant hills, and a bright, sunless ivory sky. There was enough strangeness to the trees and the sky to stop her from imagining that she was on Earth. There were people moving around in the distance, and there were black, German shepherd–sized animals that were too far away for her to see them clearly—though even in the distance the animals seemed to have too many legs. Six? Ten? The creatures seemed to be grazing.

"Lilith, come out," Jdahya said.

She took a step backward, away from all the alien vastness. The isolation room that she had hated for so long suddenly seemed safe and comforting.

"Back into your cage, Lilith?" Jdahya asked softly.

She stared at him through the hole, realized at once that he was trying to provoke her, make her overcome her fear. It would not have worked if he had not been so right. She was retreating into her cage—like a zoo animal that had been shut up for so long that the cage had become home.

She made herself step up to the opening, and then, teeth clenched, step through.

Outside, she stood beside him and drew a long, shuddering breath. She turned her head, looked at the room, then turned away quickly, resisting an impulse to flee back to it. He took her hand and led her away.

When she looked back a second time, the hole was closing and she could see that what she had come out of was actually a huge tree. Her room could not have taken more than a tiny fraction of its interior. The tree had grown from what appeared to be ordinary, pale-brown, sandy soil. Its lower limbs were heavily laden with fruit. The rest of it looked almost ordinary except for its size. The trunk was bigger around than some office buildings she remembered. And it seemed to touch the ivory sky. How tall was it? How much of it served as a building?

"Was everything inside that room alive?" she asked.

"Everything except some of the visible plumbing fixtures," Jdahya said. "Even the food you ate was produced from the fruit of one of the branches growing outside. It was designed to meet your nutritional needs."

"And to taste like cotton and paste," she muttered. "I hope I won't have to eat any more of that stuff."

"You won't. But it's kept you very healthy. Your diet in particular encouraged your body not to grow cancers while your genetic inclination to grow them was corrected."

"It has been corrected, then?"

"Yes. Correcting genes have been inserted into your cells, and your cells have accepted and replicated them. Now you won't grow cancers by accident."

That, she thought, was an odd qualification, but she let it pass for the moment. "When will you send me back to Earth?"

"You couldn't survive there now—especially not alone."

"You haven't sent any of us back yet?"

"Your group will be the first."

"Oh." This had not occurred to her—that she and others like her would be guinea pigs trying to survive on an Earth that must have greatly changed. "How is it there now?"

"Wild. Forests, mountains, deserts, plains, great oceans. It's a rich world, clean of dangerous radiation in most places. The greatest diversity of animal life is in the seas, but there are a number of small animals thriving on land: insects, worms, amphibians, reptiles, small mammals. There's no doubt your people can live there."

"When?"

"That will not be hurried. You have a very long life ahead of you, Lilith. And you have work to do here."

"You said something about that once before. What work?"

"You'll live with my family for a while—live as one of us as much as possible. We'll teach you your work."

"But *what* work?"

"You'll Awaken a small group of humans, all English-speaking, and help them learn to deal with us. You'll teach them the survival skills we teach you. Your people will all be from what you would call civilized societies. Now they'll have to learn to live in forests, build their own shelters, and raise their own food all without machines or outside help."

"Will you forbid us machines?" she asked uncertainly.

"Of course not. But we won't give them to you either. We'll give you hand tools, simple equipment, and food until you begin to make the things you need and grow your own crops. We've already armed you against the deadlier microorganisms. Beyond that, you'll have to fend for yourself—avoiding poisonous plants and animals and creating what you need."

"How can you teach us to survive on our own world? How can you know enough about it or about us?"

"How can we not? We've helped your world restore itself. We've studied your bodies, your thinking, your literature, your historical records, your many cultures...We know more of what you're capable of than you do."

Or they thought they did. If they really had had two hundred and fifty years to study, maybe they were right. "You've inoculated us against diseases?" she asked to be sure she had understood.

"No."

"But you said—"

"We've strengthened your immune system, increased your resistance to disease in general."

"How? Something else done to our genes?"

He said nothing. She let the silence lengthen until she was certain he would not answer. This was one more thing they had done to her body without her consent and supposedly for her own good. "We used to treat animals that way," she muttered bitterly.

"What?" he said.

"We did things to them—inoculations, surgery, isolation—all for their own good. We wanted them healthy and protected—sometimes so we could eat them later."

His tentacles did not flatten to his body, but she got the impression he was laughing at her. "Doesn't it frighten you to say things like that to me?" he asked.

"No," she said. "It scares me to have people doing things to me that I don't understand."

"You've been given health. The ooloi have seen to it that you'll have a chance to live on your Earth—not just to die on it."

He would not say any more on the subject. She looked around at the huge trees, some with great branching multiple trunks and foliage like long, green hair. Some of the hair seemed to move, though there was no wind. She sighed. The trees, too, then—tentacled like the people. Long, slender, green tentacles.

"Jdahya?"

His own tentacles swept toward her in a way she still found disconcerting, though it was only his way of giving her his attention or signaling her that she had it.

"I'm willing to learn what you have to teach me," she said, "but I don't think I'm the right teacher for others. There were so many humans who already knew how to live in the wilderness—so many who could probably teach you a little more. Those are the ones you ought to be talking to."

"We have talked to them. They will have to be especially careful because some of the things they 'know' aren't true anymore.

There are new plants—mutations of old ones and additions we've made. Some things that used to be edible are lethal now. Some things are deadly only if they aren't prepared properly. Some of the animal life isn't as harmless as it apparently once was. Your Earth is still your Earth, but between the efforts of your people to destroy it and ours to restore it, it has changed."

She nodded, wondering why she could absorb his words so easily. Perhaps because she had known even before her capture that the world she had known was dead. She had already absorbed that loss to the degree that she could.

"There must be ruins," she said softly.

"There were. We've destroyed many of them."

She seized his arm without thinking. "You destroyed them? There were things left and you destroyed them?"

"You'll begin again. We'll put you in areas that are clean of radioactivity and history. You will become something other than you were."

"And you think destroying what was left of our cultures will make us better?"

"No. Only different." She realized suddenly that she was facing him, grasping his arm in a grip that should have been painful to him. It was painful to her. She let go of him and his arm swung to his side in the oddly dead way in which his limbs seemed to move when he was not using them for a specific purpose.

"You were wrong," she said. She could not sustain her anger. She could not look at his tentacled, alien face and sustain anger—but she had to say the words. "You destroyed what wasn't yours," she said. "You completed an insane act."

"You are still alive," he said.

She walked beside him, silently ungrateful. Knee-high tufts of thick, fleshy leaves or tentacles grew from the soil. He stepped carefully to avoid them—which made her want to kick them. Only the fact that her feet were bare stopped her. Then she saw, to her disgust, that the leaves twisted or contracted out of the way if she stepped near one—like plants made up of snake-sized night crawlers. They seemed to be rooted to the ground. Did that make them plants?

"What are those things?" she asked, gesturing toward one with a foot.

"Part of the ship. They can be induced to produce a liquid we and our animals enjoy. It wouldn't be good for you."

"Are they plant or animal?"

"They aren't separate from the ship."

"Well, is the ship plant or animal?"

"Both, and more."

Whatever that meant. "Is it intelligent?"

"It can be. That part of it is dormant now. But even so, the ship can be chemically induced to perform more functions than you would have the patience to listen to. It does a great deal on its own without monitoring. And it..." He fell silent for a moment, his tentacles smooth against his body. Then he continued, "The human doctor used to say it loved us. There is an affinity, but it's biological—a strong, symbiotic relationship. We serve the ship's needs and it serves ours. It would die without us and we would be planetbound without it. For us, that would eventually mean death."

"Where did you get it?"

"We grew it."

"You...or your ancestors?"

"My ancestors grew this one. I'm helping to grow another."

"Now? Why?"

"We'll divide here. We're like mature asexual animals in that way, but we divide into three: Dinso to stay on Earth until it is ready to leave generations from now; Toaht to leave in this ship; and Akjai to leave in the new ship."

Lilith looked at him. "Some of you will go to Earth with us?"

"I will, and my family and others. All Dinso."

"Why?"

"This is how we grow—how we've always grown. We'll take the knowledge of shipgrowing with us so that our descendants will be able to leave when the time comes. We couldn't survive as a people if we were always confined to one ship or one world."

"Will you take . . . seeds or something?"

"We'll take the necessary materials."

"And those who leave—Toaht and Akjai—you'll never see them again?"

"I won't. At some time in the distant future, a group of my descendants might meet a group of theirs. I hope that will happen. Both will have divided many times. They'll have acquired much to give one another."

"They probably won't even know one another. They'll remember this division as mythology if they remember it at all."

"No, they'll recognize one another. Memory of a division is passed on biologically. I remember every one that has taken place in my family since we left the homeworld."

"Do you remember your homeworld itself? I mean, could you get back to it if you wanted to?"

"Go back?" His tentacles smoothed again. "No, Lilith, that's the one direction that's closed to us. This is our home-world now." He gestured around them from what seemed to be a glowing ivory sky to what seemed to be brown soil.

There were many more of the huge trees around them now, and she could see people going in and out of the trunks—naked, gray Oankali, tentacled all over, some with two arms, some, alarmingly, with four, but none with anything she recognized as sexual organs. Perhaps some of the tentacles and extra arms served a sexual function.

She examined every cluster of Oankali for humans, but saw none. At least none of the Oankali came near her or seemed to pay any attention to her. Some of them, she noticed with a shudder, had tentacles covering every inch of their heads all around. Others had tentacles in odd, irregular patches. None had quite

Jdahya's humanlike arrangement—tentacles placed to resemble eyes, ears, hair. Had Jdahya's work with humans been suggested by the chance arrangement of his head tentacles or had he been altered surgically or in some other way to make him seem more human?

"This is the way I have always looked," he said when she asked, and he would not say any more on the subject.

Minutes later they passed near a tree and she reached out to touch its smooth, slightly giving bark—like the walls of her isolation room, but darker-colored. "These trees are all buildings, aren't they?" she asked.

"These structures are not trees," he told her. "They're part of the ship. They support its shape, provide necessities for us—food, oxygen, waste disposal, transport conduits, storage and living space, work areas, many things."

They passed very near a pair of Oankali who stood so close together their head tentacles writhed and tangled together. She could see their bodies in clear detail. Like the others she had seen, these were naked. Jdahya had probably worn clothing only as a courtesy to her. For that she was grateful.

The growing number of people they passed near began to disturb her, and she caught herself drawing closer to Jdahya as though for protection. Surprised and embarrassed, she made herself move away from him. He apparently noticed.

"Lilith?" he said very quietly.

"What?"

Silence.

"I'm all right," she said. "It's just...so many people, and so strange to me."

"Normally, we don't wear anything."

"I'd guessed that."

"You'll be free to wear clothing or not as you like."

"I'll wear it!" She hesitated. "Are there any other humans Awake where you're taking me?"

"None."

She hugged herself tightly, arms across her chest. More isolation.

To her surprise, he extended his hand. To her greater surprise, she took it and was grateful.

"Why can't you go back to your homeworld?" she asked. "It... still exists, doesn't it?"

He seemed to think for a moment. "We left it so long ago... I doubt that it does still exist."

"Why did you leave?"

"It was a womb. The time had come for us to be born."

She smiled sadly. "There were humans who thought that way—right up to the moment the missiles were fired. People who believed space was our destiny. I believed it myself."

"I know—though from what the ooloi have told me, your people could not have fulfilled that destiny. Their own bodies handicapped them."

"Their... our bodies? What do you mean? We've been into space. There's nothing about our bodies that prevented—"

"Your bodies are fatally flawed. The ooloi perceived this at once. At first it was very hard for them to touch you. Then you became an obsession with them. Now it's hard for them to let you alone."

"What are you talking about?"

"You have a mismatched pair of genetic characteristics. Either alone would have been useful, would have aided the survival of your species. But the two together are lethal. It was only a matter of time before they destroyed you."

She shook her head. "If you're saying we were genetically programmed to do what we did, blow ourselves up—"

"No. Your people's situation was more like your own with the cancer my relative cured. The cancer was small. The human doctor said you would probably have recovered and been well even if humans had discovered it and removed it at that stage. You might have lived the rest of your life free of it, though she said she would have wanted you checked regularly."

"With my family history, she wouldn't have had to tell me that last."

"Yes. But what if you hadn't recognized the significance of your family history? What if we or the humans hadn't discovered the cancer?"

"It *was* malignant, I assume."

"Of course."

"Then I suppose it would eventually have killed me."

"Yes, it would have. And your people were in a similar position. If they had been able to perceive and solve their problem, they might have been able to avoid destruction. Of course, they too would have to remember to reexamine themselves periodically."

"But what was the problem? You said we had two incompatible characteristics. What were they?"

Jdahya made a rustling noise that could have been a sigh, but that did not seem to come from his mouth or throat. "You are intelligent," he said. "That's the newer of the two characteristics, and the one you might have put to work to save yourselves. You are potentially one of the most intelligent species we've found, though your focus is different from ours. Still, you had a good start in the life sciences, and even in genetics."

"What's the second characteristic?"

"You are hierarchical. That's the older and more entrenched characteristic. We saw it in your closest animal relatives and in your most distant ones. It's a terrestrial characteristic. When human intelligence served it instead of guiding it, when human intelligence did not even acknowledge it as a problem, but took pride in it or did not notice it at all . . ." The rattling sounded again. "That was like ignoring cancer. I think your people did not realize what a dangerous thing they were doing."

"I don't think most of us thought of it as a genetic problem. I didn't. I'm not sure I do now." Her feet had begun to hurt from walking so long on the uneven ground. She wanted to end both the walk and the conversation. The conversation made her uncomfortable. Jdahya sounded ... almost plausible.

"Yes," he said, "intelligence does enable you to deny facts you dislike. But your denial doesn't matter. A cancer growing in someone's body will go on growing in spite of denial. And a complex combination of genes that work together to make you intelligent as well as hierarchical will still handicap you whether you acknowledge it or not."

"I just don't believe it's that simple. Just a bad gene or two."

"It isn't simple, and it isn't a gene or two. It's many—the result of a tangled combination of factors that only begins with genes." He stopped, let his head tentacles drift toward a rough circle of huge trees. The tentacles seemed to point. "My family lives there," he said.

She stood still, now truly frightened.

"No one will touch you without your consent," he said. "And I'll stay with you for as long as you like."

She was comforted by his words and ashamed of needing comfort. How had she become so dependent on him? She shook her head. The answer was obvious. He wanted her dependent. That was the reason for her continued isolation from her own kind. She was to be dependent on an Oankali—dependent and trusting. To hell with that!

"Tell me what you want of me," she demanded abruptly, "and what you want of my people."

His tentacles swung to examine her. "I've told you a great deal."

"Tell me the price, Jdahya. What do you want? What will your people take from us in return for having saved us?"

All his tentacles seemed to hang limp, giving him an almost comical droop. Lilith found no humor in it. "You'll live," he said. "Your people will live. You'll have your world again. We already have much of what we want of you. Your cancer in particular."

"What?"

"The ooloi are intensely interested in it. It suggests abilities we have never been able to trade for successfully before."

"Abilities? From cancer?"

"Yes. The ooloi see great potential in it. So the trade has already been useful."

"You're welcome to it. But before when I asked, you said you trade...yourselves."

"Yes. We trade the essence of ourselves. Our genetic material for yours."

Lilith frowned, then shook her head. "How? I mean, you couldn't be talking about interbreeding."

"Of course not." His tentacles smoothed. "We do what you would call genetic engineering. We know you had begun to do it yourselves a little, but it's foreign to you. We do it naturally. We *must* do it. It renews us, enables us to survive as an evolving species instead of specializing ourselves into extinction or stagnation."

"We all do it naturally to some degree," she said warily. "Sexual reproduction—"

"The ooloi do it for us. They have special organs for it. They can do it for you too—make sure of a good, viable gene mix. It is part of our reproduction, but it's much more deliberate than what any mated pair of humans have managed so far.

"We're not hierarchical, you see. We never were. But we are powerfully acquisitive. We acquire new life—seek it, investigate it, manipulate it, sort it, use it. We carry the drive to do this in a minuscule cell within a cell—a tiny organelle within every cell of our bodies. Do you understand me?"

"I understand your words. Your meaning, though...it's as alien to me as you are."

"That's the way we perceived your hierarchical drives at first." He paused. "One of the meanings of Oankali is gene trader. Another is that organelle—the essence of ourselves, the origin of ourselves. Because of that organelle, the ooloi can perceive DNA and manipulate it precisely."

"And they do this...inside their bodies?"

"Yes."

"And now they're doing something with cancer cells inside their bodies?"

"Experimenting, yes."

"That sounds...a long way from safe."

"They're like children now, talking and talking about possibilities."

"What possibilities?"

"Regeneration of lost limbs. Controlled malleability. Future Oankali may be much less frightening to potential trade partners if they're able to reshape themselves and look more like the partners before the trade. Even increased longevity, though compared to what you're used to, we're very long-lived now."

"All that from cancer."

"Perhaps. We listen to the ooloi when they stop talking so much. That's when we find out what our next generations will be like."

"You leave all that to them? They decide?"

"They show us the tested possibilities. We all decide."

He tried to lead her into his family's woods, but she held back. "There's something I need to understand now," she said. "You call it a trade. You've taken something you value from us and you're giving us back our world. Is that it? Do you have all you want from us?"

"You know it isn't," he said softly. "You've guessed that much."

She waited, staring at him.

"Your people will change. Your young will be more like us and ours more like you. Your hierarchical tendencies will be modified and if we learn to regenerate limbs and reshape our bodies, we'll share those abilities with you. That's part of the trade. We're overdue for it."

"It is crossbreeding, then, no matter what you call it."

"It's what I said it was. A trade. The ooloi will make changes in your reproductive cells before conception and they'll control conception."

"How?"

"The ooloi will explain that when the time comes."

She spoke quickly, trying to blot out thoughts of more surgery or some sort of sex with the damned ooloi. "What will you make of us? What will our children be?"

"Different, as I said. Not quite like you. A little like us."

She thought of her son—how like her he had been, how like his father. Then she thought of grotesque, Medusa children. "No!" she said. "No. I don't care what you do with what you've already learned—how you apply it to yourselves—but leave us out of it. Just let us go. If we have the problem you think we do, let us work it out as human beings."

"We are committed to the trade," he said, softly implacable.

"No! You'll finish what the war began. In a few generations—"

"One generation."

"No!"

He wrapped the many fingers of one hand around her arm. "Can you hold your breath, Lilith? Can you hold it by an act of will until you die?"

"Hold my—?"

"We are as committed to the trade as your body is to breathing. We were overdue for it when we found you. Now it will be done— to the rebirth of your people and mine."

"No!" she shouted. "A rebirth for us can only happen if you let us alone! Let us begin again on our own."

Silence.

She pulled at her arm, and after a moment he let her go. She got the impression he was watching her very closely.

"I think I wish your people had left me on Earth," she whispered. "If this is what they found me for, I wish they'd left me." Medusa children. Snakes for hair. Nests of night crawlers for eyes and ears.

He sat down on the bare ground, and after a minute of surprise, she sat opposite him, not knowing why, simply following his movement.

"I can't *unfind* you," he said. "You're here. But there is...a thing I *can* do. It is...deeply wrong of me to offer it. I will never offer it again."

"What?" she asked barely caring. She was tired from the walk, overwhelmed by what he had told her. It made no sense. Good god, no wonder he couldn't go home—even if his home still existed. Whatever his people had been like when they left it, they must be very different by now—as the children of the last surviving human beings would be different.

"Lilith?" he said.

She raised her head, stared at him.

"Touch me here now," he said, gesturing toward his head tentacles, "and I'll sting you. You'll die—very quickly and without pain."

She swallowed.

"If you want it," he said.

It was a gift he was offering. Not a threat.

"Why?" she whispered.

He would not answer.

She stared at his head tentacles. She raised her hand, let it reach toward him almost as though it had its own will, its own intent. No more Awakenings. No more questions. No more impossible answers. Nothing.

Nothing.

He never moved. Even his tentacles were utterly still. Her hand hovered, wanting to fall amid the tough, flexible, lethal organs. It hovered, almost brushing one by accident.

She jerked her hand away, clutched it to her. "Oh god," she whispered. "Why didn't I do it? Why can't I do it?"

He stood up and waited uncomplaining for several minutes until she dragged herself to her feet.

"You'll meet my mates and one of my children now," he said. "Then rest and food, Lilith."

She looked at him, longing for a human expression. "Would you have done it?" she asked.

"Yes," he said.

"Why?"

"For you."

PART II

Family

PART I

Felix

1

Sleep.

She barely remembered being presented to three of Jdahya's relatives, then guided off and given a bed. Sleep. Then a small, confused awakening.

Now food and forgetting.

Food and pleasure so sharp and sweet it cleared everything else from her mind. There were whole bananas, dishes of sliced pineapple, whole figs, shelled nuts of several kinds, bread and honey, a vegetable stew filled with corn, peppers, tomatoes, potatoes, onions, mushrooms, herbs, and spices.

Where had all this been, Lilith wondered. Surely they could have given her a little of this instead of keeping her for so long on a diet that made eating a chore. Could it all have been for her health? Or had there been some other purpose—something to do with their damned gene trade?

When she had eaten some of everything, savored each new taste lovingly, she began to pay attention to the four Oankali who were with her in the small, bare room. They were Jdahya and his wife Tediin—Kaaljdahyatediin lel Kahguyaht aj Dinso. And there was Jdahya's ooloi mate Kahguyaht—Ahtrekahguyahtkaal lel Jdahyatediin aj Dinso. Finally there was the family's ooloi child Nikanj—Kaalnikanj oo Jdahyatediinkahguyaht aj Dinso.

The four sat atop familiar, featureless platforms eating Earth foods from their several small dishes as though they had been born to such a diet.

There was a central platform with more of everything on it, and the Oankali took turns filling one another's dishes. One of them could not, it seemed, get up and fill only one dish. Others were immediately handed forward, even to Lilith. She filled Jdahya's with hot stew and returned it to him, wondering when he had eaten last—apart from the orange they had shared.

"Did you eat while we were in that isolation room?" she asked him.

"I had eaten before I went in," he said. "I used very little energy while I was there so I didn't need any more food."

"How long were you there?"

"Six days, your time."

She sat down on her platform and stared at him. "That long?"

"Six days," he repeated.

"Your body has drifted away from your world's twenty-four-hour day," the ooloi Kahguyaht said. "That happens to all your people. Your day lengthens slightly and you lose track of how much time has passed."

"But—"

"How long did it seem to you?"

"A few days...I don't know. Fewer than six."

"You see?" the ooloi asked softly.

She frowned at it. It was naked as were the others except for Jdahya. This did not bother her even at close quarters as much as she had feared it might. But she did not like the ooloi. It was smug and it tended to treat her condescendingly. It was also one of the creatures scheduled to bring about the destruction of what was left of humanity. And in spite of Jdahya's claim that the Oankali were not hierarchical, the ooloi seemed to be the head of the house. Everyone deferred to it.

It was almost exactly Lilith's size—slightly larger than Jdahya and considerably smaller than the female Tediin. And it had four arms. Or two arms and two arm-sized tentacles. The big tentacles, gray and rough, reminded her of elephants' trunks—except that she could not recall ever being disgusted by the trunk of an elephant. At least the child did not have them yet—though Jdahya had assured her that it was an ooloi child. Looking at Kahguyaht, she took pleasure in the knowledge that the Oankali themselves used the neuter pronoun in referring to the ooloi. Some things deserved to be called "it."

She turned her attention back to the food. "How can you eat all this?" she asked. "I couldn't eat your foods, could I?"

"What do you think you've eaten each time we've Awakened you?" the ooloi asked.

"I don't know," she said coldly. "No one would tell me what it was."

Kahguyaht missed or ignored the anger in her voice. "It was one of our foods—slightly altered to meet your special needs," it said.

Thought of her "special needs" made her realize that this might be Jdahya's "relative" who had cured her cancer. She had somehow not thought of this until now. She got up and filled one of her small bowls with nuts—roasted, but not salted—and wondered wearily whether she had to be grateful to Kahguyaht. Automatically she filled with the same nuts, the bowl Tediin had thrust forward to her.

"Is any of our food poison to you?" she asked flatly.

"No," Kahguyaht answered. "We have adjusted to the foods of your world."

"Are any of yours poison to me?"

"Yes. A great many of them. You shouldn't eat anything unfamiliar that you find here."

"That doesn't make sense. Why should you be able to come from so far away—another world, another star system—and eat our food?"

"Haven't we had time to learn to eat your food?" the ooloi asked.

"What?"

It did not repeat the question.

"Look," she said, "how can you learn to eat something that's poison to you?"

"By studying teachers to whom it isn't poison. By studying your people, Lilith. Your bodies."

"I don't understand."

"Then accept the evidence of your eyes. We can eat anything you can. It's enough for you to understand that."

Patronizing bastard, she thought. But she said only, "Does that mean that you can learn to eat anything at all? That you can't be poisoned?"

"No. I didn't mean that."

She waited, chewing nuts, thinking. When the ooloi did not continue, she looked at it.

It was focused on her, head tentacles pointing. "The very old can be poisoned," it said. "Their reactions are slowed. They might not be able to recognize an unexpected deadly substance and remember how to neutralize it in time. The seriously injured can be poisoned. Their bodies are distracted, busy with self-repair. And the children can be poisoned if they have not yet learned to protect themselves."

"You mean...just about anything might poison you if you weren't somehow prepared for it, ready to protect yourselves against it?"

"Not just anything. Very few things, really. Things we were especially vulnerable to before we left our original home-world."

"Like what?"

"Why do you ask, Lilith? What would you do if I told you? Poison a child?"

She chewed and swallowed several peanuts, all the while staring at the ooloi, making no effort to conceal her dislike. "You invited me to ask," she said.

"No. That isn't what I was doing."

"Do you really imagine I'd hurt a child?"

"No. You just haven't learned yet not to ask dangerous questions."

"Why did you tell me as much as you did?"

The ooloi relaxed its tentacles. "Because we know you, Lilith. And, within reason, we want you to know us."

2

The ooloi took her to see Sharad. She would have preferred to have Jdahya take her, but when Kahguyaht volunteered, Jdahya leaned toward her and asked very softly, "Shall I go?"

She did not imagine that she was intended to miss the unspoken message of the gesture—that Jdahya was indulging a child. Lilith was tempted to accept the child's role and ask him to come along. But he deserved a vacation from her—and she from him. Maybe he wanted to spend some time with the big, silent Tediin. How, she wondered, did these people manage their sex lives, anyway? How did the ooloi fit in? Were its two arm-sized tentacles sexual organs? Kahguyaht had not used them in eating—had kept them either coiled against its body, under its true arms or draped over its shoulders.

She was not afraid of it, ugly as it was. So far it had inspired only disgust, anger, and dislike in her. How had Jdahya connected himself with such a creature?

Kahguyaht led her through three walls, opening all of them

by touching them with one of its large tentacles. Finally they emerged into a wide, downward-sloping, well-lighted corridor. Large numbers of Oankali walked or rode flat, slow, wheelless conveyances that apparently floated a fraction of an inch above the floor. There were no collisions, no near-misses, yet Lilith saw no order to the traffic. People walked or drove wherever they could find an opening and apparently depended on others not to hit them. Some of the vehicles were loaded with unrecognizable freight—transparent beachball-sized blue spheres filled with some liquid, two-foot-long centipede-like animals stacked in rectangular cages, great trays of oblong, green shapes about six feet long and three feet thick. These last writhed slowly, blindly.

"What are those?" she asked the ooloi.

It ignored her except to take her arm and guide her where traffic was heavy. She realized abruptly that it was guiding her with the tip of one of its large tentacles.

"What do you call these?" she asked, touching the one wrapped around her arm. Like the smaller ones it was cool and as hard as her fingernails, but clearly very flexible.

"You can call them sensory arms," it told her.

"What are they for?"

Silence.

"Look, I thought I was supposed to be learning. I can't learn without asking questions and getting answers."

"You'll get them eventually—as you need them."

In anger she pulled loose from the ooloi's grip. It was surprisingly easy to do. The ooloi did not touch her again, did not seem to notice that twice it almost lost her, made no effort to help her when they passed through a crowd and she realized she could not tell one adult ooloi from another.

"Kahguyaht!" she said sharply.

"Here." It was beside her, no doubt watching, probably laughing at her confusion. Feeling manipulated, she grasped one of its true arms and stayed close to it until they had come into a corridor that was almost empty. From there they entered a corridor that was empty. Kahguyaht ran one sensory arm along the wall for several feet, then stopped, and flatted the tip of the arm against the wall.

An opening appeared where the arm had touched and Lilith expected to be led into one more corridor or room. Instead the wall seemed to form a sphincter and pass something. There was even a sour smell to enhance the image. One of the big semitransparent green oblongs slid into view, wet and sleek.

"It's a plant," the ooloi volunteered. "We store it where it can be given the kind of light it thrives best under."

Why couldn't it have said that before, she wondered.

The green oblong writhed very slowly as the others had while the ooloi probed it with both sensory arms. After a time, the ooloi paid attention only to one end. That end, it massaged with its sensory arms.

Lilith saw that the plant was beginning to open, and suddenly she knew what was happening.

"Sharad is in that thing, isn't he?"

"Come here."

She went over to where it had sat on the floor at the now-open end of the oblong. Sharad's head was just becoming visible. The hair that she recalled as dull black now glistened, wet and plastered to his head. The eyes were closed and the look on the face peaceful—as though the boy were in a normal sleep. Kahguyaht had stopped the opening of the plant at the base of the boy's throat, but she could see enough to know Sharad was only a little older than he had been when they had shared an isolation room. He looked healthy and well.

"Will you wake him?" she asked.

"No." Kahguyaht touched the brown face with a sensory arm. "We won't be Awakening these people for a while. The human who will be guiding and training them has not yet begun his own training."

She would have pleaded with it if she had not had two years of dealing with the Oankali to tell her just how little good pleading did. Here was the one human being she had seen in those two years, in two hundred and fifty years. And she could not talk to him, could not make him know she was with him.

She touched his cheek, found it wet, slimy, cool. "Are you sure he's all right?"

"He's fine." The ooloi touched the plant where it had drawn aside and it began slowly to close around Sharad again. She watched the face until it was completely covered. The plant closed seamlessly around the small head.

"Before we found these plants," Kahguyaht said, "they used to capture living animals and keep them alive for a long while, using their carbon dioxide and supplying them with oxygen while slowly digesting nonessential parts of their bodies: limbs, skin, sensory organs. The plants even passed some of their own substance through their prey to nourish the prey and keep it alive as long as possible. And the plants were enriched by the prey's waste products. They gave a very, very long death.

Lilith swallowed. "Did the prey feel what was being done to it?"

"No. That would have hastened death. The prey . . . slept."

Lilith stared at the green oblong, writhing slowly like an obscenely fat caterpillar. "How does Sharad breathe?"

"The plant supplies him with an ideal mix of gasses."

"Not just oxygen?"

"No. It suits its care to his needs. It still benefits from the carbon dioxide he exhales and from his rare waste products. It floats in a bath of nutrients and water. These and the light supply the rest of its needs."

Lilith touched the plant, found it firm and cool. It yielded slightly under her fingers. Its surface was lightly coated with slime. She watched with amazement as her fingers sank more deeply into it and it began to engulf them. She was not frightened until she tried to pull away and discovered it would not let go— and pulling back hurt sharply.

"Wait," Kahguyaht said. With a sensory arm, it touched the plant near her hand. At once, she felt the plant begin to let go. When she was able to raise her hand, she found it numb, but otherwise unharmed. Feeling returned to the hand slowly. The print of it was still clear on the surface of the plant when Kahguyaht first rubbed its own hands with its sensory arms, then opened the wall and pushed the plant back through it.

"Sharad is very small," it said when the plant was gone. "The plant could have taken you in as well."

She shuddered. "I was in one . . . wasn't I?"

Kahguyaht ignored the question. But of course she had been in one of the plants—had spent most of the last two and a half centuries within what was basically a carnivorous plant. And the thing had taken good care of her, kept her young and well.

"How did you make them stop eating people?" she asked.

"We altered them genetically—changed some of their requirements, enabled them to respond to certain chemical stimuli from us."

She looked at the ooloi. "It's one thing to do that to a plant. It's another to do it to intelligent, self-aware beings."

"We do what we do, Lilith."

"You could kill us. You could make mules of our children—sterile monsters."

"No," it said. "There was no life at all on your Earth when our ancestors left our original homeworld, and in all that time we've never done such a thing."

"You wouldn't tell me if you had," she said bitterly.

It took her back through the crowded corridors to what she had come to think of as Jdahya's apartment. There it turned her over to the child, Nikanj.

"It will answer your questions and take you through the walls when necessary," Kahguyaht said. "It is half again your age and very knowledgeable about things other than humans. You will teach it about your people and it will teach you about the Oankali."

Half again her age, three-quarters her size, and still growing. She wished it were not an ooloi child. She wished it were not a child at all. How could Kahguyaht first accuse her of wanting to poison children, then leave her in the care of its own child?

At least Nikanj did not look like an ooloi yet.

"You do speak English, don't you?" she asked when Kahguyaht had opened a wall and left the room. The room was the one they had eaten in, empty now except for Lilith and the child. The left-over food and the dishes had been removed and she had not seen Jdahya or Tediin since her return.

"Yes," the child said. "But . . . not much. You teach."

Lilith sighed. Neither the child nor Tediin had said a word to her beyond greeting, though both had occasionally spoken in fast, choppy Oankali to Jdahya or Kahguyaht. She had wondered why. Now she knew.

"I'll teach what I can," she said.

"I teach. You teach."

"Yes."

"Good. Outside?"

"You want me to go outside with you?"

It seemed to think for a moment. "Yes," it said finally.

"Why?"

The child opened its mouth, then closed it again, head tentacles writhing. Confusion? Vocabulary problem?

"It's all right," Lilith said. "We can go outside if you like."

Its tentacles smoothed flat against its body briefly, then it took her hand and would have opened the wall and led her out but she stopped it.

"Can you show me how to make it open?" she asked.

The child hesitated, then took one of her hands and brushed it over the forest of its long head tentacles, leaving the hand slightly wet. Then it touched her fingers to the wall, and the wall began to open.

More programmed reaction to chemical stimuli. No special

areas to press, no special series of pressures. Just a chemical the Oankali manufactured within their bodies. She would go on being a prisoner, forced to stay wherever they chose to leave her. She would not be permitted even the illusion of freedom.

The child stopped her once they were outside. It struggled through a few more words. "Others," it said, then hesitated. "Others see you? Others not see human...never."

Lilith frowned, certain she was being asked a question. The child's rising inflection seemed to indicate questioning if she could depend on such clues from an Oankali. "Are you asking me whether you can show me off to your friends?" she asked.

The child turned its face to her. "Show you...off?"

"It means...to put me on display—take me out to be seen."

"Ah. Yes. I show you off?"

"All right," she said smiling.

"I talk...more human soon. You say...if I speak bad."

"Badly," she corrected.

"If I speak badly?"

"Yes."

There was a long silence. "Also, goodly?" it asked.

"No, not goodly. Well."

"Well." The child seemed to taste the word. "I speak well soon," it said.

3

Nikanj's friends poked and prodded her exposed flesh and tried to persuade her through Nikanj to take off her clothing. None of them spoke English. None seemed in the least childlike, though Nikanj said all were children. She got the feeling some would have enjoyed dissecting her. They spoke aloud very little, but there was much touching of tentacles to flesh or tentacles to other tentacles. When they saw that she would not strip, no more questions were addressed to her. She was first amused, then annoyed, then angered by their attitude. She was nothing more than an unusual animal to them. Nikanj's new pet.

Abruptly she turned away from them. She had had enough of being shown off. She moved away from a pair of children who were reaching to investigate her hair, and spoke Nikanj's name sharply.

Nikanj disentangled its long head tentacles from those of another child and came back to her. If it had not responded to its name, she would not have known it. She was going to have to learn to tell people apart. Memorize the various head-tentacle patterns, perhaps.

"I want to go back," she said.

"Why?" it asked.

She sighed, decided to tell as much of the truth as she thought it could understand. Best to find out now just how far the truth would get her. "I don't like this," she said. "I don't want to be shown off anymore to people I can't even talk to."

It touched her arm tentatively. "You . . . anger?"

"I'm angry, yes. I need to be by myself for a while."

It thought about that. "We go back," it said finally.

Some of the children were apparently unhappy about her leaving. They clustered around her and spoke aloud to Nikanj, but Nikanj said a few words and they let her pass.

She discovered she was trembling and took deep breaths to relax herself. How was a pet supposed to feel? How did zoo animals feel?

If the child would just take her somewhere and leave her for a while. If it would give her a little more of what she had thought she would never want again: Solitude.

Nikanj touched her forehead with a few head tentacles, as though sampling her sweat. She jerked her head away, not wanting to be sampled anymore by anyone.

Nikanj opened a wall into the family apartment and led her into a room that was a twin of the isolation room she thought she had left behind. "Rest here," it told her. "Sleep."

There was even a bathroom, and on the familiar table platform, there was a clean set of clothing. And replacing Jdahya was Nikanj. She could not get rid of it. It had been told to stay with her, and it meant to stay. Its tentacles settled into ugly irregular lumps when she shouted at it, but it stayed.

Defeated, she hid for a while in the bathroom. She rinsed her old clothing, though no foreign matter stuck to it—not dirt, not sweat, not grease or water. It never stayed wet for more than a few minutes. Some Oankali synthetic.

Then she wanted to sleep again. She was used to sleeping

whenever she felt tired, and not used to walking long distances or meeting new people. Surprising how quickly the Oankali had become people to her. But then, who else was there?

She crawled into the bed and turned her back to Nikanj, who had taken Jdahya's place on the table platform. Who else would there be for her if the Oankali had their way—and no doubt they were used to having their way. Modifying carnivorous plants... What had they modified to get their ship? And what useful tools would they modify human beings into? Did they know yet, or were they planning more experiments? Did they care? How would they make their changes? Or had they made them already—done a little extra tampering with her while they took care of her tumor? Had she ever had a tumor? Her family history led her to believe she had. They probably had not lied about that. Maybe they had not lied about anything. Why should they bother to lie? They owned the Earth and all that was left of the human species.

How was it that she had not been able to take what Jdahya offered?

She slept, finally. The light never changed, but she was used to that. She awoke once to find that Nikanj had come onto the bed with her and lay down. Her first impulse was to push the child away in revulsion or get up herself. Her second, which she followed, wearily indifferent, was to go back to sleep.

4

It became irrationally important to her to do two things: First, to talk to another human being. Any human would do, but she hoped for one who had been Awake longer than she had, one who knew more than she had managed to learn.

Second, she wanted to catch an Oankali in a lie. Any Oankali. Any lie.

But she saw no sign of other humans. And the closest she came to catching the Oankali lying was to catch them in half-truths—though they were honest even about this. They freely admitted that they would tell her only part of what she wanted to know. Beyond this, the Oankali seemed to tell the truth as they perceived it, always. This left her with an almost intolerable sense of hopelessness and helplessness—as though catching them in lies would make them vulnerable. As though it would make the thing they intended to do less real, easier to deny.

Only Nikanj gave her any pleasure, any forgetfulness. The ooloi child seemed to have been given to her as much as she had been given to it. It rarely left her, seemed to like her—though what "liking" a human might mean to an Oankali, she did not know. She had not even figured out Oankali emotional ties to one another. But Jdahya had cared enough for her to offer to do something he believed was utterly wrong. What might Nikanj do for her eventually?

In a very real sense, she was an experimental animal. Not a pet. What could Nikanj do for an experimental animal? Protest tearfully (?) when she was sacrificed at the end of the experiment?

But, no, it was not that kind of experiment. She was intended to live and reproduce, not to die. Experimental animal, parent to domestic animals? Or...nearly extinct animal, part of a captive breeding program? Human biologists had done that before the war—used a few captive members of an endangered animal species to breed more for the wild population. Was that what she was headed for? Forced artificial insemination. Surrogate motherhood? Fertility drugs and forced "donations" of eggs? Implantation of unrelated fertilized eggs. Removal of children from mothers at birth...Humans had done these things to captive breeders—all for a higher good, of course.

This was what she needed to talk to another human about. Only a human could reassure her—or at least understand her fear. But there was only Nikanj. She spent all her time teaching it and learning what she could from it. It kept her as busy as she would permit. It needed less sleep than she did, and when she was not asleep, it expected her to be learning or teaching. It wanted not only language, but culture, biology, history, her own life story... Whatever she knew, it expected to learn.

This was a little like having Sharad with her again. But Nikanj was much more demanding—more like an adult in its persistence. No doubt she and Sharad had been given their time together so that the Oankali could see how she behaved with a foreign child of her own species—a child she had to share quarters with and teach.

Like Sharad, Nikanj had an eidetic memory. Perhaps all

Oankali did. Anything Nikanj saw or heard once, it remembered, whether it understood or not. And it was bright and surprisingly quick to understand. She became ashamed of her own plodding slowness and haphazard memory.

She had always found it easier to learn when she could write things down. In all her time with the Oankali, though, she had never seen any of them read or write anything.

"Do you keep any records outside your own memories?" she asked Nikanj when she had worked with it long enough to become frustrated and angry. "Do you ever read or write?"

"You have not taught me those words," it said.

"Communication by symbolic marks..." She looked around for something she could mark, but they were in their bedroom and there was nothing that would retain a mark long enough for her to write words—even if she had had something to write with. "Let's go outside," she said. "I'll show you."

It opened a wall and led her out. Outside, beneath the branches of the pseudotree that contained their living quarters, she knelt on the ground and began to write with her finger in what seemed to be loose, sandy soil. She wrote her name, then experimented with different possible spellings of Nikanj's name. *Necange* didn't look right—nor did *Nekahnge*. *Nickahnge* was closer. She listened in her mind to Nikanj saying its name, then wrote *Nikanj*. That felt right, and she liked the way it looked.

"That's about what your name would look like written down," she said. "I can write the words you teach me and study them until I know them. That way I wouldn't have to ask you things over and over. But I need something to write with—and on. Thin sheets of paper would be best." She was not sure it knew what paper was, but it did not ask. "If you don't have paper, I could use thin sheets of plastic or even cloth if you can make something that will mark them. Some ink or dye—something that will make a clear mark. Do you understand?"

"You can do what you're doing with your fingers," it told her.

"That's not enough. I need to be able to keep my writing...to study it. I need—"

"No."

She stopped in midsentence, blinked at it. "This isn't anything dangerous," she said. "Some of your people must have seen our books, tapes, disks, films—our records of history, medicine, language, science, all kinds of things. I just want to make my own records of your language."

"I know about the...records your people kept. I didn't know what they were called in English, but I've seen them. We've saved many of them and learned to use them to know humans better. I don't understand them, but others do."

"May I see them?"

"No. None of your people are permitted to see them."

"Why?"

It did not answer.

"Nikanj?"

Silence.

"Then...at least let me make my own records to help me learn your language. We humans need to do such things to help us remember."

"No."

She frowned. "But...what do you mean, 'no'? We do."

"I cannot give you such things. Not to write or to read."

"Why!"

"It is not allowed. The people have decided that it should not be allowed."

"That doesn't answer anything. What was their reason?"

Silence again. It let its sensory tentacles droop. This made it look smaller—like a furry animal that had gotten wet.

"It can't be that you don't have—or can't make—writing materials," she said.

"We can make anything your people could," it said. "Though we would not want to make most of their things."

"This is such a simple thing…" She shook her head. "Have you been told not to tell me why?"

It refused to answer. Did that mean not telling her was its own idea, its own childish exercise of power? Why shouldn't the Oankali do such things as readily as humans did?

After a time, it said, "Come back in. I'll teach you more of our history." It knew she liked stories of the long, multispecies Oankali history, and the stories helped her Oankali vocabulary. But she was in no mood to be cooperative now. She sat down on the ground and leaned back against the pseudotree. After a moment, Nikanj sat down opposite her and began to speak.

"Six divisions ago, on a white-sun water world, we lived in great shallow oceans," it said. "We were many-bodied and spoke with body lights and color patterns among ourself and among ourselves…"

She let it go on, not questioning when she did not understand, not wanting to care. The idea of Oankali blending with a species of intelligent, schooling, fishlike creatures was fascinating, but she was too angry to give it her full attention. Writing materials. Such small things, and yet they were denied to her. Such *small* things!

When Nikanj went into the apartment to get food for them both, she got up and walked away. She wandered, freer than she ever had before through the parklike area outside the living quarters—the pseudotrees. Oankali saw her, but seemed to pay no more than momentary attention to her. She had become absorbed in looking around when abruptly Nikanj was beside her.

"You must stay with me," it said in a tone that reminded her of a human mother speaking to her five-year-old. That, she thought, was about right for her rank in its family.

After that incident she slipped away whenever she could. Either she would be stopped, punished, and/or confined, or she would not be.

She was not. Nikanj seemed to get used to her wandering.

Abruptly, it ceased to show up at her elbow minutes after she had escaped it. It seemed willing to give her an occasional hour or two out of its sight. She began to take food with her, saving easily portable items from her meals—a highly seasoned rice dish wrapped in an edible, high-protein envelope, nuts, fruit or quatasayasha, a sharp, cheeselike Oankali food that Kahguyaht had said was safe. Nikanj had acknowledged its acceptance of her wandering by advising her to bury any uneaten food she did not want. "Feed it to the ship," was the way it put the suggestion.

She would fashion her extra jacket into a bag and put her lunch into it, then wander alone, eating and thinking. There was no real comfort in being alone with her thoughts, her memories, but somehow the illusion of freedom lessened her despair.

Other Oankali tried to talk with her sometimes, but she could not understand enough of their language to hold a conversation. Sometimes even when they spoke slowly, she would not recognize words she should have known and did know moments after the encounter had ended. Most of the time she wound up resorting to gestures—which did not work very well—and feeling impenetrably stupid. The only certain communication she managed was in enlisting help from strangers when she was lost.

Nikanj had told her that if she could not find her way "home" she was to go to the nearest adult and say her name with new Oankali additions: Dhokaaltediinjdahyalilith eka Kahguyaht aj Dinso. The *Dho* used as prefix indicated an adopted non-Oankali. *Kaal* was a kinship group name. Then Tediin's and Jdahya's names with Jdahya's last because he had brought her into the family. *Eka* meant child. A child so young it literally had no sex—as very young Oankali did not. Lilith had accepted this designation hopefully. Surely sexless children were not used in breeding experiments. Then there was Kahguyaht's name. It was her third "parent," after all. Finally there was the trade status name. The Dinso group was staying on Earth, changing itself by taking part of humanity's genetic heritage, spreading its own genes like a disease among unwilling humans...Dinso. It wasn't a surname. It was a terrible promise, a threat.

Yet if she said this long name—all of it—people immediately understood not only who she was but where she should be, and they pointed her toward "home." She was not particularly grateful to them.

On one of these solitary walks, she heard two Oankali use one of their words for humans—kaizidi—and she slowed down to listen. She assumed the two were talking about her. She often supposed people she walked among were discussing her as though she were an unusual animal. These two confirmed her fears when they fell silent at her approach and continued their conversation silently with mutual touching of head tentacles. She had all but forgotten this incident when, several walks later, she heard another group of people in the same area speaking again of a kaizidi—a male they called Fukumoto.

Again everyone fell silent at her approach. She had tried to freeze and listen, just hidden by the trunk of one of the great pseudotrees, but the moment she stopped there, conversation went silent among the Oankali. Their hearing, when they chose to focus their attention on it, was acute. Nikanj had complained early on in her stay about the loudness of her heartbeat.

She walked on, ashamed in spite of herself of having been caught eavesdropping. There was no sense to such a feeling. She was a captive. What courtesy did a captive owe beyond what was necessary for self-preservation?

And where was Fukumoto?

She replayed in her mind what she remembered of the fragments she had heard. Fukumoto had something to do with the Tiej kinship group—also a Dinso people. She knew vaguely where their area was, though she had never been there.

Why had people in Kaal been discussing a human in Tiej? What had Fukumoto done? And how could she reach him?

She would go to Tiej. She would do her wandering there if

she could—if Nikanj did not appear to stop her. It still did that occasionally, letting her know that it could follow her anywhere, approach her anywhere, and seem to appear from nowhere. Maybe it liked to see her jump.

She began to walk toward Tiej. She might manage to see the man today if he happened to be outside—addicted to wandering as she was. And if she saw him, he might speak English. If he spoke English, his Oankali jailers might not prevent him from speaking to her. If the two of them spoke together, he might prove as ignorant as she was. And if he were not ignorant, if they met and spoke and all went well, the Oankali might decide to punish her. Solitary confinement again? Suspended animation? Or just closer confinement with Nikanj and its family? If they did either of the first two she would simply be relieved of a responsibility she did not want and could not possibly handle. If they did the third, what difference would it really make? What difference balanced against the chance to see and speak with one of her own kind again, finally?

None at all.

She never considered going back to Nikanj and asking it or its family to let her meet Fukumoto. They had made it clear to her that she was not to have contact with humans or human artifacts.

The walk to Tiej was longer than she had expected. She had not yet learned to judge distances aboard the ship. The horizon, when it was not obscured by pseudotrees and hill-like entrances to other levels, seemed startlingly close. But how close, she could not have said.

At least no one stopped her. Oankali she passed seemed to assume that she belonged wherever she happened to be. Unless Nikanj appeared, she would be able to wander in Tiej for as long as she liked.

She reached Tiej and began her search. The pseudotrees in Tiej were yellow-brown rather than the gray-brown of Kaal, and their bark looked rougher—more like what she expected of tree bark. Yet people opened them in the way to come and go. She peered through the openings they made when she got the chance. This trip, she felt, would be worthwhile if she could just catch a glimpse of Fukumoto—of any human Awake and aware. Anyone at all.

She had not realized until she actually began looking how important it was for her to find someone. The Oankali had removed her so completely from her own people—only to tell her they planned to use her as a Judas goat. And they had done it all so softly, without brutality, and with patience and gentleness so corrosive of any resolve on her part.

She walked and looked until she was too tired to continue. Finally, discouraged and more disappointed than even she thought reasonable, she sat down against a pseudotree and ate the two oranges she had saved from the lunch she had eaten earlier in Kaal.

Her search, she admitted finally, had been ridiculous. She could have stayed in Kaal, daydreamed about meeting another human, and gotten more satisfaction from it. She could not even be certain how much of Tiej she had covered. There were no signs that she could read. Oankali did not use such things. Their kinship group areas were clearly scent-marked. Each time they opened a wall, they enhanced the local scent markers—or they identified themselves as visitors, members of a different kinship group. Ooloi could change their scent, and did when they left home to mate. Males and females kept the scents they were born with and never lived outside their kinship area. Lilith could not read scent signs. As far as she was concerned Oankali had no odor at all.

That was better, she supposed, than their having a foul odor and forcing her to endure it. But it left her bereft of signposts.

She sighed and decided to go back to Kaal—if she could find her way back. She looked around, confirmed her suspicions that she was already disoriented, lost. She would have to ask someone to aim her toward Kaal.

She got up, moved away from the pseudotree she had been leaning against, and scratched a shallow hole in the soil—it actually was soil, Nikanj had told her. She buried her orange peelings, knowing they would be gone within a day, broken down by tendrils of the ship's own living matter.

Or that was what was supposed to happen.

As she shook out her extra jacket and brushed herself off, the ground around the buried peelings began to darken. The color change recaptured her attention and she watched as the soil slowly became mud and turned the same orange that the peelings had been. This was an effect she had never seen before.

The soil began to smell, to stink in a way she found hard to connect with oranges. It was probably the smell that drew the Oankali. She looked up and found two of them standing near her, their head tentacles swept toward her in a point.

One of them spoke to her, and she tried hard to understand the words—did understand some of them, but not fast enough or completely enough to catch the sense of what was being said.

The orange spot on the ground began to bubble and grow. Lilith stepped away from it. "What's happening?" she asked. "Do either of you speak English?"

The larger of the two Oankali—Lilith thought this one was female—spoke in a language neither Oankali nor English. They confused her at first. Then she realized the language sounded like Japanese.

"Fukumoto-san?" she asked hopefully.

There was another burst of what must have been Japanese, and she shook her head. "I don't understand," she said in Oankali. Those words she had learned quickly through repetition. The only Japanese words that came quickly to mind were stock phrases from a trip she had made years before to Japan: *Konichiwa, arigato gozaimaso, sayonara*...

Other Oankali had gathered to watch the bubbling ground. The orange mass had grown to be about three feet across and almost perfectly circular. It had touched one of the fleshy, ten-tacled pseudoplants and the pseudoplant darkened and lashed about as though in agony. Seeing its violent twisting Lilith forgot that it was not an individual organism. She focused on the fact that it was alive and she had probably caused it pain. She had not merely caused an interesting effect, she had caused harm.

She made herself speak in slow, careful Oankali. "I can't change this," she said, wanting to say that she couldn't repair the damage. "Will you help?"

An ooloi stepped up, touched the orange mud with one of its sensory arms, held the arm still in the mud for several seconds. The bubbling slowed, then stopped. By the time the ooloi with-drew, the bright orange coloring was also beginning to fade to normal.

The ooloi said something to a big female and she answered, gesturing toward Lilith with her head tentacles.

Lilith frowned suspiciously at the ooloi. "Kahguyaht?" she asked, feeling foolish. But the pattern of this ooloi's head tentacles was the same as Kahguyaht's.

The ooloi pointed its head tentacles toward her. "How have you managed," it asked her, "to remain so promising and yet so ignorant?"

Kahguyaht.

"What are you doing here?" she demanded.

Silence. It shifted its attention to the healing ground, seemed to examine it once more, then said something loudly to the gathered people. Most of them went smooth and began to disperse. She suspected it had made a joke at her expense.

"So you finally found something to poison," it said to her.

She shook her head. "I just buried a few orange peelings. Nikanj told me to bury my leavings."

"Bury anything you like in Kaal. When you leave Kaal, and you want to throw something away, give it to an ooloi. And don't leave Kaal again until you're able to speak to people. Why are you here?"

Now she refused to answer.

"Fukumoto-san died recently," it said. "No doubt that's why you heard talk of him. You did hear people talking about him, didn't you?"

After a moment she nodded.

"He was one hundred and twenty years old. He spoke no English."

"He was human," she whispered.

"He lived here awake for almost sixty years. I don't think he saw another human more than twice."

She stepped closer to Kahguyaht, studying it. "And it doesn't occur to you that that was a cruelty?"

"He adjusted very well."

"But still—"

"Can you find your way home, Lilith?"

"We're an adaptable species," she said, refusing to be stopped, "but it's wrong to inflict suffering just because your victim can endure it."

"Learn our language. When you have, one of us will introduce you to someone who, like Fukumoto, has chosen to live and die among us instead of returning to Earth."

"You mean Fukumoto chose—"

"You know almost nothing," it said. "Come on. I'll take you home—and speak to Nikanj about you."

That made her speak up quickly. "Nikanj didn't know where I was going. It might be tracking me right now."

"No, it isn't. I was. Come on."

5

Kahguyaht took her beneath a hill onto a lower level. There it ordered her onto a small, slow-moving flat vehicle. The transport never moved faster than she could have run, but it got them home surprisingly quickly, no doubt taking a more direct route than she had.

Kahguyaht would not speak to her during the trip. She got the impression it was angry, but she didn't really care. She only hoped it wasn't too angry with Nikanj. She had accepted the possibility that she might be punished somehow for her Tiej trip, but she had not intended to make trouble for Nikanj.

Once they were home, Kahguyaht took Nikanj into the room she and Nikanj shared, leaving her in what she had come to think of as the dining room. Jdahya and Tediin were there, eating Oankali food this time, the products of plants that would have been deadly to her.

She sat down silently and after a while, Jdahya brought her nuts, fruit, and some Oankali food that had a vaguely meaty taste and texture, though it was actually a plant product.

"Just how much trouble am I in?" she asked as he handed her her dishes.

He smoothed his tentacles. "Not so much, Lilith."

She frowned. "I got the impression Kahguyaht was angry."

Now the smooth tentacles became irregular, raised knots. "That was not exactly anger. It is concerned about Nikanj."

"Because I went to Tiej?"

"No." His lumps became larger, uglier. "Because this is a hard time for it—and for you. Nikanj has left you for it to stumble over."

"What?"

Tediin said something in rapid, incomprehensible Oankali, and Jdahya answered her. The two of them spoke together for a few minutes. Then Tediin spoke in English to Lilith.

"Kahguyaht must teach . . . same-sex child. You see?"

"And I'm part of the lesson," Lilith answered bitterly.

"Nikanj or Kahguyaht," Tediin said softly.

Lilith frowned, looked to Jdahya for an explanation.

"She means if you and Nikanj weren't supposed to be teaching each other, you would be learning from Kahguyaht."

Lilith shuddered. "Good god," she whispered. And seconds later, "Why couldn't it be you?"

"Ooloi generally handle the teaching of new species."

"Why? If I have to be taught, I'd rather you did it."

His head tentacles smoothed.

"You like him or Kahguyaht?" Tediin asked. Her unpracticed English, acquired just from hearing others speak was much better than Lilith's Oankali.

"No offense," Lilith said, "but I prefer Jdahya."

"Good," Tediin said, her own head smooth, though Lilith did not understand why. "You like him or Nikanj?"

Lilith opened her mouth, then hesitated. Jdahya had left her completely to Nikanj for so long—deliberately, no doubt. And Nikanj . . . Nikanj was appealing—probably because it was a child. It was no more responsible for the thing that was to happen to the remnants of humanity than she was. It was simply doing—or trying to do—what the adults around it said should be done. Fellow victim?

No, not a victim. Just a child, appealing in spite of itself. And she liked it in spite of herself.

"You see?" Tediin asked, smooth all over now.

"I see." She took a deep breath. "I see that everyone including Nikanj wants me to prefer Nikanj. Well you win. I do." She turned to Jdahya. "You people are manipulative as hell, aren't you?"

Jdahya concentrated on eating.

"Was I that much of a burden?" she asked him.

He did not answer.

"Will you help me to be less of a burden in one way, at least?"

He aimed some of his tentacles at her. "What do you want?"

"Writing materials. Paper. Pencils or pens—whatever you've got."

"No."

There was no give behind the refusal. He was part of the family conspiracy to keep her ignorant—while trying as hard as they could to educate her. Insane.

She spread both hands before her, shaking her head. *"Why?"*

"Ask Nikanj."

"I have! It won't tell me."

"Perhaps it will now. Have you finished eating?"

"I've had enough—in more ways than one."

"Come on. I'll open the wall for you."

She unfolded herself from her platform and followed him to the wall.

"Nikanj can help you remember without writing," he told her as he touched the wall with several head tentacles.

"How?"

"Ask it."

She stepped through the hole as soon as it was large enough, and found herself intruding on the two ooloi who refused to notice her beyond the automatic sweep of some of their head tentacles. They were talking—arguing—in very fast Oankali. She was, no doubt, the reason for their dispute.

She looked back, hoping to step back through the wall and leave them. Let one of them tell her later what had been decided. She didn't imagine it would be anything she would be eager to hear. But the wall had sealed itself—abnormally quickly.

Nikanj seemed to be holding its own, at least. At one point, it beckoned to her with a sharp movement of head tentacles. She moved to stand beside it, willing to offer whatever moral support she could against Kahguyaht.

Kahguyaht stopped whatever it had been saying and faced her. "You haven't understood us at all, have you?" it asked in English.

"No," she admitted.

"Do you understand me now?" it asked in slow Oankali.

"Yes."

Kahguyaht turned its attention back to Nikanj and spoke rapidly. Straining to understand, Lilith thought it said something close to, "Well, at least we know she's capable of learning."

"I'm capable of learning even faster with paper and pencil," she said. "But with or without them, I'm capable of telling you what I think of you in any one of three human languages!"

Kahguyaht said nothing for several seconds. Finally it turned, opened a wall, and left the room.

When the wall had closed, Nikanj lay down on the bed and crossed its arms over its chest, hugging itself.

"Are you all right?" she asked.

"What are the other two languages?" it asked softly.

She managed a smile. "Spanish and German. I used to speak a little German. I still know a few obscenities."

"You are . . . not fluent?"

"I am in Spanish."

"But why not in German?"

"Because it's been years since I've studied it or spoken it—years before the war, I mean. We humans...if we don't use a language, we forget it."

"No. You don't."

She looked at its tightly contracted body tentacles and decided it did not look happy. It really was concerned over her failure to learn quickly and retain everything. "Are you going to let me have writing materials?" she asked.

"No. It will be done our way. Not yours."

"It ought to be done the way that works. But what the hell. You want to spend two or three times as long teaching me, you go right ahead."

"I don't."

She shrugged, not caring whether it missed the gesture or failed to understand it.

"Ooan was upset with me, Lilith, not with you."

"But because of me. Because I'm not learning fast enough."

"No. Because...because I'm not teaching you as it thinks I should. It fears for me."

"Fears...? Why?"

"Come here. Sit here. I will tell you."

After a time, she shrugged again and went to sit beside it.

"I'm growing up," it told her. "Ooan wants me to hurry with you so that you can be given your work and I can mate."

"You mean...the faster I learn, the sooner you mate?"

"Yes. Until I have taught you, shown that I can teach you, I won't be considered ready to mate."

There it was. She was not just its experimental animal. She was, in some way she did not fully understand, its final exam. She sighed and shook her head. "Did you ask for me Nikanj, or did we just get dumped on one another?"

It said nothing. It doubled one of its arms backward in a way natural to it, but still startling to Lilith, and rubbed its armpit. She tilted her head to one side to examine the place it was rubbing.

"Do you grow the sensory arms after you've mated or before?" she asked.

"They will come soon whether I mate or not."

"*Should* they grow in after you're mated?"

"Mates like them to come in afterward. Males and females mature more quickly than ooloi. They like to feel that they have . . . how do you say? Helped their ooloi out of childhood."

"Helped raise them," Lilith said, "or helped rear them."

". . . rear?"

"The word has multiple meanings."

"Oh. There's no logic to such things."

"There probably is, but you'd need an etymologist to explain it. Is there going to be trouble between you and your mates?"

"I don't know. I hope not. I'll go to them when I can. I've told them that." It paused. "Now I must tell you something."

"What?"

"Ooan wanted me to act and say nothing . . . to . . . surprise you. I won't do that."

"*What!*"

"I must make small changes—a few small changes. I must help you reach your memories as you need them."

"What do you mean? What is it you want to change?"

"Very small things. In the end, there will be a tiny alteration in your brain chemistry."

She touched her forehead in an unconsciously protective gesture. "Brain chemistry?" she whispered.

"I would like to wait, do it when I'm mature. I could make it pleasurable for you then. It should be pleasurable. But Ooan . . . I understand what it feels. It says I have to change you now."

"I don't want to be changed!"

"You would sleep through it the way you did when Ooan Jdahya corrected your tumor."

"Ooan Jdahya? Jdahya's ooloi parent did that? Not Kahguyaht?"

"Yes. It was done before my parents were mated."

"Good." No reason at all to be grateful to Kahguyaht.

"Lilith?" Nikanj laid a many-fingered hand—a sixteen-fingered hand—on her arm. "It will be like this. A touch. Then a . . . a small puncture. That's all you'll feel. When you wake up the change will be made."

"*I don't want to be changed!*"

There was a long silence. Finally it said, "Are you afraid?"

"I don't have a disease! Forgetting things is normal for most humans! I don't need anything done to my brain!"

"Would it be so bad to remember better? To remember the way Sharad did—the way I do?"

"What's frightening is the idea of being tampered with." She drew a deep breath. "Listen, no part of me is more definitive of who I am than my brain. I don't want—"

"Who you are won't be changed. I'm not old enough to make the experience pleasant for you, but I'm old enough to function as an ooloi in this way. If I were unfit, others would have noticed by now."

"If everyone's so sure you're fit, why do you have to test yourself with me?"

It refused to answer, remained silent for several minutes. When it tried to pull her down beside it, she broke away and got up, paced around the room. Its head tentacles followed her with more than their usual lazy sweep. They kept sharply pointed at her and eventually she fled to the bathroom to end the staring.

There, she sat on the floor, arms folded, hands clutching her forearms.

What would happen now? Would Nikanj follow orders and surprise her sometime when she was asleep? Would it turn her over to Kahguyaht? Or would they both—please heaven—*let her alone*!

6

She had no idea how much time passed. She found herself thinking of Sam and Ayre, her husband and son, both taken from her before the Oankali, before the war, before she realized how easily her life—any human life—could be destroyed.

There had been a carnival—a cheap little vacant-lot carnival with rides and noise and scabby ponies. Sam had decided to take Ayre to see it while Lilith spent time with her pregnant sister. It had been an ordinary Saturday on a broad, dry street in bright sunshine. A young girl, just learning to drive, had rammed head-on into Sam's car. She had swerved to the wrong side of the road, had perhaps somehow lost control of the car she was driving. She'd had only a learner's permit and was not supposed to drive alone. She died for her mistake. Ayre died—was dead when the ambulance arrived, though paramedics tried to revive him.

Sam only half died.

He had head injuries—brain damage. It took him three months to finish what the accident had begun. Three months to die.

He was conscious some of the time—more or less—but he did

not know anyone. His parents came from New York to be with him. They were Nigerians who had lived in the United States long enough for their son to be born and grow up there. Still, they had not been pleased at his marriage to Lilith. They had let Sam grow up as an American, but had sent him to visit their families in Lagos when they could. They had hoped he would marry a Yoruban girl. They had never seen their grandchild. Now they never would.

And Sam did not know them.

He was their only son, but he stared through them as he stared through Lilith, his eyes empty of recognition, empty of him. Sometimes Lilith sat alone with him, touched him, gained the empty attention of those eyes briefly. But the man himself had already gone. Perhaps he was with Ayre, or caught between her and Ayre—between this world and the next.

Or was he aware, but isolated in some part of his mind that could not make contact with anyone outside—trapped in the narrowest, most absolute solitary confinement—until, mercifully, his heart stopped.

That was brain damage—one form of brain damage. There were other forms, many worse. She saw them in the hospital over the months of Sam's dying.

He was lucky to have died so quickly.

She had never dared speak that thought aloud. It had come to her even as she wept for him. It came to her again now. He was lucky to have died so quickly.

Would she be equally lucky?

If the Oankali damaged her brain, would they have the decency to let her die—or would they keep her alive, a prisoner, permanently locked away in that ultimate solitary confinement?

She became aware abruptly that Nikanj had come into the bathroom silently and sat down opposite her. It had never intruded on her this way before. She stared at it, outraged.

"It isn't my ability to cope with your physiology that anyone questions," it said softly. "If I couldn't do that, my defects would have been noticed long ago."

"Get out of here!" she shouted. "Get away from me!"

It did not move. It continued to speak in the same soft voice. "Ooan says humans won't be worth talking to for at least a generation." Its tentacles writhed. "I don't know how to be with someone I can't talk to."

"Brain damage isn't going to improve my conversation," she said bitterly.

"I would rather damage my own brain than yours. I won't damage either." It hesitated. "You know you must accept me or Ooan."

She said nothing.

"Ooan is an adult. It can give you pleasure. And it is not as . . . as angry as it seems."

"I'm not looking for pleasure. I don't even know what you're talking about. I just want to be let alone."

"Yes. But you must trust me or let Ooan surprise you when it's tired of waiting."

"You won't do that yourself—won't just spring it on me?"

"No."

"Why not?"

"There's something wrong with doing it that way—surprising people. It's . . . treating them as though they aren't people, as though they aren't intelligent."

Lilith laughed bitterly. "Why should you suddenly start to worry about that?"

"Do you want me to surprise you?"

"Of course not!"

Silence.

After a while, she got up and went to the bed platform. She lay down and eventually managed to fall asleep.

She dreamed of Sam and awoke in a cold sweat. Empty, empty eyes. Her head ached. Nikanj had stretched out beside her as usual. It looked limp and dead. How would it be to awaken with

Kahguyaht there instead, lying beside her like a grotesque lover instead of an unhappy child? She shuddered, fear and disgust almost overwhelming her. She lay still for several minutes, calming herself, forcing herself to make a decision, then to act on it before fear could silence her.

"Wake up!" she said harshly to Nikanj. The raw sound of her own voice startled her. "Wake up and do whatever it is you claim you have to do. Get it over with."

Nikanj sat up instantly, rolled her over onto her side and pulled away the jacket she had been sleeping in to expose her back and neck. Before she could complain or change her mind, it began.

On the back of her neck, she felt the promised touch, a harder pressure, then the puncture. It hurt more than she had expected, but the pain ended quickly. For a few seconds she drifted in painless semiconsciousness.

Then there were confused memories, dreams, finally nothing.

7

When she awoke, at ease and only mildly confused, she found herself fully clothed and alone. She lay still, wondering what Nikanj had done to her. Was she changed? How? Had it finished with her? She could not move at first, but by the time this penetrated her confusion, she found the paralysis wearing off. She was able to use her muscles again. She sat up carefully just in time to see Nikanj coming through a wall.

Its gray skin was as smooth as polished marble as it climbed onto the bed beside her. "You're so complex," it said, taking both her hands. It did not point its head tentacles at her in the usual way, but placed its head close to hers and touched her with them. Then it sat back, pointing at her. It occurred to her distantly that this behavior was unusual and should have alarmed her. She frowned and tried to feel alarmed.

"You're filled with so much life and death and potential for change," Nikanj continued. "I understand now why some people took so long to get over their fear of your kind."

She focused on it. "Maybe it's because I'm still drugged out of my mind, but I don't know what you're talking about."

"Yes. You'll never really know. But when I'm mature, I'll try to show you a little." It brought its head close to hers again and touched her face and burrowed into her hair with its tentacles.

"What are you *doing*?" she asked, still not really disturbed.

"Making sure you're all right. I don't like what I had to do to you."

"What did you do? I don't feel any different—except a little high."

"You understand me."

It dawned on her slowly that Nikanj had come to her speaking Oankali and she had responded in kind—had responded without really thinking. The language seemed natural to her, as easy to understand as English. She remembered all that she had been taught, all that she had picked up on her own. It was even easy for her to spot the gaps in her knowledge—words and expressions she knew in English, but could not translate into Oankali; bits of Oankali grammar that she had not really understood; certain Oankali words that had no English translation, but whose meaning she had grasped.

Now she was alarmed, pleased, and frightened. She stood slowly, testing her legs, finding them unsteady, but functional. She tried to clear the fog from her mind so that she could examine herself and trust her findings.

"I'm glad the family decided to put the two of us together," Nikanj was saying. "I didn't want to work with you. I tried to get out of it. I was afraid. All I could think of was how easy it would be for me to fail and perhaps damage you."

"You mean...you mean you weren't sure of what you were doing just now?"

"That? Of course I was sure. And your 'just now' took a long time. Much longer than you usually sleep."

"But what did you mean about failing—"

"I was afraid I could never convince you to trust me enough to let me show you what I could do—show you that I wouldn't hurt you. I was afraid I would make you hate me. For an ooloi to do that...it would be very bad. Worse than I can tell you."

"But Kahguyaht doesn't think so."

"Ooan says humans—any new trade partner species—can't be treated the way we must treat each other. It's right up to a point. I just think it goes too far. We were bred to work with you. We're Dinso. We should be able to find ways through most of our differences."

"Coercion," she said bitterly. "That's the way you've found."

"No. Ooan would have done that. I couldn't have. I would have gone to Ahajas and Dichaan and refused to mate with them. I would have looked for mates among the Akjai since they'll have no direct contact with humans."

It smoothed its tentacles again. "But now when I go to Ahajas and Dichaan, it will be to mate—and you'll go with me. We'll send you to your work when you're ready. And you'll be able to help me through my final metamorphosis." It rubbed its armpit. "Will you help?"

She looked away from it. "What do you want me to do?"

"Just stay with me. There will be times when having Ahajas and Dichaan near me would be tormenting. I would be...sexually stimulated, and unable to do anything about it. Very stimulated. You can't do that to me. Your scent, your touch is different, neutral."

Thank god, she thought.

"It would be bad for me to be alone while I change. We need others close to us, more at that time than at any other."

She wondered what it would look like with its second pair of arms, what it would be like as a mature being. More like Kahguyaht? Or maybe more like Jdahya and Tediin. How much did sex determine personality among the Oankali? She shook her head. Stupid question. She did not know how much sex determined personality even among human beings.

"The arms," she said, "they're sexual organs, aren't they?"

"No," Nikanj told her. "They protect sexual organs: the sensory hands."

"But . . ." She frowned. "Kahguyaht doesn't have anything like a hand at the end of its sensory arms." In fact, it had nothing at all at the end of its sensory arms. There was only a blunt cap of hard, cool skin—like a large callus.

"The hand is inside. Ooan will show you if you ask."

"Never mind."

It smoothed. "I'll show you myself—when I have something to show. Will you stay with me while they grow?"

Where else was she going? "Yes. Just make sure I know anything I might need to know about you and them before they start."

"Yes. I'll sleep most of the time, but still, I'll need someone there. If you're there, I'll know and I'll be all right. You . . . you might have to feed me."

"That's all right." There was nothing unusual about the way Oankali ate. Not on the surface, anyway. Several of their front teeth were pointed, but their size was well within the human range. She had, twice, on her walks, seen Oankali females extend their tongues all the way down to their throat orifices, but normally, the long gray tongues were kept inside the mouths and used as humans used tongues.

Nikanj made a sound of relief—a rubbing together of body tentacles in a way that sounded like stiff paper being crumpled. "Good," it said. "Mates know what we feel when they stay near us, they know the frustration. Sometimes they think it's funny."

Lilith was surprised to find herself smiling. "It is, sort of."

"Only for the tormentors. With you there, they'll torment me less. But before all that . . ." It stopped, aimed a loose point at her. "Before that, I'll try to find an English-speaking human for you. One as much like you as possible. Ooan will not stand in the way of your meeting one now."

8

A day, Lilith had decided long ago, was what her body said it was. Now it became what her newly improved memory said it was as well. A day was long activity, then long sleep. And now, she remembered every day that she had been awake. And she counted the days as Nikanj searched for an English-speaking human for her. It went alone to interview several. Nothing she said could induce it to take her along or at least tell her about the people it had talked to.

Finally Kahguyaht found someone. Nikanj had a look, then accepted its parent's judgment. "It will be one of the humans who has chosen to stay here," Nikanj told her.

She had expected that from what Kahguyaht had said earlier. It was still hard to believe, though. "Is it a man or a woman?" she asked.

"Male. A man."

"How . . . how could he not want to go home?"

"He's been here among us for a long time. He's only a little older than you are, but he was Awakened young and kept Awake. A Toaht family wanted him and he was willing to stay with them."

Willing? What kind of choice had they given him? Probably the same kind they had given her, and he had been years younger. Only a boy, perhaps. What was he now? What had they created from their human raw material? "Take me to him," she said.

For the second time, Lilith rode one of the flat transports through the crowded corridors. This transport moved no faster than the first one she had ridden. Nikanj did not steer it except occasionally to touch one side or the other with head tentacles to make it turn. They rode for perhaps a half hour before she and Nikanj dismounted. Nikanj touched the transport with several head tentacles to send it away.

"Won't we need it to go back?" she asked.

"We'll get another," Nikanj said. "Maybe you'll want to stay here awhile."

She looked at it sharply. What was this? Step two of the captive breeding program? She glanced around at the retreating transport. Maybe she had been too quick to agree to see this man. If he were thoroughly enough divorced from his humanity to want to stay here, who knew what else he might be willing to do.

"It's an animal," Nikanj said.

"What?"

"The thing we rode. It's an animal. A tilio. Did you know?"

"No, but I'm not surprised. How does it move?"

"On a thin film of a very slippery substance."

"Slime?"

Nikanj hesitated. "I know that word. It's...inadequate, but it will serve. I've seen Earth animals who use slime to move. They are inefficient compared to the tilio, but I can see similarities. We shaped the tilio from larger, more efficient creatures."

"It doesn't leave a slime trail."

"No. The tilio has an organ at its rear that collects most of what it spreads. The ship takes in the rest."

"Nikanj, do you ever build machinery? Tamper with metal and plastic instead of living things?"

"We do that when we have to. We...don't like it. There's no trade."

She sighed. "Where is the man? What's his name, by the way?"

"Paul Titus."

Well, that didn't tell her anything. Nikanj took her to a nearby wall and stroked it with three long head tentacles. The wall changed from off-white to dull red, but it did not open.

"What's wrong?" Lilith asked.

"Nothing. Someone will open it soon. It's better not to go in if you don't know the quarters well. Better to let the people who live there know you are waiting to go in."

"So what you did is like knocking," she said, and was about to demonstrate knocking for it when the wall began to open. There was a man on the other side, dressed only in a pair of ragged shorts.

She stared at him. A human being—tall, stocky, as dark as she was, clean shaved. He looked wrong to her at first—alien and strange, yet familiar, compelling. He was beautiful. Even if he had been bent and old, he would have been beautiful.

She glanced at Nikanj, saw that it had become statue-still. It apparently had no intention of moving or speaking soon.

"Paul Titus?" she asked.

The man opened his mouth, closed it, swallowed, nodded. "Yes," he said finally.

The sound of his voice—deep, definitely human, definitely male—fed a hunger in her. "I'm Lilith Iyapo," she said. "Did you know we were coming or is this a surprise to you?"

"Come in," he said, touching the wall opening. "I knew. And you don't know how welcome you are." He glanced at Nikanj. "Kaalnikanj oo Jdahyatediinkahguyaht aj Dinso, come in. Thank you for bringing her."

Nikanj made a complex gesture of greeting with its head

tentacles and stepped into the room—the usual bare room. Nikanj went to a platform in a corner and folded itself into a sitting position on it. Lilith chose a platform that allowed her to sit almost with her back to Nikanj. She wanted to forget it was there, observing, since it clearly did not intend to do anything but observe. She wanted to give all her attention to the man. He was a miracle—a human being, an adult who spoke English and looked more than a little like one of her dead brothers.

His accent was as American as her own and her mind overflowed with questions. Where had he lived before the war? How had he survived? Who was he beyond a name? Had he seen any other humans? Had he—

"Have you really decided to stay here?" she demanded abruptly. It was not the first question she had intended to ask.

The man sat cross-legged in the middle of a platform large enough to be a serving table or a bed.

"I was fourteen when they woke me up," he said. "Everyone I knew was dead. The Oankali said they'd send me back to Earth eventually if I wanted to go. But once I had been here for a while, I knew this was where I wanted to be. There's nothing that I care about left on Earth."

"Everyone lost relatives and friends," she said. "As far as I know, I'm the only member of my family still alive."

"I saw my father, my brother—their bodies. I don't know what happened to my mother. I was dying myself when the Oankali found me. They tell me I was. I don't remember, but I believe them."

"I don't remember their finding me either." She twisted around. "Nikanj, did your people do something to us to keep us from remembering?"

Nikanj seemed to rouse itself slowly. "They had to," it said. "Humans who were allowed to remember their rescue became uncontrollable. Some died in spite of our care."

Not surprising. She tried to imagine what she had done when

in the middle of the shock of realizing that her home, her family, her friends, her world were all destroyed. She was confronted with a collecting party of Oankali. She must have believed she had lost her mind. Or perhaps she did lose it for a while. It was a miracle that she had not killed herself trying to escape them.

"Have you eaten?" the man asked.

"Yes," she said, suddenly shy.

There was a long silence. "What were you before?" he asked. "I mean, did you work?"

"I had gone back to school," she said. "I was majoring in anthropology." She laughed bitterly. "I suppose I could think of this as fieldwork—but how the hell do I get out of the field?"

"Anthropology?" he said, frowning. "Oh yeah, I remember reading some stuff by Margaret Mead before the war. So you wanted to study what? People in tribes?"

"Different people anyway. People who didn't do things the way we did them."

"Where were you from?" he asked.

"Los Angeles."

"Oh, yeah. Hollywood, Beverly Hills, movie stars...I always wanted to go there."

One trip would have shattered his illusions. "And you were from...?"

"Denver."

"Where were you when the war started?"

"Grand Canyon—shooting the rapids. That was the first time we'd ever really done anything, gone anywhere really good. We froze afterward. And my father used to say nuclear winter was nothing but politics."

"I was in the Andes in Peru," she said, "hiking toward Machu Picchu. I hadn't been anywhere either, really. At least not since my husband—"

"You were married?"

"Yes. But he and my son...were killed—before the war, I

mean. I had gone on a study tour of Peru. Part of going back to college. A friend talked me into taking that trip. She went too... and died."

"Yeah." He shrugged uncomfortably. "I was sort of looking forward to going to college myself. But I had just gotten through the tenth grade when everything blew up."

"The Oankali must have taken a lot of people out of the southern hemisphere," she said, thinking. "I mean we froze too, but I heard the southern freeze was spotty. A lot of people must have survived."

He drifted into his own thoughts. "It's funny," he said. "You started out years older than me, but I've been Awake for so long... I guess I'm older than you are now."

"I wonder how many people they were able to get out of the northern hemisphere—other than the soldiers and politicians whose shelters hadn't been bombed open." She turned to ask Nikanj and saw that it was gone.

"He left a couple of minutes ago," the man said. "They can move really quietly and fast when they want to."

"But—"

"Hey, don't worry. He'll come back. And if he doesn't, I can open the walls or get food for you if you want anything."

"You can?"

"Sure. They changed my body chemistry a little when I decided to stay. Now the walls open for me just like they do for them."

"Oh." She wasn't sure she liked being left with the man this way—especially if he was telling the truth. If he could open walls and she could not, she was his prisoner.

"They're probably watching us," she said. And she spoke in Oankali, imitating Nikanj's voice: "Now let's see what they'll do if they think they're alone."

The man laughed. "They probably are. Not that it matters."

"It matters to me. I'd rather have watchers where I can keep an eye on them, too."

The laughter again. "Maybe he thought we might be kind of inhibited if he stayed around."

She deliberately ignored the implications of this. "Nikanj isn't male," she said. "It's ooloi."

"Yeah, I know. But doesn't yours seem male to you?"

She thought about that. "No. I guess I've taken their word for what they are."

"When they woke me up, I thought the ooloi acted like men and women while the males and females acted like eunuchs. I never really lost the habit of thinking of ooloi as male or female."

That, Lilith thought, was a foolish way for someone who had decided to spend his life among the Oankali to think—a kind of deliberate, persistent ignorance.

"You wait until yours is mature," he said. "You'll see what I mean. They change when they've grown those two extra things." He lifted an eyebrow. "You know what those things are?"

"Yes," she said. He probably knew more, but she realized that she did not want to encourage him to talk about sex; not even Oankali sex.

"Then you know they're not arms, no matter what they tell us to call them. When those things grow in, ooloi let everyone know who's in charge. The Oankali need a little women's and men's lib up here."

She wet her lips. "It wants me to help it through its metamorphosis."

"Help it. What did you tell it?"

"I said I would. It didn't sound like much."

He laughed. "It isn't hard. Puts them in debt to you, though. Not a bad idea to have someone powerful in debt to you. It proves you can be trusted, too. They'll be grateful and you'll be a lot freer. Maybe they'll fix things so you can open your own walls."

"Is that what happened with you?"

He moved restlessly. "Sort of." He got up from his platform, touched all ten fingers to the wall behind him, and waited as the wall opened. Behind the wall was a food storage cabinet of the kind she had often seen at home. Home? Well, what else was it? She lived there.

He took out sandwiches, something that looked like a small pie—that was a pie—and something that looked like French fries.

Lilith stared at the food in surprise. She had been content with the foods the Oankali had given her—good variety and flavor once she began staying with Nikanj's family. She had missed meat occasionally, but once the Oankali made it clear they would neither kill animals for her nor allow her to kill them while she lived with them, she had not minded much. She had never been a particular eater, had never thought of asking the Oankali to make the food they prepared look more like what she was used to.

"Sometimes," he said, "I want a hamburger so bad I dream about them. You know the kind with cheese and bacon and dill pickles and—"

"What's in your sandwich?" she asked.

"Fake meat. Mostly soybean, I guess. And quat."

Quatasayasha, the cheeselike Oankali vegetable. "I eat a lot of quat myself," she said.

"Then have some. You don't really want to sit there and watch me eat, do you?"

She smiled and took the sandwich he offered. She was not hungry at all, but eating with him was companionable and safe. She took a few of his French fries, too.

"Cassava," he told her. "Tastes like potatoes, though. I'd never heard of cassava before I got it here. Some tropical plant the Oankali are raising."

"I know. They mean for those of us who go back to Earth to raise it and use it. You can make flour from it and use it like wheat flour."

He stared at her until she frowned. "What's the matter?" she asked.

His gaze slid away from her and he stared downward at

nothing. "Have you really thought about what it will be like?" he asked softly. "I mean...Stone Age! Digging in the ground with a stick for roots, maybe eating bugs, rats. Rats survived, I hear. Cattle and horses didn't. Dogs didn't. But rats did."

"I know."

"You said you had a baby."

"My son. Dead."

"Yeah. Well, I'll bet when he was born, you were in a hospital with doctors and nurses all around helping you and giving you shots for the pain. How would you like to do it in a jungle with nothing around but bugs and rats and people who feel sorry for you but can't do shit to help you?"

"I had natural childbirth," she said. "It wasn't any fun, but it went okay."

"What do you mean? No painkiller?"

"None. No hospital either. Just something called a birthing center—a place for pregnant women who don't like the idea of being treated as though they were sick."

He shook his head, smiled crookedly. "I wonder how many women they had to go through before they came up with you. A lot, I'll bet. You're probably just what they want in ways I haven't even thought of."

His words bit more deeply into her than she let him see. With all the questioning and testing she had gone through, the two and a half years of round-the-clock observation—the Oankali must know her in some ways better than any human being ever had. They knew how she would react to just about everything they put her through. And they knew how to manipulate her, maneuver her into doing whatever they wanted. Of course they knew she had had certain practical experiences they considered important. If she had had an especially difficult time giving birth—if she had had to be taken to the hospital in spite of her wishes, if she had needed a caesarean—they would probably have passed over her to someone else.

"Why are you going back?" Titus asked. "Why do you want to spend your life living like a cavewoman?"

"I don't."

His eyes widened. "Then why don't you—"

"We don't have to forget what we know," she said. She smiled to herself. "I couldn't forget if I wanted to. We don't have to go back to the Stone Age. We'll have a lot of hard work, sure, but with what the Oankali will teach us and what we already know, we'll at least have a chance."

"They don't teach for free! They didn't save us out of kindness! It's all trade with them. You know what you'll have to pay down there!"

"What have you paid to stay up here?"

Silence.

He ate several more bites of food. "The price," he said softly, "is just the same. When they're finished with us there won't be any real human beings left. Not here. Not on the ground. What the bombs started, they'll finish."

"I don't believe it has to be like that."

"Yeah. But then, you haven't been Awake long."

"Earth is a big place. Even if parts of it are uninhabitable, it's still a damn big place."

He looked at her with such open, undisguised pity that she drew back angrily. "Do you think they don't know what a big place it is?" he asked.

"If I thought that, I wouldn't have said anything to you and whoever's listening. They know how I feel."

"And they know how to make you change your mind."

"Not about that. Never about that."

"Like I said, you haven't been Awake long."

What had they done to him, she wondered. Was it just that they had kept him Awake so long—Awake and for the most part without human companions? Awake and aware that everything he had ever known was dead, that nothing he could have on Earth now could measure up to his former life. How had that gone down with a fourteen-year-old?

"If you wanted it," he said, "they'd let you stay here...with me."

"What, permanently?"

"Yeah."

"No."

He put down the small pie that he had not offered to share with her and came over to her. "You know they expect you to say no," he said. "They brought you here so you could say it and they could be sure all over again that they were right about you." He stood tall and broad, too close to her, too intense. She realized unhappily that she was afraid of him. "Surprise them," he continued softly. "Don't do what they expect—just for once. Don't let them play you like a puppet."

He had put his hands on her shoulders. When she drew back reflexively, he held on to her in a grip that was almost painful.

She sat still and stared at him. Her mother had looked at her the way she was looking at him now. She had caught herself giving her son the same look when she thought he was doing something he knew was wrong. How much of Titus was still fourteen, still the boy the Oankali had awakened and impressed and enticed and inducted into their own ranks?

He let her go. "You could be safe here," he said softly. "Down on Earth...how long will you live? How long will you want to live? Even if you don't forget what you know, other people will forget. Some of them will want to be cavemen—drag you around, put you in a harem, beat the shit out of you." He shook his head. "Tell me I'm wrong. Sit there and tell me I'm wrong."

She looked away from him, realizing that he was probably right. What was waiting for her on Earth? Misery? Subjugation? Death? Of course there were people who would toss aside civilized restraint. Not at first, perhaps, but eventually—as soon as they realized they could get away with it.

He took her by the shoulders again and this time tried

awkwardly to kiss her. It was like what she could recall of being kissed by an eager boy. That didn't bother her. And she caught herself responding to him in spite of her fear. But there was more to this than grabbing a few minutes of pleasure.

"Look," she said when he drew back. "I'm not interested in putting on a show for the Oankali."

"What difference do they make? It's not like human beings were watching us."

"It is to me."

"Lilith," he said, shaking his head, "they will *always* be watching."

"The other thing I'm not interested in doing is giving them a human child to tamper with."

"You probably already have."

Surprise and sudden fear kept her silent, but her hand moved to her abdomen where her jacket concealed her scar.

"They didn't have enough of us for what they call a normal trade," he said. "Most of the ones they have will be Dinso—people who want to go back to Earth. They didn't have enough for the Toaht. They had to make more."

"While we slept? Somehow they—"

"Somehow!" he hissed. "*Anyhow*! They took stuff from men and women who didn't even know each other and put it together and made babies in women who never knew the mother or the father of their kid—and who maybe never got to know the kid. Or maybe they grew the baby in another kind of animal. They have animals they can adjust to—to incubate human fetuses, as they say. Or maybe they don't even worry about men and women. Maybe they just scrape some skin from one person and make babies out of it—cloning, you know. Or maybe they use one of their prints—and don't ask me what a print is. But if they've got one of you, they can use it to make another you even if you've been dead for a hundred years and they haven't got anything at all left of your body. And that's just the start. They can make people in ways I don't even know how to talk about. Only thing they can't do, it seems, is let us alone. Let us do it our own way."

His hands were almost gentle on her. "At least they haven't until now." He shook her abruptly. "You know how many kids I got? They say, 'Your genetic material has been used in over seventy children.' And I've never even seen a woman in all the time I've been here."

He stared at her for several seconds and she feared him and pitied him and longed to be away from him. The first human being she had seen in years and all she could do was long to be away from him.

Yet it would do no good to fight him physically. She was tall, had always thought of herself as strong, but he was much bigger—six-four, six-five, and stocky.

"They've had two hundred and fifty years to fool around with us," she said. "Maybe we can't stop them, but we don't have to help them."

"The hell with them." He tried to unfasten her jacket.

"*No!*" she shouted, deliberately startling him. "Animals get treated like this. Put a stallion and a mare together until they mate, then send them back to their owners. What do they care? They're just animals!"

He tore her jacket off then fumbled with her pants.

She threw her weight against him suddenly and managed to shove him away.

He stumbled backward for several steps, caught himself, came at her again.

Screaming at him, she swung her legs over the platform she had been sitting on and came down standing on the opposite side of it. Now it was between them. He strode around it.

She sat on it again and swung her legs over, keeping it between them.

"Don't make yourself their dog!" she pleaded. "Don't do this!"

He kept coming, too far gone to care what she said. He actually seemed to be enjoying himself. He cut her off from the bed by coming over it himself. He cornered her against a wall.

"How many times have they made you do this before?" she asked desperately. "Did you have a sister back on Earth? Would you know her now? Maybe they've made you do it with your sister."

He caught her arm, jerked her to him.

"Maybe they've made you do it with your mother!" she shouted.

He froze and she prayed she had hit a nerve.

"Your mother," she repeated. "You haven't seen her since you were fourteen. How would you know if they brought her to you and you—"

He hit her.

Staggered by shock and pain, she collapsed against him and he half pushed and half threw her away as though he had found himself clutching something loathsome.

She fell hard, but was not quite unconscious when he came to stand over her.

"I never got to do it before," he whispered. "Never once with a woman. But who knows who they mixed the stuff with." He paused, stared at her where she had fallen. "They said I could do it with you. They said you could stay here if you wanted to. And you had to go and mess it up!" He kicked her hard. The last sound she heard before she lost consciousness was his ragged, shouted curse.

9

She awoke to voices—Oankali near her, not touching her. Nikanj and one other.

"Go away now," Nikanj was saying. "She is regaining consciousness."

"Perhaps I should stay," the other said softly. Kahguyaht. She had thought once that all Oankali sounded alike with their quiet androgynous voices, but now she couldn't mistake Kahguyaht's deceptively gentle tones. "You may need help with her," it said.

Nikanj said nothing.

After a while Kahguyaht rustled its tentacles and said, "I'll leave. You're growing up faster than I thought. Perhaps she's good for you after all."

She was able to see it step through a wall and leave. Not until it was gone did she become aware of the aching of her own body—her jaw, her side, her head, and in particular, her left arm. There was no sharp pain, nothing startling. Only dull, throbbing pain, especially noticeable when she moved.

"Be still," Nikanj told her. "Your body is still healing. The pain will be gone soon."

She turned her face away from it, ignoring the pain.

There was a long silence. Finally it said, "We didn't know." It stopped, corrected itself. "I didn't know how the male would behave. He has never lost control so completely before. He hasn't lost control at all for several years."

"You cut him off from his own kind," she said through swollen lips. "You kept him away from women for how long? Fifteen years? More? In some ways you kept him fourteen for all those years."

"He was content with his Oankali family until he met you."

"What did he know? You never let him see anybody else!"

"It wasn't necessary. His family took care of him."

She stared at it, feeling more strongly than ever, the difference between them—the unbridgeable alienness of Nikanj. She could spend hours talking to it in its own language and fail to communicate. It could do the same with her, although it could force her to obey whether she understood or not. Or it could turn her over to others who would use force against her.

"His family thought you should have mated with him," it said. "They knew you wouldn't stay with him permanently, but they believed you would share sex with him at least once."

Share sex, she thought sadly. Where had it picked up that expression? She had never said it. She liked it, though. Should she have shared sex with Paul Titus? "And maybe gotten pregnant," she said aloud.

"You would not have gotten pregnant," Nikanj said.

And it had her full attention. "Why not?" she demanded.

"It isn't time for you to have children yet."

"Have you done something to me? Am I sterile?"

"Your people called it birth control. You are slightly changed. It was done while you slept, as it was done to all humans at first. It will be undone eventually."

"When?" she asked bitterly. "When you're ready to breed me?"

"No. When you're ready. Only then."

"Who decides? You?"

"You, Lilith. You."

Its sincerity confused her. She felt that she had learned to read its emotions through posture, sensory tentacle position, tone of voice . . . It seemed not only to be telling the truth—as usual—but to be telling a truth it considered important. Yet Paul Titus, too, had seemed to be telling the truth. "Does Paul really have over seventy children?" she asked.

"Yes. And he's told you why. The Toaht desperately need more of your kind to make a true trade. Most humans taken from Earth must be returned to it. But Toaht must have at least an equal number stay here. It seemed best that the ones born here be the ones to stay." Nikanj hesitated. "They should not have told Paul what they were doing. But that's always a difficult thing to realize—and sometimes we realize it too late."

"He had a right to know!"

"Knowing frightened him and made him miserable. You discovered one of his fears—that perhaps one of his female relatives had survived and been impregnated with his sperm. He's been told that this did not happen. Sometimes he believes; sometimes he doesn't."

"He still had a right to know. I would want to know."

Silence.

"Has it been done to me, Nikanj?"

"No."

"And . . . will it be?"

It hesitated, then spoke softly. "The Toaht have a print of you— of every human we brought aboard. They need the genetic diversity. We're keeping prints of the humans they take away, too. Millenia after your death, your body might be reborn aboard the ship. It won't be you. It will develop an identity of its own."

"A clone," she said tonelessly. Her left arm throbbed, and she rubbed it without actually focusing on the pain.

"No," Nikanj said. "What we've preserved of you isn't living tissue. It's memory. A gene map, your people might call it—though they couldn't have made one like those we remember and use. It's more like what they would call a mental blueprint. A plan for the assembly of one specific human being: You. A tool for reconstruction."

It let her digest this, said nothing more to her for several minutes. So few humans could do that—just let someone have a few minutes to think.

"Will you destroy my print if I ask you to?" she asked.

"It's a memory, Lilith, a complete memory carried by several people. How would I destroy such a thing?"

A literal memory, then, not some kind of mechanical recording or written record. Of course.

After a while, Nikanj said, "Your print may never be used. And if it is, the reconstruction will be as much at home aboard the ship as you were on Earth. She'll grow up here and the people she grows up among will be her people. You know they won't harm her."

She sighed. "I don't know any such thing. I suspect they'll do what they think is best for her. Heaven help her."

It sat beside her and touched her aching left arm with several head tentacles. "Did you really need to know that?" it asked. "Should I have told you?"

It had never asked such a question before. Her arm hurt more than ever for a moment, then felt warm and pain-free. She managed not to jerk away, though Nikanj had not paralyzed her.

"What are you doing?" she asked.

"You were having pain in that arm. There's no need for you to suffer."

"I hurt all over."

"I know. I'll take care of it. I just wanted to talk to you before you slept again."

She lay still for a moment, glad that the arm was no longer

throbbing. She had barely been aware of this individual pain before Nikanj stopped it. Now she realized it had been among the worst of the many. The hand, the wrist, the lower arm.

"You had a bone broken in your wrist," Nikanj told her. "It will be completely healed by the time you awaken again." And it repeated its question. "Did you really need to know, Lilith?"

"Yes," she said. "It concerned me. I needed to know."

It said nothing for a while and she did not disturb its thoughts. "I will remember that," it said softly, finally.

And she felt as though she had communicated something important. Finally.

"How did you know my arm was bothering me?"

"I could see you rubbing it. I knew it was broken and that I had done very little to it. Can you move your fingers?"

She obeyed, amazed to see the fingers move easily, painlessly.

"Good. I'll have to make you sleep again now."

"Nikanj, what happened to Paul?"

It shifted the focus of some of its head tentacles from her arm to her face. "He's asleep."

She frowned. "Why? I didn't hurt him. I couldn't have."

"He was . . . enraged. Out of control. He attacked members of his family. They say he would have killed them if he could have. When they restrained him, he wept and spoke incoherently. He refused to speak Oankali at all. In English, he cursed his family, you, everyone. He had to be put to sleep—perhaps for a year or more. The long sleeps are healing to nonphysical wounds."

"A year . . . ?"

"He'll be all right. He won't age. And his family will be waiting for him when he Awakes. He is very attached to them—and they to him. Toaht family bonds are . . . beautiful, and very strong."

She rested her right arm across her forehead. "His family," she said bitterly. "You keep saying that. His *family* is dead! Like mine. Like Fukumoto's. Like just about everyone's. That's half our problem. We haven't got any real family bonds."

"He has."

"He has *nothing*! He has no one to teach him to be a man, and he damn sure can't be an Oankali, so don't talk to me about his family!"

"Yet they are his family," Nikanj insisted softly. "They have accepted him and he has accepted them. He has no other family, but he has them."

She made a sound of disgust and turned her face away. What did Nikanj tell others about her? Did it talk about her family? According to her new name, she had been adopted, after all. She shook her head, confused and disturbed.

"He beat you, Lilith," Nikanj said. "He broke your bones. If you had gone untreated, you might have died of what he did."

"He did what you and his so-called family set him up to do!"

It rustled its tentacles. "That's truer than I would like. It's hard for me to influence people now. They think I'm too young to understand. I did warn them, though, that you wouldn't mate with him. Since I'm not yet mature, they didn't believe me. His family and my parents overruled me. That won't happen again."

It touched the back of her neck, pricking the skin with several sensory tentacles. She realized what it was doing as she felt herself beginning to lose consciousness.

"Put me back, too," she demanded while she could still talk. "Let me sleep again. Put me where they've put him. I'm no more what your people think than he was. Put me back. Find someone else!"

10

But the ease of her awakening, when it came, told her that her sleep had been ordinary and relatively brief, returning her all too quickly to what passed for reality. At least she was not in pain.

She sat up, found Nikanj lying stone-still next to her. As usual, some of its head tentacles followed her movements lazily as she got up and went to the bathroom.

Trying not to think, she bathed, worked to scrub off an odd, sour smell that her body had acquired—some residual effect of Nikanj's healing, she supposed. But the smell would not wash away. Eventually she gave up. She dressed and went back out to Nikanj. It was sitting up on the bed, waiting for her.

"You won't notice the smell in a few days," it said. "It isn't as strong as you think."

She shrugged, not caring.

"You can open walls now."

Startled, she stared at it, then went to a wall and touched it with the fingertips of one hand. The wall reddened as Paul Titus' wall had under Nikanj's touch.

"Use all your fingers," it told her.

She obeyed, touching the fingers of both hands to the wall. The wall indented, then began to open.

"If you're hungry," Nikanj said, "you can get food for yourself now. Within these quarters, everything will open for you."

"And beyond these quarters?" she asked.

"The walls will let you out and back in again. I've changed them a little too. But no other walls will open for you."

So she could walk the corridors or walk among the trees, but she couldn't get into anything Nikanj didn't want her in. Still, that was more freedom than she had had before it put her to sleep.

"Why did you do this?" she asked, staring at it.

"To give you what I could. Not another long sleep or solitude. Only this. You know the layout of the quarters now, and you know Kaal. And the people nearby know you."

So she could be trusted out alone again, she thought bitterly. And within the quarters, she could be depended on not to do the local equivalent of spilling the drain-cleaner or starting a fire. She could even be trusted not to annoy the neighbors. Now she could keep herself occupied until someone decided it was time to send her off to the work she did not want and could not do—the work that would probably get her killed. How many more Paul Tituses could she survive, after all?

Nikanj lay down again and seemed to tremble. It was trembling. Its body tentacles exaggerated the movement and made its whole body seem to vibrate. She neither knew nor cared what was wrong with it. She left it where it was and went out to get food.

In one compartment in the seemingly empty little living-room-dining-room-kitchen, she found fresh fruit: oranges, bananas, mangoes, papayas, and melons of different kinds. In other compartments she found nuts, bread, and honey.

Picking and choosing, she made herself a meal. She had

intended to take it outside, to eat—the first meal she had not had to ask for or wait for. The first meal she would eat under the pseudotrees without first having to be let out like a pet animal.

She opened a wall to go out, then stopped. The wall began to close after a moment. She sighed and turned away from it.

Angrily, she reopened the food compartments, took out extra food and went back in to Nikanj. It was still lying down, still trembling. She put a few pieces of fruit down next to it.

"Your sensory arms have already begun, haven't they?" she asked.

"Yes."

"Do you want anything to eat?"

"Yes." It took an orange and bit into it, eating skin and all. It hadn't done that before.

"We generally peel them," she said.

"I know. Wasteful."

"Look, do you need anything? Want me to find one of your parents?"

"No. This is normal. I'm glad I changed you when I did. I wouldn't trust myself to do it now. I knew this was coming."

"Why didn't you tell me it was so close?"

"You were too angry."

She sighed, tried to understand her own feelings. She was still angry—angry, bitter, frightened . . .

And yet she had come back. She had not been able to leave Nikanj trembling in its bed while she enjoyed her greater freedom.

Nikanj finished the orange and began on a banana. It did not peel this either.

"Can I see?" she asked.

It raised one arm, displaying ugly, lumpy, mottled flesh perhaps six inches beneath the arm.

"Does it hurt?"

"No. There isn't a word in English for the way it makes me feel. The closest would be . . . sexually aroused."

She stepped away from it, alarmed.

"Thank you for coming back."

She nodded. "You're not supposed to feel aroused with just me here."

"I'm becoming sexually mature. I'll feel this way from time to time as my body changes even though I don't yet have the organs I would use in sex. It's a little like feeling an amputated limb as though it were still there. I've heard humans do that."

"I've heard that we do, too, but—"

"I would feel aroused if I were alone. You don't make me feel it any more than I would if I were alone. Yet your presence helps me." It drew its head and body tentacles into knots. "Give me something else to eat."

She gave it a papaya and all the nuts she had brought in. It ate them quickly.

"Better," it said. "Eating dulls the feeling sometimes."

She sat down on the bed and asked, "What happens now?"

"When my parents realize what's happening to me, they'll send for Ahajas and Dichaan."

"Do you want me to look for them—your parents, I mean?"

"No." It rubbed the bed platform beneath its body. "The walls will alert them. Probably they already have. Wall tissues respond to beginning metamorphosis very quickly."

"You mean the walls will feel different or smell different or something?"

"Yes."

"Yes, what? Which one?"

"All that you said, and more." It changed the subject abruptly. "Lilith, sleep during metamorphosis can be very deep. Don't be afraid if sometimes I don't seem to see or hear."

"All right."

"You'll stay with me?"

"I said I would."

"I was afraid...good. Lie here with me until Ahajas and Dichaan come."

She was tired of lying down, but she stretched out beside it.

"When they come to carry me to Lo, you help them. That will tell them the first thing they need to know about you."

11

Leavetaking.

There was no real ceremony. Ahajas and Dichaan arrived and Nikanj immediately retreated into a deep sleep. Even its head tentacles hung limp and still.

Ahajas alone could have carried it. She was big like most Oankali females—slightly larger than Tediin. She and Dichaan were brother and sister as usual in Oankali matings. Males and females were closely related and ooloi were outsiders. One translation of the world *ooloi* was "treasured strangers." According to Nikanj, this combination of relatives and strangers served best when people were bred for specific work—like opening a trade with an alien species. The male and female concentrated desirable characteristics and the ooloi prevented the wrong kind of concentrations. Tediin and Jdahya were cousins. They had both not particularly liked their siblings. Unusual.

Now Ahajas lifted Nikanj as though it were a young child and held it easily until Dichaan and Lilith took its shoulders. Neither Ahajas nor Dichaan showed surprise at Lilith's participation.

"It has told us about you," Ahajas said as they carried Nikanj down to the lower corridors. Kahguyaht preceded them, opening walls. Jdahya and Tediin followed.

"It's told me a little about you, too," Lilith replied uncertainly. Things were moving too fast for her. She had not gotten up that day with the idea that she would be leaving Kaal—leaving Jdahya and Tediin who had become comfortable and familiar to her. She did not mind leaving Kahguyaht, but it had told her when it brought Ahajas and Dichaan to Nikanj that it would be seeing her again soon. Custom and biology dictated that as same-sex parent, Kahguyaht was permitted to visit Nikanj during its metamorphosis. Kahguyaht, like Lilith, smelled neutral and could not increase Nikanj's discomfort or stir inappropriate desires in it.

Lilith helped to arrange Nikanj on the flat tilio that sat waiting for them in a public corridor. Then she stood alone, watching as the five conscious Oankali came together, touching and entangling head and body tentacles. Kahguyaht stood between Tediin and Jdahya. Ahajas and Dichaan stood together and made their contacts with Tediin and Jdahya. It was almost as though they were avoiding Kahguyaht too. The Oankali could communicate this way, could pass messages from one to another almost at the speed of thought—or so Nikanj had said. Controlled multisensory stimulation. Lilith suspected it was the closest thing to telepathy she would ever see practiced. Nikanj had said it might be able to help her perceive this way when it was mature. But its maturity was months away. Now she was alone again—the alien, the uncomprehending outsider. That was what she would be again in the home of Ahajas and Dichaan.

When the group broke up, Tediin came over to Lilith, took both Lilith's arms. "It has been good having you with us," she said in Oankali. "I've learned from you. It's been a good trade."

"I've learned too," Lilith said honestly. "I wish I could stay here." Rather than go with strangers. Rather than be sent to teach a lot of frightened, suspicious humans.

"No," Tediin said. "Nikanj must go. You would not like to be separated from it."

She had nothing to say to that. It was true. Everyone, even Paul Titus inadvertently, had pushed her toward Nikanj. They had succeeded.

Tediin let her go and Jdahya came to speak to her in English. "Are you afraid?" he asked.

"Yes," she said.

"Ahajas and Dichaan will welcome you. You're rare—a human who can live among us, learn about us, and teach us. Everyone is curious about you."

"I thought I would be spending most of my time with Nikanj."

"You will be, for a while. And when Nikanj is mature, you'll be taken for training. But there'll be time for you to get to know Ahajas and Dichaan and others."

She shrugged. Nothing he said settled her nervousness now.

"Dichaan has said he would adjust the walls of their home to you so that you can open them. He and Ahajas can't change you in any way, but they can adjust your new surroundings."

So at least she wouldn't have to go back to the house pet stage, asking every time she wanted to enter or leave a room or eat a snack. "I'm grateful for that, at least," she said.

"It's trade," Jdahya said. "Stay close to Nikanj. Do what it has trusted you to do."

12

Kahguyaht came to see her a few days later. She had been installed in the usual bare room, this one with one bed and two table platforms, a bathroom, and Nikanj who slept so much and so deeply that it too seemed part of the room rather than a living being.

Kahguyaht was almost welcome. It relieved her boredom, and, to her surprise, it brought gifts: a block of tough, thin, white paper—more than a ream—and a handful of pens that said Paper Mate, Parker, and Bic. The pens, Kahguyaht said, had been duplicated from prints taken of centuries-gone originals. This was the first time she had seen anything she knew to be a print re-creation. And it was the first time she had realized that the Oankali re-created non-living things from prints. She could find no difference between the print copies and the remembered originals.

And Kahguyaht gave her a few brittle, yellowed books—treasures she had not imagined: A spy novel, a Civil War novel, an ethnology textbook, a study of religion, a book about cancer and one about human genetics, a book about an ape being taught sign language and one about the space race of the 1960s.

Lilith accepted them all without comment.

Now that it knew she was serious about looking after Nikanj, it was easier to get along with, more likely to answer if she asked it a question, less ready with its own sarcastic rhetorical questions. It returned several times to sit with her as she attended Nikanj and, in fact, became her teacher, using its body and Nikanj's to help her understand more of Oankali biology. Nikanj slept through most of this. Most often it slept so deeply that its head tentacles did not follow movement.

"It will remember all that happens around it," Kahguyaht said. "It still perceives in all the ways that it would if it were awake. But it cannot respond now. It is not aware now. It is...recording." Kahguyaht lifted one of Nikanj's limp arms to observe the development of the sensory arms. There was nothing to be seen yet but a large, dark, lumpy swelling—a frightening-looking growth.

"Is that the arm itself," she asked, "or will the arm come out of that?"

"That is the arm," Kahguyaht said. "While it's growing, don't touch it unless Nikanj asks you to."

It did not look like anything Lilith would want to touch. She looked at Kahguyaht and decided to take a chance on its new civility. "What about the sensory hand?" she asked. "Nikanj mentioned that there was such a thing."

Kahguyaht said nothing for several seconds. Finally, in a tone she could not interpret, it said, "Yes. There is such a thing."

"If I've asked something that I shouldn't, just tell me," she said. Something about that odd tone of voice made her want to move away from it, but she kept still.

"You haven't," Kahguyaht said, its voice neutral now. "In fact, it's important that you know about the...sensory hand." It extended one of its sensory arms, long and gray and rough-skinned, still reminding her of a blunt, closed elephant's trunk.

"All the strength and resistance to harm of this outer covering is to protect the hand and its related organs," it said. "The arm is closed, you see?" It showed her the rounded tip of the arm, capped by a semitransparent material that she knew was smooth and hard.

"When it's like this, it's merely another limb." Kahguyaht coiled the end of the arm, wormlike, reached out, touched Lilith's head, then held before her eyes a single strand of hair, pulled straight in a twist of the arm. "It is very flexible, very versatile, but only another limb." The arm drew back from Lilith, releasing the hair. The semitransparent material at the end began to change, to move in circular waves away to the sides of the tip and something slender and pale emerged from the center of the tip. As she watched, the slender thing seemed to thicken and divide. There were eight fingers—or rather, eight slender tentacles arranged around a circular palm that looked wet and deeply lined. It was like a starfish—one of the brittle stars with long, slender, snake-like arms.

"How does it seem to you?" Kahguyaht asked.

"On Earth, we had animals that looked like that," she replied. "They lived in the seas. We called them starfish."

Kahguyaht smoothed its tentacles. "I've seen them. There is a similarity." It turned the hand so that she could see it from different angles. The palm, she realized, was covered with tiny projections very like the tube feet of a starfish. They were almost transparent. And the lines she had seen on the palm were actually orifices—openings to a dark interior.

There was a faint odor to the hand—oddly flowery. Lilith did not like it and drew back from it after a moment of looking.

Kahguyaht retracted the hand so quickly that it seemed to vanish. It lowered the sensory arm. "Humans and Oankali tend to bond to one ooloi," it told her. "The bond is chemical and not strong in you now because of Nikanj's immaturity. That's why my scent makes you uncomfortable."

"Nikanj didn't mention anything like that," she said suspiciously.

"It healed your injuries. It improved your memory. It couldn't do those things without leaving its mark. It should have told you."

"Yes. It should have. What is this mark? What will it do to me?"

"No harm. You'll want to avoid deep contact—contact that involves penetration of the flesh—with other ooloi, you understand? Perhaps for a while after Nikanj matures, you'll want to avoid all contact with most people. Follow your feelings. People will understand."

"But . . . how long will it last?"

"It's different with humans. Some linger in the avoidance stage much longer than we would. The longest I've known it to last is forty days."

"And during that time, Ahajas and Dichaan—"

"You won't avoid them, Lilith. They're part of the household. You'll be comfortable with them."

"What happens if I don't avoid people, if I ignore my feelings?"

"If you managed to do that, you'd make yourself sick, at least. You might manage to kill yourself."

". . . that bad."

"Your body will tell you what to do. Don't worry." It shifted its attention to Nikanj. "Nikanj will be most vulnerable when the sensory hands begin to grow. It will need a special food then. I'll show you."

"All right."

"You'll actually have to put the food into its mouth."

"I've already done that with the few things it's wanted to eat."

"Good." Kahguyaht rustled its tentacles. "I didn't want to accept you, Lilith. Not for Nikanj or for the work you'll do. I believed that because of the way human genetics were expressed in culture, a human male should be chosen to parent the first group. I think now that I was wrong."

"Parent?"

"That's the way we think of it. To teach, to give comfort, to feed and clothe, to guide them through and interpret what will be, for them, a new and frightening world. To parent."

"You're going to set me up as their *mother*?"

"Define the relationship in any way that's comfortable to you. We have always called it parenting." It turned toward a wall as though to open it, then stopped, faced Lilith again. "It's a good thing that you'll be doing. You'll be in a position to help your own people in much the same way you're helping Nikanj now."

"They won't trust me or my help. They'll probably kill me."

"They won't."

"You don't understand us as well as you think you do."

"And you don't understand us at all. You never will, really, though you'll be given much more information about us."

"Then put me back to sleep, dammit, and choose someone you think is brighter! I never wanted this job!"

It was silent for several seconds. Finally, it said, "Do you really believe I was disparaging your intelligence?"

She glared at it, refusing to answer.

"I thought not. Your children will know us, Lilith. You never will."

PART III

Nursery

1

The room was slightly larger than a football field. Its ceiling was a vault of soft, yellow light. Lilith had caused two walls to grow at a corner of it so that she had a room, enclosed except for a doorway where the walls would have met. There were times when she brought the walls together, sealing herself away from the empty vastness outside—away from the decisions she must make. The walls and floor of the great room were hers to reshape as she pleased. They would do anything she was able to ask of them except let her out.

She had erected her cubicle enclosing the doorway of a bathroom. There were eleven more bathrooms unused along one long wall. Except for the narrow, open doorways of these facilities, the great room was featureless. Its walls were pale green and its floors pale brown. Lilith had asked for color and Nikanj had found someone who could teach it how to induce the ship to produce color. Stores of food and clothing were encapsulated within the walls in various unmarked cabinets within Lilith's room and at both ends of the great room.

The food, she had been told, would be replaced as it was used—replaced by the ship itself which drew on its own substance to make print reconstructions of whatever each cabinet had been taught to produce.

The long wall opposite the bathrooms concealed eighty sleeping human beings—healthy, under fifty, English-speaking, and frighteningly ignorant of what was in store for them.

Lilith was to choose and Awaken no fewer than forty. No wall would open to let her or those she Awakened out until at least forty human beings were ready to meet the Oankali.

The great room was darkening slightly. Evening. Lilith found surprising comfort and relief in having time divided visibly into days and nights again. She had not realized how she had missed the slow change of light, how welcome the darkness would be.

"It's time for you to get used to having planetary night again," Nikanj had told her.

On impulse, she had asked if there were anywhere in the ship where she could look at the stars.

Nikanj had taken her, on the day before it put her into this huge, empty room, down several corridors and ramps, then by way of something very like an elevator. Nikanj said it corresponded closer to a gas bubble moving harmlessly through a living body. Her destination turned out to be a kind of observation bubble through which she could see not only stars, but the disk of the Earth, gleaming like a full moon in the black sky.

"We're still beyond the orbit of your world's satellite," it told her as she searched hungrily for familiar continental outlines. She believed she had found a few of them—part of Africa and the Arabian peninsula. Or that was what it looked like, hanging there in the middle of a sky that was both above and beneath her feet. There were more stars out there than she had ever seen, but it was Earth that drew her gaze. Nikanj let her look at it until her own tears blinded her. Then it wrapped a sensory arm around her and led her to the great room.

She had been in the great room alone for three days now, thinking, reading, writing her thoughts. All her books, papers, and pens had been left for her. With them were eighty dossiers— short biographies made up of transcribed conversations, brief histories, Oankali observations and conclusions, and pictures. The human subjects of the dossiers had no living relatives. They were all strangers to one another and to Lilith.

She had read just over half the dossiers, searching not only for likely people to Awaken, but for a few potential allies—people she could Awaken first and perhaps come to trust. She needed to share the burden of what she knew, what she must do. She needed thoughtful people who would hear what she had to say and not do anything violent or stupid. She needed people who could give her ideas, push her mind in directions she might otherwise miss. She needed people who could tell her when they thought she was being a fool—people whose arguments she could respect.

On another level, she did not want to Awaken anyone. She was afraid of these people, and afraid for them. There were so many unknowns, in spite of the information in the dossiers. Her job was to weave them into a cohesive unit and prepare them for the Oankali—prepare them to be the Oankali's new trade partners. That was impossible.

How could she Awaken people and tell them they were to be part of the genetic engineering scheme of a species so alien that the humans would not be able to look at it comfortably for a while? How would she Awaken these people, these survivors of war, and tell them that unless they could escape the Oankali, their children would not be human?

Better to tell them little or none of that for a while. Better not to Awaken them at all until she had some idea how to help them, how not to betray them, how to get them to accept their captivity, accept the Oankali, accept anything until they were sent to Earth. Then to run like hell at the first opportunity.

Her mind slipped into the familiar track: There was no escape from the ship. None at all. The Oankali controlled the ship with their own body chemistry. There were no controls that could be memorized or subverted. Even the shuttles that traveled between Earth and the ship were like extensions of Oankali bodies.

No human could do anything aboard the ship except make trouble and be put back into suspended animation—or be killed. Therefore, the only hope was Earth. Once they were on Earth— somewhere in the Amazon basin, she had been told—they would at least have a chance.

That meant they must control themselves, learn all she could teach them, all the Oankali could teach them, then use what they had learned to escape and keep themselves alive.

What if she could make them understand that? And what if it turned out that that was exactly what the Oankali wanted her to do? Of course, they knew it was what she *would* do. They knew her. Did that mean they were planning their own betrayal: No trip to Earth. No chance to run. Then why had they made her spend a year being taught to live in a tropical forest? Perhaps the Oankali were simply very certain of their ability to keep humans corralled even on Earth.

What could she do? What could she tell the humans but "Learn and Run!" What other possibility for escape was there?

None at all. Her only other personal possibility was to refuse to Awaken anyone—hold out until the Oankali gave up on her and went looking for a more cooperative subject. Another Paul Titus, perhaps—someone who had truly given up on humanity and cast his lot with the Oankali. A man like that could make Titus' predictions self-fulfilling. He could undermine what little civilization might be left in the minds of those he Awoke. He could make them a gang. Or a herd.

What would she make them?

She lay on her bed platform, staring at a picture of a man. Five-seven, his statistics said. One hundred and forty pounds, thirty-two years old, missing the third, fourth, and fifth fingers of his left hand. He had lost the fingers in a childhood accident with a lawn mower, and he was self-conscious about the incomplete hand. His name was Victor Dominic—Vidor Domonkos, really. His parents had come to the United States from Hungary just before he was born. He had been a lawyer. The Oankali suspected he had been a good one. They had found him intelligent, talkative, understandably suspicious of unseen questioners, and very creative at lying to them. He had probed constantly for their identity, but was, like Lilith, one of the few native English-speakers who had never expressed the suspicion that they might be extraterrestrials.

He had been married three times already, but had fathered no children due to a biological problem the Oankali believed they had corrected. Not fathering children had bothered him intensely, and he had blamed his wives, all the while refusing to see a doctor himself.

Apart from this, the Oankali had found him reasonable and formidable. He had never broken down in his unexplained solitary confinement, had never wept or attempted suicide. He had, however, promised to kill his captors if he ever got the chance. He had said this only once, calmly, more as though he were making a casual remark than as though he were seriously threatening murder.

Yet his Oankali interrogator had been disturbed by the words, and had put Victor Dominic back to sleep at once.

Lilith liked the man. He had brains and, except for the foolishness with his wives, self-control—exactly what she needed. But she also feared him.

What if he decided she was one of his captors? She was bigger, and now certainly stronger than he was, but that did not have to matter. He would have too many chances to attack when she was off guard.

Better to Awaken him later when she had allies. She put his dossier to one side on the smaller of two piles—people she definitely wanted, but did not dare to Awaken first. She sighed and picked up a new dossier.

Leah Bede. Quiet, religious, slow—slow-moving, not slow-witted, though the Oankali had not been particularly impressed by her intelligence. It was her patience and self-sufficiency that had impressed them. They had not been able to make her obey. She had outwaited them in stolid silence. Outwaited Oankali! She had starved herself almost to death when they stopped feeding her to coerce her cooperation. Finally, they had drugged her, gotten the information they wanted, and, after a period of letting her regain weight and strength, they had put her back to sleep. Why, Lilith wondered. Why hadn't the Oankali not simply drugged her as soon as they realized she was stubborn? Why had they not drugged Lilith herself? Perhaps because they wanted to see how far human beings had to be pushed before they broke. Perhaps they even wanted to see *how* each individual broke. Or perhaps the Oankali version of stubbornness was so extreme from a human point of view that very few humans tried their patience. Lilith had not. Leah had.

The photo of Leah was a pale, lean, tired-looking woman, though an ooloi had noted that she had a physiological tendency to be heavy.

Lilith hesitated, then put Leah's folder atop Victor's. Leah, too, sounded like a good potential ally, but not a good one to Awaken first. She sounded as though she could be an intensely loyal friend—unless she got the idea Lilith was one of her captors.

Anyone Lilith Awakened might get that idea—almost certainly would get it the moment Lilith opened a wall or caused new walls to grow, thus proving she had abilities they did not. The Oankali had given her information, increased physical strength, enhanced memory, and an ability to control the walls and the suspended animation plants. These were her tools. And every one of them would make her seem less human.

"What else shall we give you?" Ahajas had asked her when Lilith saw her last. Ahajas had worried about her, found her too small to be impressive. She had discovered that humans were impressed by size. The fact that Lilith was taller and heavier than most women seemed not enough. She was not taller and heavier than most men. But there was nothing to be done about it.

"Nothing you could give me would be enough," Lilith had answered.

Dichaan had heard this and come over to take Lilith's hands. "You want to live," he told her. "You won't squander your life."

They were squandering her life.

She picked up the next folder and opened it.

Joseph Li-Chin Shing. A widower whose wife had died before the war. The Oankali had found him quietly grateful for that. After his own period of stubborn silence, he had discovered that he didn't mind talking to them. He seemed to accept the reality that his life was, as he said, "on hold" until he found out what had happened in the world and who was running things now. He constantly probed for answers to these questions. He admitted that he remembered deciding, not long after the war, that it was time for him to die. He believed that he had been captured before he could attempt suicide. Now, he said, he had reason to live—to see who had caged him and why and how he might want to repay them.

He was forty years old, a small man, once an engineer, a citizen of Canada, born in Hong Kong. The Oankali had considered making him a parent of one of the human groups they meant to establish. But they had been put off by his threat. It was, the Oankali questioner thought, soft, but potentially quite deadly. Yet the Oankali recommended him to her—to any first parent. He was intelligent, they said, and steady. Someone who could be depended on.

Nothing special about his looks, Lilith thought. He was a small, ordinary man, yet the Oankali had been very interested in him. And the threat he had made was surprisingly conservative—deadly only if Joseph did not like what he found out. He would not like it, Lilith thought. But he would also be bright enough to realize that the time to do something about it would be when they were all on the ground, not while they were caged in the ship.

Lilith's first impulse was to Awaken Joseph Shing—Awaken him at once and end her solitude. The impulse was so strong that she sat still for several moments, hugging herself, holding herself rigid against it. She had promised herself that she would not Awaken anyone until she had read all the dossiers, until she had had time to think. Following the wrong impulse now could kill her.

She went through several more dossiers without finding anyone she thought compared with Joseph, though some of the people she found would definitely be Awakened.

There was a woman named Celene Ivers who had spent much of her short interrogation period crying over the death of her husband and her twin daughters, or crying over her own unexplained captivity and her uncertain future. She had wished herself dead over and over, but had never made any attempt at suicide. The Oankali had found her very pliable, eager to please—or rather, fearful of displeasing. Weak, the Oankali had said. Weak and sorrowing, not stupid, but so easily frightened that she could be induced to behave stupidly.

Harmless, Lilith thought. One person who would not be a threat, no matter how strongly she suspected Lilith of being her jailer.

There was Gabriel Rinaldi, an actor, who had confused the Oankali utterly for a while because he played roles for them instead of letting them see him as he was. He was another they had finally stopped feeding on the theory that sooner or later hunger would bring out the true man. They were not entirely sure that it had. Gabriel must have been good. He was also very good-looking. He had never tried to harm himself or threatened to harm the Oankali. And for some reason, they had never drugged him. He was, the Oankali said, twenty-seven, thin, physically stronger than he looked, stubborn and not as bright as he liked to think.

That last, Lilith thought, could be said of most people. Gabriel, like the others who had defeated or come near defeating the Oankali, was potentially valuable. She did wonder whether she would ever be able to trust Gabriel, but his dossier remained with those she meant to Awaken.

There was Beatrice Dwyer who had been completely unreachable while she was naked, but whom clothing had transformed into a bright, likable person who seemed actually to have made a friend of her interrogator. That interrogator, an experienced ooloi, had attempted to have Beatrice accepted as a first parent. Other interrogators had observed her and disagreed for no stated reason. Maybe it was just the woman's extreme physical modesty. Nevertheless, one ooloi had been completely won over.

There was Hilary Ballard, poet, artist, playwright, actress, singer, frequent collector of unemployment compensation. She really was bright; she had memorized poetry, plays, songs—her own and those of more established writers. She had something that would help future human children remember who they were. The Oankali thought she was unstable, but not dangerously so. They had had to drug her because she injured herself trying to break free of what she called her cage. She had broken both her arms.

And that was not dangerously unstable?

No, it probably was not. Lilith herself had panicked at being caged. So had a great many other people. Hilary's panic had simply been more extreme than most. She probably should not be given crucial work to do. The survival of the group should never depend on her—but then it should not depend on any one person. The fact that it did was not the fault of human beings.

There was Conrad Loehr—called Curt—who had been a cop in New York, and who had survived only because his wife had finally dragged him off to Colombia where her family lived. They had not gone anywhere for years before that. The wife had been killed in one of the riots that began shortly after the last missile exchange. Thousands had been killed even before it began to get cold. Thousands had simply trampled one another or torn one another apart in panic. Curt had been picked up with seven children, none of them his own, whom he had been guarding. His own four children, left back in the States with his relatives, were all dead. Curt Loehr, the Oankali said, needed people to look after. People stabilized him, gave him purpose. Without them, he might have been a criminal—or dead. He had, alone in his isolation room, done his best to tear out his own throat with his fingernails.

Derick Wolski had been working in Australia. He was single, twenty-three, had no strong idea what he wanted to do with his life, had done nothing so far except go to school and work at temporary or part-time jobs. He'd fried hamburgers, driven a delivery truck, done construction work, sold household products door to door—badly—bagged groceries, helped clean office buildings, and on his own, done some nature photography. He'd quit everything except the photography. He liked the outdoors, liked animals. His father thought that sort of thing was nonsense, and he had been afraid his father might be right. Yet, he had been photographing Australian wildlife when the war began.

Tate Marah had just quit another job. She had some genetic problem that the Oankali had controlled, but not cured. But her real problem seemed to be that she did things so well that she quickly became bored. Or she did them so badly that she abandoned them before anyone noticed her incompetence. People had to see her as a formidable presence, bright, dominant, well off.

Her family had had money—had owned a very successful real estate business. Part of her problem, the Oankali believed, was that she did not *have* to do anything. She had great energy, but needed some external pressure, some challenge to force her to focus it.

How about the preservation of the human species?

She had attempted suicide twice before the war. After the war, she fought to live. She had been alone, vacationing in Rio de Janeiro when war came. It had not been a good time to be a North American, she felt, but she had survived and managed to help others. She had that in common with Curt Loehr. Under Oankali interrogation, she had engaged in verbal fencing and game playing that eventually exasperated the ooloi questioner. But in the end, the ooloi had admired her. It thought she was more like an ooloi than like a female. She was good at manipulating people—could do it in ways they did not seem to mind. That had bored her too in the past. But boredom had not driven her to do harm to anyone except herself. There had been times when she withdrew from people to protect them from the possible consequences of her own frustration. She had withdrawn from several men this way, occasionally pairing them off with female friends. Couples she brought together tended to marry.

Lilith put Tate Marah's dossier down slowly, left it by itself on the bed. The only other one that was by itself was Joseph Shing's. Tate's dossier fell open, once again displaying the woman's small, pale, deceptively childlike face. The face was smiling slightly, not as though posing for a picture, but as though sizing up the photographer. In fact, Tate had not known the picture was being made. And the pictures were not photographs. They were paintings, impressions of the inner person as well as the outer physical reality. Each contained print memories of their subjects. Oankali interrogators had painted these pictures with sensory tentacles or sensory arms, using deliberately produced bodily fluids. Lilith knew this, but the pictures looked like, even felt like photos. They had been done on some kind of plastic, not on paper. The pictures looked alive enough to speak. In each one, there was nothing except the head and shoulders of the subject against a gray background. None of them had that blank, wanted-poster look that snapshots could have produced. These pictures had a lot to say even to non-Oankali observers about who their subjects were—or who the Oankali thought they were.

Tate Marah, they thought, was bright, somewhat flexible, and not dangerous except perhaps to the ego.

Lilith left the dossiers, left her private cubicle, and began building another near it.

The walls that would not open to let her out responded to her touch now by growing inward along a line of her sweat or saliva drawn along the floor. Thus the old walls extruded new ones, and the new ones would open or close, advance or retreat as she directed. Nikanj had made very sure she knew how to direct them. And when it finished instructing her, its mates, Dichaan and Ahajas, told her to seal herself in if her people attacked her. They had both spent time interrogating isolated humans and they seemed more worried about her than Nikanj did. They would get her out, they promised. They would not leave her to die for someone else's miscalculation.

Which was fine if she could spot the trouble and seal herself in in time.

Better to choose the right people, bring them along slowly, and Awaken new ones only when she was sure of the ones already Awake.

She drew two walls to within about eighteen inches of each other. That left a narrow doorway—one that would preserve as much privacy as possible without a door. She also turned one wall inward, forming a tiny entrance hall that concealed the room itself from casual glances. There would be nothing among the people she Awoke to borrow or steal, and anyone who thought now was a good time to play Peeping Tom would have to be disciplined by the group. Lilith might be strong enough now to handle troublemakers herself, but she did not want to do that unless she had to. It would not help the people become a community, and if they could not unite, nothing else they did would matter.

Within the new room, Lilith raised a bed platform, a table

platform, and three chair platforms around the table. The table and chairs would be at least a small change from what they were all used to in the Oankali isolation rooms. A more human arrangement.

Creating the room took some time. Afterward Lilith gathered all but eleven of the dossiers and sealed them inside her own table platform. Some of these eleven would be her core group, first Awake, and first to show her just how much of a chance she had to survive and do what was necessary.

Tate Marah first. Another woman. No sexual tension.

Lilith took the picture, went to the long, featureless stretch of wall opposite the rest rooms and stood for a moment, staring at the face.

Once people were Awake, she would have no choice but to live with them. She could not put them to sleep again. And in some ways, Tate Marah would probably be hard to live with.

Lilith rubbed her hand across the surface of the picture, then placed the picture flat against the wall. She began at one end of the wall and walked slowly toward the other, far away, keeping the face of the picture against the wall. She closed her eyes as she moved, remembering that it had been easier when she practiced this with Nikanj if she ignored her other senses as much as possible. All her attention should be focused on the hand that held the picture flat against the wall. Male and female Oankali did this with head tentacles. Oankali did it with their sensory arms. Both did it from memory, without pictures impregnated with prints. Once they read someone's print or examined someone and took a print, they remembered it, could duplicate it. Lilith would never be able to read prints or duplicate them. That required Oankali organs of perception. Her children would have them, Kahguyaht had said.

She stopped now and then to rub one sweaty hand over the picture, renewing her own chemical signature.

More than halfway down the hall, she began to feel a response, a slight bulging of the surface against the picture, against her hand.

She stopped at once, not certain at first that she had felt anything at all. Then the bulge was unmistakable. She pressed against it lightly, maintaining the contact until the wall began to open beneath the picture. Then she drew back to let the wall disgorge its long, green plant. She went to a space at one end of the great room, opened a wall, and took out a jacket and a pair of pants. These people would probably welcome clothing as eagerly as she had.

The plant lay, writhing slowly, still surrounded by the foul odor that had followed it through the wall. She could not see well enough through its thick, fleshy body to know which end concealed Tate Marah's head, but that did not matter. She drew her hands along the length of the plant as though unzipping it, and it began to come apart.

There was no possibility this time of the plant trying to swallow her. She would be no more palatable to it now than Nikanj would.

Slowly, the face and body of Tate Marah became visible. Small breasts. Figure like that of a girl who had barely reached puberty. Pale, translucent skin and hair. Child's face. Yet Tate was twenty-seven.

She would not awaken until she was lifted completely clear of the suspended animation plant. Her body was wet and slippery, but not heavy. Sighing, Lilith lifted her clear.

2

Get away from me!" Tate said the moment she opened her eyes. "Who are you? What are you doing?"

"Trying to get you dressed," Lilith said. "You can do it yourself now—if you're strong enough."

Tate was beginning to tremble, beginning to react to being awakened from suspended animation. It was surprising that she had been able to speak her few coherent words before succumbing to the reaction.

Tate made a tight, shuddering fetal knot of her body and lay moaning. She gasped several times, gulping air as she might have gulped water.

"Shit!" she whispered minutes later when the reaction began to wane. "Oh shit. It wasn't a dream, I see."

"Finish dressing," Lilith told her. "You knew it wasn't a dream."

Tate looked up at Lilith, then down at her own half naked body. Lilith had managed to get pants on her, but had only gotten one of her arms into the jacket. She had managed to work that arm free as she suffered through the reaction. She picked up the jacket, put it on, and in a moment, had discovered how to close it. Then she turned to watch silently as Lilith closed the plant, opened the wall nearest to it, and pushed the plant through. In seconds the only sign left of it was a rapidly drying spot on the floor.

"And in spite of all that," Lilith said, facing Tate, "I'm a prisoner just as you are."

"More like a trustee," Tate said quietly.

"More like. I have to Awaken at least thirty-nine more people before any of us are allowed out of this room. I chose to start with you."

"Why?" She was incredibly self-possessed—or seemed to be. She had only been Awakened twice before—average among people not chosen to parent a group—but she behaved almost as though nothing unusual were happening. That was a relief to Lilith, a vindication of her choice of Tate.

"Why did I begin with you?" Lilith said. "You seemed least likely to try to kill me, least likely to fall apart, and most likely to be able to help with the others as they Awaken."

Tate seemed to think about that. She fiddled with her jacket, reexamining the way the front panels adhered to one another, the way they pulled apart. She felt the material itself, frowning.

"Where the hell are we?" she asked.

"Some distance beyond the orbit of the moon."

Silence. Then finally, "What was that big green slug-thing you pushed into the wall?"

"A...a plant. Our captors—our rescuers—use them for keeping people in suspended animation. You were in the one you saw. I took you out of it."

"Suspended animation?"

"For over two hundred and fifty years. The Earth is just about ready to have us back now."

"We're going back!"

"Yes."

Tate looked around at the vast, empty room. "Back to what?"

"Tropical forest. Somewhere in the Amazon basin. There are no more cities."

"No. I didn't think there would be." She drew a deep breath. "When are we fed?"

"I put some food in your room before I Awoke you. Come on."

Tate followed. "I'm hungry enough to eat even that plaster of Paris garbage they served me when I was Awake before."

"No more plaster. Fruit, nuts, a kind of stew, bread, something like cheese, coconut milk..."

"Meat? A steak?"

"You can't have everything."

Tate was too good to be true. Lilith worried for a moment that at some point she would break—begin to cry or be sick or scream or beat her head against the wall—lose that seemingly easy control. But whatever happened to her, Lilith would try to help. Just these few minutes of apparent normality were worth a great deal of trouble. She was actually speaking with and being understood by another human being—*after so long.*

Tate dove into the food, eating until she was satisfied, not wasting time talking. She had not, Lilith thought, asked one very important question. Of course there was a great deal she had not asked, but one thing in particular made Lilith wonder.

"What's your name, by the way?" Tate asked, finally resting from her eating. She sipped coconut milk tentatively, then drank it all.

"Lilith Iyapo."

"Lilith. Lil?"

"Lilith, I've never had a nickname. Never wanted one. Is there anything apart from your name that you'd like to be called?"

"No. Tate will do. Tate Marah. They told you my name, didn't they?"

"Yes."

"I thought so. All those damn questions. They kept me Awake

and in solitary for . . . it must have been two or three months. Did they tell you that? Or were you watching?"

"I was either asleep or in solitary myself, but yes, I knew about your confinement. It was three months in all. Mine was just over two years."

"It took them that long to make a trustee of you, did it?"

Lilith frowned, took a few nuts and ate them. "What do you mean by that?" she asked.

For an instant, Tate looked uncomfortable, uncertain. The expression appeared and vanished so quickly that Lilith could have missed it through just a moment's inattention.

"Well, why should they keep you awake and alone for so long?" Tate demanded.

"I wouldn't talk to them at first. Then later when I began to talk, apparently a number of them were interested in me. They weren't trying to make a trustee of me at that point. They were trying to decide whether I was fit to be one. If I had had a vote, I'd still be asleep."

"Why wouldn't you talk to them? Were you military?"

"God, no. I just didn't like the idea of being locked up, questioned, and ordered around by I-didn't-know-who. And Tate, it's time you knew who—even though you've been careful not to ask."

She drew a deep breath, rested her forehead on her hand and stared down at the table. "I asked them. They wouldn't tell me. After a while I got scared and stopped asking."

"Yeah. I did that too."

"Are they . . . Russians?"

"They're not human."

Tate did not move, did not say anything for so long that Lilith continued.

"They call themselves Oankali, and they look like sea creatures, though they are bipedal. They . . . are you taking any of this in?"

"I'm listening."

Lilith hesitated. "Are you believing?"

Tate looked up at her, seemed to smile a little. "How can I?"

Lilith nodded. "Yeah. But you'll have to sooner or later, of course, and I'm supposed to do what I can to prepare you. The Oankali are ugly. Grotesque. But we can get used to them, and they won't hurt us. Remember that. Maybe it will help when the time comes."

3

For three days, Tate slept a great deal, ate a great deal, and asked questions that Lilith answered completely honestly. Tate also talked about her life before the war. Lilith saw that it seemed to relax her, ease that shell of emotional control she usually wore. That made it worthwhile. It meant Lilith felt obligated to talk a little about herself—her past before the war—something she would not normally have been inclined to do. She had learned to keep her sanity by accepting things as she found them, adapting herself to new circumstances by putting aside the old ones whose memories might overwhelm her. She had tried to talk to Nikanj about humans in general, only occasionally bringing in personal anecdotes. Her father, her brothers, her sister, her husband and son...She chose now to talk about her return to college.

"Anthropology," Tate said disparagingly. "Why did you want to snoop through other people's cultures? Couldn't you find what you wanted in your own?"

Lilith smiled and noticed that Tate frowned as though this were the beginning of a wrong answer. "I started out wanting to do exactly that," Lilith said. "Snoop. Seek. It seemed to me that my culture—ours—was running headlong over a cliff. And, of course, as it turned out, it was. I thought there must be saner ways of life."

"Find any?"

"Didn't have much of a chance. It wouldn't have mattered much anyway. It was the cultures of the U.S. and the U.S.S.R. that counted."

"I wonder."

"What?"

"Human beings are more alike than different—damn sure more alike than we like to admit. I wonder if the same thing wouldn't have happened eventually, no matter which two cultures gained the ability to wipe one another out along with the rest of the world."

Lilith gave a bitter laugh. "You might like it here. The Oankali think a lot like you do."

Tate turned away, suddenly disturbed. She wandered over to look at the new third and fourth rooms Lilith had grown on either side of the second restroom. One of them was back to back with her own room, and in part, an extension of one of her walls. She had watched the walls growing—watched first with disbelief, then anger, refusing to believe she was not being tricked somehow. Then she began to keep her distance from Lilith, to watch Lilith suspiciously, to be jumpy and silent.

That had not lasted long. Tate was adaptable if nothing else. "I don't understand," she had said softly, though by then, Lilith had explained why she could control the walls, how she could find and Awaken specific individuals.

Now, Tate wandered back and said again, "I don't understand. None of this makes sense!"

"I had an easier time believing," Lilith said. "An Oankali sealed himself in my isolation room and refused to leave until I got used to him. You can't look at them and doubt that they're alien."

"Maybe *you* can't."

"I won't argue with you about it. I've been Awake a lot longer than you have. I've lived among the Oankali and I accept them as what they are."

"What they say they are."

Lilith shrugged. "I want to start Awakening more people. Two new ones today. Will you help me?"

"Who are you Awakening?"

"Leah Bede and Celene Iver."

"Two more women? Why don't you wake up a man?"

"I will eventually."

"You're still thinking about your Paul Titus, aren't you?"

"He wasn't mine." She wished she had not told Tate about him.

"Awaken a man next, Lilith. Awaken the guy who was found protecting the kids."

Lilith turned to look at her. "On the theory that if you fall off a horse, you should immediately get back on?"

"Yes."

"Tate, once he's Awake, he stays Awake. He's six-three, he weighs two-twenty, he's been a cop for seven years, and he's used to ordering people around. He can't save us or protect us here, but he can damn sure screw us up. All he has to do to hurt us is refuse to believe we're on a ship. After that, everything he does will be wrong and potentially deadly."

"So what? You're going to wait until you can Awaken him to a kind of harem?"

"No. Once we've got Leah and Celene awake and reasonably stable, I'm going to Awaken Curt Loehr and Joseph Shing."

"Why wait?"

"I'm going to get Celene out first. You take care of her while I get Leah out. I think Celene might be someone for Curt to take care of."

She went to her room, brought back pictures of both women,

and was about to begin hunting for Celene when Tate caught her arm.

"We're being watched, aren't we?" she asked.

"Yes. I don't know that we're watched every minute, but now, when we're both Awake, yes, I'm sure they're watching."

"If there's trouble, will they help?"

"If they decide it's bad enough. I think there were some who would have let Titus rape me. I don't think they would have let him kill me. They might have been too slow to prevent it, though."

"Wonderful," Tate muttered bitterly. "We're on our own."

"Exactly."

Tate shook her head. "I don't know whether I should be shedding the constraints of civilization and getting ready to fight for my life or keeping and enhancing them for the sake of our future."

"We'll do what's necessary," Lilith said. "Sooner or later, that will probably mean fighting for our lives."

"I hope you're wrong," Tate said. "What have we learned if all we can do now is go on fighting among ourselves?" She paused. "You didn't have kids, did you Lilith?"

Lilith began to walk slowly along the wall, eyes closed, Celene's picture flat between the wall and her hand. Tate walked along beside her, distracting her.

"Wait until I call you," Lilith told her. "Searching like this takes all my attention."

"It's really hard for you to talk about your life before, isn't it?" Tate said, with sympathy Lilith did not begin to trust.

"Pointless," Lilith said. "Not hard. I lived in those memories for my two years of solitary. By the time the Oankali showed up in my room, I was ready to move into the present and stay there. My life before was a lot of groping around, looking for I-didn't-know-what. And, as for kids, I had a son. He was killed in an auto accident before the war." Lilith took a deep breath. "Let me alone now. I'll call you when I've found Celene."

Tate moved away, settled against the opposite wall near one of the rest rooms. Lilith closed her eyes and began inching along again. She let herself lose track of time and distance, felt as though she were almost flowing along the wall. The illusion was familiar—as physically pleasing and emotionally satisfying as a drug—a needed drug at this moment.

"If you have to do something, it might as well feel good," Nikanj had told her. It had become very interested in her physical pleasures and pains once its sensory arms were fully grown. Happily, it had paid more attention to pleasure than to pain. It had studied her as she might have studied a book—and it had done a certain amount of rewriting.

The bulge in the wall felt large and distinct when her fingers found it. But when she opened her eyes and looked, she could not see any irregularity.

"There's nothing there!" Tate said over her right shoulder.

Lilith jumped, dropped the picture, refused to turn and glare at Tate as she bent to pick it up. "Get away from me!" she said quietly.

Grudgingly, Tate moved back several steps. Lilith could have found the spot again without any particular concentration, without having Tate move away, but Tate had to learn to accept Lilith's authority in anything to do with controlling the walls or dealing with the Oankali and their ship. What the hell did she think she was doing, coming back, creeping along behind Lilith? What was she looking for? Some trick?

Lilith rubbed one hand on the face of the picture and placed it against the wall. She found the bulge at once, though it was still too slight to be seen. It had ceased to grow with the removal of the picture, but had not yet vanished. Now Lilith rubbed it gently with the picture, encouraging it to grow. When she could see the protrusion, she stepped away and waited, gesturing for Tate to come.

Standing together, they watched the wall disgorge the long,

translucent green plant. Tate made a sound of disgust and stepped back as the smell drifted to her.

"You want to look at it before I open it?" Lilith asked.

Tate came closer and stared at the plant. "Why is it moving?"

"So that every part of it is exposed to the light for a while. If you could mark it, you would see that it's very slowly turning over. The movement is supposed to be good for the people inside, too. It exercises their muscles and changes their position."

"It doesn't really look like a slug," Tate said. "Not when someone's in it." She went to it, stroked it with several fingers, then looked at her fingers.

"Be careful," Lilith told her. "Celene isn't very big. The plant probably wouldn't mind taking someone else in."

"Would you be able to get me out?"

"Yes." She smiled. "The first Oankali to show these to me didn't warn me. I put my hand on the plant and almost panicked when I realized the plant was holding me and growing around my hand."

Tate tried this, and the plant obligingly began to swallow her hand. She tugged at her hand, then looked at Lilith, obviously afraid. "Make it let go!"

Lilith touched the plant around her captive hand and the plant released her. "Now," Lilith said, moving to one end of the plant. She drew her hands along the length of the plant. It opened in its usual slow way, and she lifted Celene out and put her on the floor where Tate could look after her.

"Get some clothes on her before she wakes up if you can," she told Tate.

But by the time Celene was fully awake, Lilith had Leah Bede out of the wall and out of her plant. She dressed Leah quickly. Not until both women were fully awake and looking around did Lilith push the two plants back through the wall. When that was done, she turned, meaning to sit down with Leah and Celene and answer their questions.

Instead, she was suddenly staggered by Leah's weight as the

woman leaped onto her back and began strangling her. Lilith began to fall. Time seemed to slow down for her.

If she fell on Leah, the woman would probably injure her back or her head. The injury might be only superficial, but could be serious. It would be wrong to let a potentially useful person be lost for one act of stupidity.

Lilith managed to fall on her side so that only Leah's arm and shoulder struck the floor. Lilith reached up and took Leah's hands from her throat. It was not difficult. Lilith was even able to go on taking care not to cause injury. She also took care not to let Leah see how easy it was for Lilith to defeat her. She gasped as she tore Leah's hands from her throat, though she was nowhere near desperate for air yet. And she allowed Leah's hands to move in her own as Leah struggled.

"Will you stop it!" she shouted. "I'm a prisoner here just like you. I can't let you out. I can't get out myself. Do you understand?"

Leah stopped struggling. Now she glared up at Lilith. "Get off me." Her voice was naturally deep and throaty. Now it was almost a growl.

"I intend to," Lilith said. "But don't jump me again. I'm not your enemy."

Leah made a wordless sound.

"Save your strength," Lilith said. "We've got a lot of rebuilding to do."

"Rebuilding?" Leah growled.

"The war," Lilith said. "Remember?"

"I wish I could forget." The growl had softened.

"You kill me here and you'll prove you haven't had enough war yet. You'll prove you're not fit to take part in the rebuilding."

Leah said nothing. After a moment, Lilith released her.

Both women stood up warily.

"Who decides whether or not I'm fit?" Leah asked. "You?"

"Our jailers."

Unexpectedly, Celene whispered, "Who are they?" Her face was already streaked with tears. She and Tate had come up silently to join the discussion—or watch the fight.

Lilith glanced at Tate, and Tate shook her head. "And you were afraid Awakening a man would cause violence," she said.

"I still am," Lilith told her. She looked at Celene, then Leah. "Let's get something to eat. I'll answer any questions I can."

She took them to the room that would be Celene's and watched their eyes widen when they saw, not the expected bowls of god-knew-what, but recognizable food.

It was easier to talk to them when they'd eaten their fill, when they were relatively relaxed and comfortable. They refused to believe they were on a ship beyond the moon's orbit. Leah laughed aloud when she heard that they were being held by extraterrestrials.

"Either you're a liar or you're crazy," she said.

"It's true," Lilith said softly.

"It's crap."

"The Oankali modified me," Lilith told her, "so that I can control the walls and the suspended animation plants. I can't do it as well as they can, but I can Awaken people, feed them, clothe them, and give them a certain amount of privacy. You shouldn't get so wrapped up in doubting me that you ignore the things you see me do. And remember two things in particular that I've told you. We are on a ship. Act as though you believe that even if you don't. There is no place to run on a ship. Even if you could get out of this room, there would be nowhere to go, nowhere to hide, nowhere to be free. On the other hand, if we endure our time here, we'll get our world back. We'll be put down on Earth as the first of the returning human colonists."

"Just do as we're told and wait, huh?" Leah said.

"Unless you like it here well enough to stay."

"I don't believe a word you say."

"Believe what you want! I'm telling you how to act if you ever want to feel the ground under your feet again!"

Celene began to cry quietly and Lilith frowned at her. "What's the matter with you?"

Celene shook her head. "I don't know what to believe. I don't even know why I'm still alive."

Tate sighed and shook her head in disgust.

"You are alive," Lilith said coldly. "We have no medical supplies here. If you want to commit suicide, you might succeed. If you want to hang around and help get things started back on Earth . . . well, that seems a lot more worth succeeding at."

"Did you have any children?" Celene asked, clearly expecting the answer to be no.

"Yes," Lilith made herself reach out, take the woman's hand, though already she disliked her. "All the people I have to Awaken are here without their families. We're all alone. We've got each other, and nobody else. We'll become a community—friends, neighbors, husbands, wives—or we won't."

"When will there be men?" Celene demanded.

"In a day or two. I'll Awaken two men next."

"Why not now?"

"No. I'll get rooms ready for them, get food and clothing out for them—the way I have for you and Leah."

"You mean you build the rooms?"

"It's more accurate to say I grow them. You'll see."

"You grow the food, too?" Leah asked, one eyebrow raised.

"Food and clothing is stored along the walls at each end of the big room. They're replaced as we use them. I can open the storage cabinets, but I can't open the wall behind them. Only the Oankali can do that."

There was silence for a moment. Lilith began gathering her own fruit peelings and seeds. "Any garbage goes into one of the toilets," she said. "You don't have to worry about stopping them up. They're more than they appear to be. They'll digest anything that isn't alive."

"Digest!" Celene said, horrified. "They...they're alive themselves?"

"Yes. The ship is alive and so is almost everything in it. The Oankali use living matter the way we used machinery." She started away toward the nearest bathroom, then stopped. "The other thing I meant to tell you," she said focusing on Leah and Celene, "is that we're being watched—just as we were all watched in our isolation rooms. I don't think the Oankali will bother us this time—not until forty or more of us are Awake and getting along fairly well together. They will come in, though, if we start to murder each other. And the would-be murderers—or actual murderers—will be kept here on the ship for the rest of their lives."

"So you're protected from us," Leah said. "Convenient."

"We're protected from one another," Lilith said. "We're an endangered species—almost extinct. If we're going to survive, we need protection."

4

Lilith did not release Curt Loehr from his suspended animation plant until Joseph Shing's plant lay beside it. Then, quickly, she opened both plants, lifted Joseph out and dragged Loehr out. She set Leah and Tate to work dressing Curt and worked alone to dress Joseph since Celene would not touch him while he was naked. Both men were fully clothed by the time they struggled to full consciousness.

After the initial misery of Awakening, they sat up and looked around. "Where are we?" Curt demanded. "Who's in charge here?"

Lilith winced. "I am," she said. "I Awoke you. We're all prisoners here, but it's my job to Awaken people."

"And who are you working for?" Joseph demanded. He had a slight accent and Curt, hearing it, turned to stare, then to glare at him.

Lilith introduced them quickly. "Conrad Loehr of New York, this is Joseph Shing of Vancouver." Then she introduced each of the women.

Celene had already settled close to Curt, and once she was

introduced, she added: "Back when things were normal, everyone called me Cele."

Tate rolled her eyes and Leah frowned. Lilith managed not to smile. She had been right about Celene. Celene would put herself under Curt's protection if he let her. That would keep Curt occupied. Lilith caught a faint smile on Joseph's face.

"We have food if you two are hungry," Lilith said, slipping into what was becoming a standard speech. "While we eat, I'll answer your questions."

"One answer now," Curt said. His question: "Who are you working for? Which side?"

He had not seen her push his suspended animation plant back into the wall. She had not turned her back on him since he had been fully Awake.

"Down on Earth," she said carefully, "there are no people left to draw lines on maps and say which sides of those lines are the right sides. There is no government left. No human government, anyway."

He frowned, then glared at her as he had earlier at Joseph. "You're saying we've been captured by...something that isn't human?"

"Or rescued," Lilith said.

Joseph stepped up to her. "You've seen them?"

Lilith nodded.

"You believed they are extraterrestrials?"

"Yes."

"And you believe we are on some kind of...what? Space ship?"

"A very, very large one, almost like a small world."

"What proof can you show us?"

"Nothing that you couldn't perceive as a trick if you wanted to."

"Please show us anyway."

She nodded, not minding. Each pair or group of new people would have to be handled slightly differently. She explained what she could of the changes that had been made in her body chemistry, then, with both men watching, she grew another room. Twice she stopped to allow them to inspect the walls. She said nothing when they attempted to control the walls as she did, and then attempted to break them. The living tissue of the walls resisted them, ignored them. Their strength was meaningless. Finally they watched silently as Lilith completed the room.

"It's like the stuff my cell was made of when I was Awake before," Curt said. "What the hell is it? Some kind of plastic?"

"Living matter," Lilith said. "More plant than animal." She let their surprised silence last for a moment, then led them into the room where she and Leah had left the food. Tate was already there, eating a hot rice and bean dish.

Celene handed Curt one of the large edible bowls of food and Lilith offered one to Joseph. But Joseph kept focused on the subject of the living ship. He refused to eat himself or let Lilith eat in peace until he knew everything she did about the way the ship worked. He seemed annoyed that she knew so little.

"Do you believe what she says?" Leah asked him when he finally gave up the interrogation and tasted his cold food.

"I believe that Lilith believes," he said. "I haven't decided yet what I believe." He paused. "It does seem important, though, for us to behave as though we are in a ship—unless we find out for certain that we aren't. A ship in space could be an excellent prison even if we could get out of this room."

Lilith nodded gratefully. "That's it," she said. "That's what's important. If we endure this place, behave as though it's a ship no matter what anyone thinks individually, we can survive here until we're sent to Earth."

And she went on to tell them about the Oankali, about the plan to reseed Earth with human communities. Then she told them about the gene trade because she had decided they must know. If she waited too long to tell them, they might feel betrayed by her silence. But telling them now gave them plenty of time to reject the idea, then slowly begin to think about it and realize what it could mean.

Tate and Leah laughed at her, refused absolutely to believe that any manipulation of DNA could mix humans with extraterrestrial aliens.

"As far as I know," Lilith told them, "I haven't seen any human-Oankali combinations. But because of the things I *have* seen, because of the changes the Oankali have made in *me*, I believe they can tamper with us genetically, and I believe they intend to. Whether they'll blend with us or destroy us...that I don't know."

"Well, I haven't seen *anything*," Curt said. He had been quiet for a long time, listening, slipping his arm around Celene when she sat near him and looked frightened. "Until I do see something—and I don't mean more moving walls—this is all bullshit."

"I'm not sure I'd believe no matter what I saw," Tate said.

"It isn't hard to believe our captors intend to do some kind of genetic tampering," Joseph said. "They could do that whether they were human or extraterrestrial. There was a lot of work being done in genetics before the war. That may have devolved into some kind of eugenics program afterward. Hitler might have done something like that after World War Two if he had had the technology and if he had survived." He took a deep breath. "I think our best bet now is to learn all we can. Get facts. Keep our eyes open. Then later we can make the best possible use of any opportunities we might have to escape."

Learn and run, Lilith thought almost gleefully. She could have hugged Joseph. Instead, she took a bite of her cold food.

5

Two days later when Lilith saw that Curt was not likely to cause trouble—at least, not soon—she Awakened Gabriel Rinaldi and Beatrice Dwyer. She asked Joseph to help her with Gabriel and turned Beatrice over to Leah and Curt. Celene was still useless when it came to getting people dressed and oriented. Tate was apparently becoming bored with the process of Awakening people.

"I think we ought to double our numbers every time," she told Lilith. "That way we go through less repetition, get things done faster, get down to Earth faster."

At least now she was beginning to accept the idea that she was not already on Earth, Lilith thought. That was something.

"I'm probably already Awakening people too fast," Lilith told her. "We've got to be able to work together before we reach Earth. It isn't enough for us just to refrain from killing one another. Down in the forest, we'll probably be more interdependent than most of us have ever been. We might be a little better at that if we give each new set of people time to fit in and a growing structure to fit into."

"What structure?" Tate began to smile. "You mean like a family . . . with you as Mama?"

Lilith only looked at her.

After a time, Tate shrugged. "Just wake up a group of them, sit them down, tell them what's going on—they won't believe you, of course—take questions, feed them, and the next day, start on the next batch. Quick and easy. They can't learn to work together if they aren't Awake."

"I've always heard that small classes worked better than large ones," Lilith said. "This is too important to rush."

The argument ended as Lilith's arguments with Tate usually ended. No resolution. Lilith continued to Awaken people slowly and Tate continued to disapprove.

After three days, Beatrice Dwyer and Gabriel Rinaldi seemed to be settling in. Gabriel paired with Tate. Beatrice avoided the men sexually, but joined in the endless discussions of their situation, first refusing to believe it, then finally accepting it along with the group's learn-and-run philosophy.

Now, Lilith decided, was the time to Awaken two more people. She Awoke two every two or three days, no longer worrying about Awakening men since there had been no real trouble. She did deliberately Awaken a few more women than men in the hope of minimizing violence.

But as the number of people grew, so did the potential for disagreement. There were several short, vicious fist-fights. Lilith tried to keep out of them, allowing people to sort things out for themselves. Her only concern was that the fights do no serous harm. Curt helped with this in spite of his cynicism. Once as they pulled two struggling, bleeding men apart, he told her she might have made a pretty good cop.

There was one fight that Lilith could not keep out of—one

begun for a foolish reason as usual. A large, angry, not particularly bright woman named Jean Pelerin demanded an end to the meatless diet. She wanted meat, she wanted it *now*, and Lilith had better produce it if she knew what was good for her.

Everyone else had accepted, however grudgingly, the absence of meat. "The Oankali don't eat it," Lilith had told them. "And because we can get along without it, they won't give it to us. They say once we're back on Earth, we'll be free to keep and kill animals again—though the ones we're used to are mostly extinct."

Nobody liked the idea. So far she had not Awakened a single voluntary vegetarian. But until Jean Pelerin, no one had tried to do anything about it.

Jean lunged at Lilith, punching, kicking, obviously intending to overwhelm at once.

Surprised, but far from overwhelmed, Lilith struck back. Two short, quick jabs.

Jean collapsed, unconscious, bleeding from her mouth.

Frightened, still angry, Lilith checked to see that the woman was breathing and not badly hurt. She stayed with her until Jean had regained consciousness enough to glare at Lilith. Then, without a word, Lilith left her.

Lilith went to her room, sat thinking for a few moments about the strength Nikanj had given her. She had pulled her punches, not intending to knock Jean unconscious. She was no longer concerned about Jean now, but it bothered her that she no longer knew her own strength. She could kill someone by accident. She could maim someone. Jean did not know how lucky she was with her headache and her split lip.

Lilith slipped to the floor, took off her jacket, and began doing exercises to burn off excess energy and emotion. Everyone knew she exercised. Several other people had begun doing it as well. For Lilith, it was a comfortable, mindless activity that gave her something to do when there was nothing she could do about her situation.

Some people would attack her. She had probably not yet experienced the worst of them. She might have to kill. They might kill her. People who accepted her now might turn away from her if she seriously injured or killed someone.

On the other hand, what could she do? She had to defend herself. What would people say if she had beaten a man as easily as she beat Jean? Nikanj had said she could do it. How long would it be before someone forced her to find out for sure?

"May I come in?"

Lilith stopped her exercising, put her jacket on, and said, "Come."

She was still seated on the floor, breathing deeply, perversely enjoying the slight ache in her muscles when Joseph Shing came around her new curving entrance-hall partition and into the room. She leaned against the bed platform and looked up at him. Because it was him, she smiled.

"You aren't hurt at all?" he asked.

She shook her head. "A couple of bruises."

He sat down next to her. "She's telling people you're a man. She says only a man can fight that way."

To her own surprise, Lilith laughed aloud.

"Some people aren't laughing," he said. "That new man, Van Weerden said he didn't think you were human at all."

She stared at him, then got up to go out, but he caught her hand and held it.

"It's all right. They're not standing out there muttering to themselves and believing fantasy. In fact, I don't think Van Weerden really believes it. They only want someone to focus their frustration on."

"I don't want to be that someone," she muttered.

"What choice have you?"

"I know." She sighed. She let him pull her down beside him again. She found it impossible to delude herself when he was around. This caused her enough pain sometimes to make her wonder why she encouraged him to stay around. Tate, with typical malice, had said, "He's old, he's short, and he's ugly. Haven't you got any discrimination at all?"

"He's forty," Lilith had said. "He doesn't seem ugly to me, and if he can deal with my size, I can deal with his."

"You could do better."

"I'm content." She never told Tate that she had almost made Joseph the first person she Awakened. She shook her head over Tate's halfhearted attempts to lure Joseph away. It wasn't as though Tate wanted him. She just wanted to prove she could have him—and in the process, try him out. Joseph seemed to find the whole sequence funny. Other people were less relaxed about similar situations. That caused some of the most savage fights. An increasing number of bored, caged humans could not help finding destructive things to do.

"You know," she told him, "you could become a target yourself. Some people could decide to take their anger at me out on you."

"I know kung fu," he said examining her bruised knuckles.

"Do you really?"

He smiled. "No, just a little tai chi for exercise. Not so much sweating."

She decided he was telling her she smelled—which she did. She started to get up to go wash, but he would not let her go.

"Can you talk to them?" he asked.

She looked at him. He was growing a thin black beard. All the men were growing beards since no razors had been provided. Nothing hard or sharp had been provided.

"You mean talk to the Oankali?" she asked.

"Yes."

"They hear us all the time."

"But if you ask for something, will they provide it?"

"Probably not. I think it was a major concession for them just to give us all clothing."

"Yes. I thought you might say that. Then you should do what

Tate wants you to do. Awaken a large number of people at once. There's too little to do here. Get people busy helping one another, teaching one another. There are fourteen of us now. Awaken ten more tomorrow."

Lilith shook her head. "Ten? But—"

"It will take some of the negative attention off you. Busy people have less time for fantasizing and fighting."

She moved away from his side to sit facing him. "What is it, Joe? What's wrong?"

"People being people, that's all. You're probably not in any danger now, but you will be soon. You must know that."

She nodded.

"When there are forty of us, will the Oankali take us out of here or—"

"When there are forty of us, and the Oankali decide we're ready, they'll come in. Eventually, they'll take us to be taught to live on Earth. They have a . . . an area of the ship that they've made over into a fragment of Earth. They've grown a small tropical forest there—like the forest we'll be sent to on Earth. We'll be trained there."

"You've seen this place?"

"I spent a year there."

"Why?"

"First learning, then proving I'd learned. Knowing and using the knowledge aren't the same thing."

"No." He thought for a moment. "The presence of the Oankali will bring them together, but it might turn them even more strongly against you. Especially if the Oankali really scare them."

"The Oankali will scare them."

"That bad?"

"That alien. That ugly. That powerful."

"Then . . . don't come into the forest with us. Try to get out of it."

She smiled sadly. "I speak their language, Joe, but I've never yet been able to convince them to change one of their decisions."

"Try, Lilith!"

His intensity surprised her. Had he really seen something she had missed—something he wouldn't tell her? Or was he simply understanding her position for the first time? She had known for a long time that she might be doomed. She had had time to get used to the idea and to understand that she must struggle not against nonhuman aliens, but against her own kind.

"Will you talk to them?" Joseph asked.

She had to think for a moment to realize he meant the Oankali. She nodded. "I'll do what I can," she said. "You and Tate may be right about Awakening people faster, too. I think I'm ready to try that."

"Good. You have a fair core group around you. The new ones you Awaken can work things out in the forest. There they should have more to do."

"Oh, they'll have plenty to do. The tedium of some of it, though . . . wait until I teach you to weave a basket or a hammock or to make your own garden tools and use them to grow your food."

"We'll do what's necessary," he said. "If we can't, then we won't survive." He paused, looked away from her. "I've been a city man all my life. I might not survive."

"If I do, you will," she said grimly.

He broke the mood by laughing quietly. "That's foolishness— but it's a lovely foolishness. I feel the same way about you. You see what comes of being shut up together and having so little to do. Good things as well as bad. How many people will you Awaken tomorrow?"

She had bent her body almost in thirds, arms clasped around doubled knees, head resting on knees. Her body shook with humorless laughter. He had awakened her one night, seemingly out of the blue and asked her if he might come to bed with her. She had had all she could do to stop herself from grabbing him and pulling him in.

But they had not talked about their feelings until now. Every-one knew. Everyone knew everything. She knew, for instance, that people said he slept with her to get special privileges or to escape their prison. Certainly, he was not someone she would have noticed on prewar Earth. And he would not have noticed her. But here, there had been a pull between them from the moment he Awoke, intense, inescapable, acted upon, and now, spoken.

"I'll Awaken ten people as you said," she told him finally. "It seems a good number. It will occupy everyone I would dare to trust to look after a newly Awakened person. As for the others... I don't want them free to wander around and cause trouble or get together and cause trouble. I'll double them with you, Tate, Leah, and me."

"Leah?" he said.

"Leah's all right. Surly, moody, stubborn. And hardworking, loyal, and hard to scare. I like her."

"I think she likes you," he said. "That surprises me. I would have expected her to resent you."

Behind him, the wall began to open.

Lilith froze, then sighed and deliberately stared at the floor. When she looked up again, seemingly to look at Joseph, she could see Nikanj coming through the opening.

6

She moved over beside Joseph who, leaning against the bed platform, had noticed nothing. She took his hand, held it for a moment between her own, wondering if she were about to lose him. Would he stay with her after tonight? Would he speak to her tomorrow beyond absolute necessity? Would he join her enemies, confirming to them things they only suspected now? What the hell did Nikanj want anyway? Why couldn't it stay out as it had said it would. There: She had finally caught it in a lie. She would not forgive it if that lie destroyed Joseph's feelings for her.

"What is it?" Joseph was saying as Nikanj strode across the room in utter silence and sealed the doorway.

"For God knows what reason, the Oankali have decided to give you a preview," she said softly, bitterly. "You aren't in any physical danger. You won't be hurt." Let Nikanj make a lie of that and she would force it to put her back into suspended animation.

Joseph looked around sharply, froze when he saw Nikanj. After a moment of what Lilith suspected was absolute terror, he jerked himself to his feet and stumbled back against the wall, cornering himself between the wall and the bed platform.

"What is it!" Lilith demanded in Oankali. She stood to face Nikanj. "Why are you here?"

Nikanj spoke in English. "So that he could endure his fear now, privately, and be of help to you later."

A moment after hearing the quiet androgynous, human sounding voice speak in English, Joseph came out of his corner. He moved to Lilith's side, stood staring at Nikanj. He was trembling visibly. He said something in Chinese—the first time Lilith had heard him speak the language—then somehow, stilled his trembling. He looked at her.

"You know this one?"

"Kaalnikanjl oo Jdahyatediinkahguyaht aj Dinso," she said, staring at Nikanj's sensory arms, remembering how much more human it had looked without them. "Nikanj," she said when she saw Joseph frowning.

"I didn't believe," he said softly. "I couldn't, even though you said it."

She did not know what to say. He was handling the situation better than she had. Of course he had been warned and he was not being kept isolated from other humans. Still, he was doing well. He was as adaptable as she had suspected.

Moving slowly, Nikanj reached the bed and boosted itself up with one hand, folding its legs under it as it settled. Its head tentacles focused sharply on Joseph. "There's no hurry," it said. "We'll talk for a while. If you're hungry, I'll get you something."

"I'm not hungry," Joseph said. "Others may be, though."

"They must wait. They should spend a little time waiting for Lilith, understanding that they're helpless without her."

"They're just as helpless with me," Lilith said softly. "You've made them dependent on me. They may not be able to forgive me for that."

"Become their leader, and there'll be nothing to forgive."

Joseph looked at her as though Nikanj had finally said something to distract him from the strangeness of its body.

"Joe," she said, "it doesn't mean leader. It means Judas goat."

"You can make their lives easier," Nikanj said. "You can help them accept what is to happen to them. But whether you lead them or not, you can't prevent it. It would happen even if you died. If you lead them, more of them will survive. If you don't, you may not survive yourself."

She stared at it, remembered lying next to it when it was weak and helpless, remembered breaking bits of food into small pieces and slowly, carefully feeding it those pieces.

After a time its head and body tentacles drew themselves into knotted lumps and it hugged itself with its sensory arms. It spoke to her in Oankali: "I want you to live! Your mate is right! Some of these people are already plotting against you!"

"I told you they would plot against me," she said in English. "I told you they would probably kill me."

"You didn't tell me you would help them!"

She leaned against her table platform, head down. "I'm trying to live," she whispered. "You know I am."

"You could clone us," Joseph said. "Is that right?"

"Yes."

"You could take reproductive cells from us and grow human embryos in artificial wombs?"

"Yes."

"You can even re-create us from some kind of gene map or print."

"We can do that too. We have already done these things. We must do them to understand a new species better. We must compare them to normal human conception and birth. We must compare the children we have made to those we took from Earth. We're very careful to avoid damaging new partner-species."

"Is that what you call it?" Joseph muttered in bitter revulsion.

Nikanj spoke very softly. "We revere life. We had to be certain we had found ways for you to live with the partnership, not simply to die of it."

"You don't need us!" Joseph said. "You've created your own human beings. Poor bastards. Make them your partners."

"We...do need you." Nikanj spoke so softly that Joseph leaned forward to hear. "A partner must be biologically interesting, attractive to us, and you are fascinating. You are horror and beauty in rare combination. In a very real way, you've captured us, and we can't escape. But you're more than only the composition and the workings of your bodies. You are your personalities, your cultures. We're interested in those too. That's why we saved as many of you as we could."

Joseph shuddered. "We've seen how you saved us—your prison cells and your suspended animation plants, and now this."

"Those are the simplest things we do. And they leave you relatively untouched. You are what you were on Earth—minus any disease or injury. With a little training, you can go back to Earth and sustain yourselves comfortably."

"Those of us who survive this room and the training room."

"Those of you who survive."

"You could have done this another way!"

"We've tried other ways. This way is best. There is incentive not to do harm. No one who has killed or severely injured another will set foot on Earth again."

"They'll be kept here?"

"For the rest of their lives."

"Even..." Joseph glanced at Lilith, then faced Nikanj again. "Even if the killing is in self-defense?"

"She is exempt," Nikanj said.

"What?"

"She knows. We've given her abilities that at least one of you must have. They make her different, and therefore they make her a target. It would be self-defeating for us to forbid her to defend herself."

"Nikanj," Lilith said, and when she saw that she had its attention she spoke in Oankali. "Exempt him."

"No."

Flat refusal. That was that, and she knew it. But she could not help trying. "He's a target because of me," she said. "He could be killed because of me."

Nikanj spoke in Oankali. "And I want him to live because of you. But I didn't make the decision to keep humans who kill away from Earth—and I didn't exempt you. It was a consensus. I can't exempt him."

"Then . . . strengthen him the way you did me."

"He would be more likely to kill then."

"And less likely to die. I mean give him more resistance to injury. Help him heal faster if he is injured. Give him a chance!"

"What are you talking about?" Joseph said to her angrily. "Speak English!"

She opened her mouth, but Nikanj spoke first. "She's speaking for you. She wants you protected."

He looked at Lilith for confirmation. She nodded. "I'm afraid for you. I wanted you exempted too. It says it can't do that. So I've asked it to . . ." She stopped, looked from Nikanj to Joseph. "I've asked it to strengthen you, give you at least a chance."

He frowned at her. "Lilith, I'm not large, but I'm stronger than you think. I can take care of myself."

"I didn't speak in English because I didn't want to hear you say that. Of course you can't take care of yourself. No one person could against what might happen out there. I only wanted to give you more of a chance than you have now."

"Show him your hand," Nikanj said.

She hesitated, fearing that he would begin to see her as alien or too close to aliens—too much changed by them. But now that Nikanj had drawn attention to her hand, she could not conceal it. She raised her no-longer-bruised knuckles and showed them to Joseph.

He examined her hand minutely, then looked at the other one just to be certain he had not made a mistake. "They did this?" he asked. "Enabled you to heal so quickly?"

"Yes."

"What else?"

"Made me stronger than I was—and I was strong before—and enabled me to control interior walls and suspended animation plants. That's all."

He faced Nikanj. "How did you do this?"

Nikanj rustled its tentacles. "For the walls, I altered her body chemistry slightly. For the strength, I gave her more efficient use of what she already has. She should have been stronger. Her ancestors were stronger—her nonhuman ancestors in particular. I helped her fulfill her potential."

"How?"

"How do you move and coordinate the fingers of your hands? I'm an ooloi bred to work with humans. I can help them do anything their bodies are capable of doing. I made biochemical changes that caused her regular exercises to be much more effective than they would have been otherwise. There is also a slight genetic change. I haven't added or subtracted anything, but I have brought out latent ability. She is as strong and as fast as her nearest animal ancestors were." Nikanj paused, perhaps noticing the way Joseph was looking at Lilith. "The changes I've made are not hereditary," it said.

"You said you changed her genes!" Joseph charged.

"Body cells only. Not reproductive cells."

"But if you cloned her..."

"I will not clone her."

There was a long silence. Joseph looked at Nikanj, then stared long at Lilith. She spoke when she thought she had endured his stare long enough.

"If you want to go out and join the others, I'll open the wall," she said.

"Is that what you think?" he asked.

"That's what I fear," she whispered.

"Could you have prevented what was done to you?"

"I didn't try to prevent it." She swallowed. "They were going to give me this job no matter what I said. I told them they might as well kill me themselves. Even that didn't stop them. So when Nikanj and its mates offered me as much as they could offer, I didn't even have to think about it. I welcomed it."

After a time, he nodded.

"I'll give you some of what I gave her," Nikanj said. "I won't increase your strength, but I will enable you to heal faster, recover from injuries that might otherwise kill you. Do you want me to do this?"

"You're giving me a choice?"

"Yes."

"The change is permanent?"

"Unless you ask to be changed back."

"Side effects?"

"Psychological."

Joseph frowned. "What do you mean, psycho...Oh. So that's why you won't give me the strength."

"Yes."

"But you trust...Lilith."

"She has been Awake and living with my families for years. We know her. And, of course, we're always watching."

After a time, Joseph took Lilith's hands. "Do you see?" he asked gently. "Do you understand why they chose you—someone who desperately doesn't want the responsibility, who doesn't want to lead, who is a woman?"

The condescension in his voice first startled, then angered her. "Do I see, Joe? Oh, yes. I've had plenty of time to see."

He seemed to realize how he had sounded. "You have, yes—not that it helps to know."

Nikanj had shifted its attention from one of them to the other.

Now it focused on Joseph. "Shall I make the change in you?" it asked.

Joseph released Lilith's hands. "What is it? Surgery? Something to do with blood or bone marrow?"

"You will be made to sleep. When you awake, the change will have been made. There won't be any pain or illness, no surgery in the usual sense of the word."

"How will you do it?"

"These are my tools." It extended both sensory arms. "Through them, I'll study you, then make the necessary adjustments. My body and yours will produce any substances I need."

Joseph shuddered visibly. "I...I don't think I could let you touch me."

Lilith looked at him until he turned to face her. "I was shut up for days with one of them before I could touch him," she said. "There were times...I'd rather take a beating than go through anything like that again."

Joseph moved closer to her, his manner protective. It was easier for him to give comfort than to ask for it. Now he managed to do both at once.

"How long are you going to stay here now?" he demanded of Nikanj.

"Not much longer. I'll come back. You'll probably feel less afraid when you see me again." It paused. "Eventually you must touch me. You must show at least that much control before I change you."

"I don't know. Maybe I don't want you to change me. I don't really understand what it is you do with those...those tentacles."

"Sensory arms, we call them in English. They're more than arms—much more—but the term is convenient." It focused its attention on Lilith and spoke in Oankali. "Do you think it would help if he saw a demonstration?"

"I'm afraid he would be repelled," she said.

"He's an unusual male. I think he might surprise you."

"No."

"You should trust me. I know a great deal about him."

"No! Leave him to me."

It stood up, unfolding itself dramatically. When she saw that it was about to leave, she almost relaxed. Then in a single swift sweep of motion, it stepped to her and looped a sensory arm around her neck forming an oddly comfortable noose. She was not afraid. She had been through this often enough to be used to it. Her first thoughts were concern for Joseph and anger at Nikanj.

Joseph had not moved. She stood between the two of them.

"It's all right," she told him. "It wanted you to see. This is all the contact it would need."

Joseph stared at the coil of sensory arm, looked from the arm to Nikanj and back to the arm again where it rested against Lilith's flesh. After a moment, he raised his hand toward it. He stopped. His hand twitched, drew back, then slowly reached out again. With only a moment's hesitation, he touched the cool, hard flesh of the sensory arm. His fingers rested on its hornlike tip and that tip twisted to grasp his wrist.

Now Lilith was no longer their intermediary. Joseph stood rigid and silent, sweating, but not trembling, his hand upright, fingers clawlike, a noose of sensory tentacles settled in a painless, unbreakable grip around the wrist.

With a sound that could have been the beginning of a scream, Joseph collapsed.

Lilith stepped to him quickly, but Nikanj caught him. He was unconscious. She said nothing until she had helped Nikanj put him on the bed. Then she caught it by the shoulders and turned it to face her.

"Why couldn't you let him alone!" she demanded. "I'm supposed to be in charge of them. Why didn't you just leave him to me?"

"Do you know," it said, "that no undrugged human has ever done that before? Some have touched us by accident this soon after meeting us, but no one has done it deliberately. I told you he was unusual."

"Why couldn't you let him alone!"

It unfastened Joseph's jacket and began to remove it. "Because there are already two human males speaking against him, trying to turn others against him. One has decided he's something called a faggot and the other dislikes the shape of his eyes. Actually, both are angry about the way he's allied himself with you. They would prefer to have you without allies. Your mate needs any extra protection I can give him now."

She listened, appalled. Joseph had talked about the danger to her. Had he known how immediate his own danger was?

Nikanj threw the jacket aside and lay down beside Joseph. It wrapped one sensory tentacle around Joseph's neck and the other around his waist, drawing Joseph's body close against its own.

"Did you drug him, or did he faint?" she asked—then wondered why she cared.

"I drugged him as soon as I grasped his arm. He had reached his breaking point, though. He might have fainted on his own. This way, he can be angry with me for drugging him, not for making him look weak in front of you."

She nodded. "Thank you."

"What is a faggot?" it asked.

She told it.

"But they know he's not that. They know he's mated with you."

"Yes. Well, there's been some doubt about me, too, I hear."

"None of them really believe it."

"Yet."

"Serve them by leading them, Lilith. Help us send as many of them home as we can."

She stared at it for a long time, feeling frightened and empty. It sounded so sincere—not that that mattered. How could she become the leader of people who saw her as their jailer? On some level, a leader had to be trusted. Yet every act she performed that proved the truth of what she said also made her loyalties, and even her humanity suspect.

She sat down on the floor, cross-legged and at first stared at nothing. Eventually, her eyes were drawn to Nikanj holding Joseph on the bed. The pair did not move, though once she heard Joseph sigh. Was he no longer completely unconscious, then? Was he already learning the lesson all adult ooloi eventually taught? So much in only one day.

"Lilith?"

She jumped. Both Joseph and Nikanj had spoken her name, though clearly, only Nikanj was enough awake to know what it was saying. Joseph, drugged and under the influence of multiple neural links, would shadow everything Nikanj said or did unless Nikanj split its attention enough to stop him. Nikanj did not bother.

"I have adjusted him, even strengthened him a little, though he'll have to exercise to be able to use that to his best advantage. He will be more difficult to injure, faster to heal, and able to survive and recover from injuries that would have killed him before." Joseph, unknowing, spoke every word exactly in unison with Nikanj.

"Stop that!" Lilith said sharply.

Nikanj altered its connection without missing a beat. "Lie here with us," it said, speaking alone. "Why should you be down there by yourself?"

She thought there could be nothing more seductive than an ooloi speaking in that particular tone, making that particular suggestion. She realized she had stood up without meaning to and taken a step toward the bed. She stopped, stared at the two of them. Joseph's breathing now became a gentle snore and he seemed to sleep comfortably against Nikanj as she had awakened to find him sleeping comfortably against her many times. She did not pretend outwardly or to herself that she would resist Nikanj's invitation—or that she wanted to resist it. Nikanj could give her an intimacy with Joseph that was beyond ordinary human experience. And what it gave, it also experienced. This was what had captured Paul Titus, she thought. This, not sorrow over his losses or fear of a primitive Earth.

She clenched her fists, holding back. "This won't help me," she said. "It will just make it harder for me when you're not around."

Nikanj freed one sensory arm from Joseph's waist and extended it toward her.

She stayed where she was for a moment longer, proving to herself that she was still in control of her behavior. Then she tore off her jacket and seized the ugly, ugly elephant's trunk of an organ, letting it coil around her as she climbed onto the bed. She sandwiched Nikanj's body between her own and Joseph's, placing it for the first time in the ooloi position between two humans. For an instant, this frightened her. This was the way she might someday be made pregnant with an other-than-human child. Not now while Nikanj wanted other work from her, but someday. Once it plugged into her central nervous system it could control her and do whatever it wanted.

She felt it tremble against her, and knew it was in.

7

She did not lose consciousness. Nikanj did not want to cheat itself of sensation. Even Joseph was conscious, though utterly controlled, unafraid because Nikanj kept him tranquil. Lilith was not controlled. She could lift a free hand across Nikanj to take Joseph's cool, seemingly lifeless hand.

"No," Nikanj said softly into her ear—or perhaps it stimulated the auditory nerve directly. It could do that—stimulate her senses individually or in any combination to make perfect hallucinations. "Only through me," its voice insisted.

Lilith's hand tingled. She released Joseph's hand and immediately received Joseph as a blanket of warmth and security, a compelling, steadying presence.

She never knew whether she was receiving Nikanj's approximation of Joseph, a true transmission of what Joseph was feeling, some combination of truth and approximation, or just a pleasant fiction.

What was Joseph feeling from her?

It seemed to her that she had always been with him. She had

no sensation of shifting gears, no "time alone" to contrast with the present "time together." He had always been there, part of her, essential.

Nikanj focused on the intensity of their attraction, their union. It left Lilith no other sensation. It seemed, itself, to vanish. She sensed only Joseph, felt that he was aware only of her.

Now their delight in one another ignited and burned. They moved together, sustaining an impossible intensity, both of them tireless, perfectly matched, ablaze in sensation, lost in one another. They seemed to rush upward. A long time later, they seemed to drift down slowly, gradually, savoring a few more moments wholly together.

Noon, evening, dusk, darkness.

Her throat hurt. Her first solitary sensation was pain—as though she had been shouting, screaming. She swallowed painfully and raised her hand to her throat, but Nikanj's sensory arm was there ahead of her and brushed her hand away. It laid its exposed sensory hand across her throat. She felt it anchor itself, sensory fingers stretching, clasping. She did not feel the tendrils of its substance penetrate her flesh, but in a moment the pain in her throat was gone.

"All that and you only screamed once," it told her.

"How'd you let me do even that?" she asked.

"You surprised me. I've never made you scream before."

She let it withdraw from her throat, then moved languidly to stroke it. "How much of that experience was Joseph's and mine?" she asked. "How much did you make up?"

"I've never made up an experience for you," it said. "I won't have to for him either. You both have memories filled with experiences."

"That was a new one."

"A combination. You had your own experiences and his. He had his and yours. You both had me to keep it going much longer than it would have otherwise. The whole was...overwhelming."

She looked around. "Joseph?"

"Asleep. Very deeply asleep. I didn't induce it. He's tired. He's all right, though."

"He...felt everything I felt?"

"On a sensory level. Intellectually, he made his interpretations and you made yours."

"I wouldn't call them intellectual."

"You understand me."

"Yes." She moved her hand over its chest, taking a perverse pleasure in feeling its tentacles squirm, then flatten under her hand.

"Why do you do that?" it asked.

"Does it bother you?" she asked stilling her hand.

"No."

"Let me do it, then. I didn't used to be able to."

"I have to go. You should wash, then feed your people. Seal your mate in. Be certain you're the first to talk to him when he wakes."

She watched it climb over her, joints bending all wrong, and lower itself to the floor. She caught its hand before it could head for a wall. Its head tentacles pointed at her loosely in unspoken question.

"Do you like him?" she asked.

The point focused briefly on Joseph. "Ahajas and Dichaan are mystified," it said. "They thought you would choose one of the big dark ones because they're like you. I said you would choose this one—because he's like you."

"What?"

"During his testing, his responses were closer to yours than anyone else I'm aware of. He doesn't look like you but he's like you."

"He might..." She forced herself to voice the thought. "He might not want anything more to do with me when he realizes what I helped you do with him."

"He'll be angry—and frightened and eager for the next time and determined to see that there won't be a next time. I've told you, I know this one."

"How do you know him so well? What have you had to do with him before?"

Its head and body smoothed so that even with its sensory arms, it resembled a slender, hairless, sexless human.

"He was the subject of one of my first acts of adult responsibility," it said. "I knew you by then, and I set out to find someone for you. Not another Paul Titus, but someone you would want. Someone who would want you. I examined memory records of thousands of males. This one might have been taught to parent a group himself, but when I showed other ooloi the match, they agreed that the two of you should be together."

"You . . . You chose him for me?"

"I offered you to one another. The two of you did your own choosing." It opened a wall and left her.

8

People gathered around silently, radiating hostility when Lilith called them out to eat. Most were already out, waiting for her sullenly, impatiently, hungrily. Lilith ignored their annoyance.

"It's about time," Peter Van Weerden muttered as she opened the various wall cabinets and people began to come forward and take food. This was the man who claimed she was not human, she recalled.

"If you're through screwing, that is," Jean Pelerin added.

Lilith turned to look at Jean and managed to examine the woman's bruised, swollen face before Jean turned away.

Troublemakers. Only two of them out in the open so far. How long would that last?

"I'll be Awakening ten more people tomorrow," she said before anyone could leave. "You'll all be helping with them singly or in pairs." She paced alongside the food wall, automatically drawing her fingers around the circular cabinet openings, keeping them from closing while people chose what they wanted. Even the

newest people were used to this, but Gabriel Rinaldi complained
mildly.

"It's ridiculous for you to have to do that, Lilith. Make them
stay open."

"That's the idea," she said. "They stay open for two or three
minutes, then they close unless I touch them again." She stopped,
took the last bowl of hot, spicy beans from one cabinet, and let
it close. The cabinet would not begin to refill itself until the wall
was sealed. She put the beans on the floor to one side for her
own meal later. People sat around on the floor, eating from edible
dishes. There was comfort in eating together—one of their few
comforts. Groups formed and people talked quietly among themselves. Lilith was taking fruit for herself when Peter spoke from
his group nearby. His group of Jean, Curt Loehr, and Celene Ivers.

"If you ask me, the walls are fixed that way to keep us from
thinking about what we ought to do to our jailor," Peter said.

Lilith waited, wondering whether anyone would defend her.
No one did, though silence spread to other groups.

She drew a deep breath, walked over to Peter's group. "Things
can change," she said quietly. "Maybe you can turn everybody
here against me. That would make me a failure." She raised her
voice slightly, though even her quiet words had carried. "That
would mean all of you put back into suspended animation so that
you can be separated and put through all this again with other
people." She paused. "If that's what you want—to be split up, to
begin again alone, to go through this however many times it takes
for you to let yourself get all the way through it, keep trying. You
might succeed."

She left him, took her food and joined Tate, Gabriel, and Leah.

"Not bad," Tate said when people had resumed their own conversations. "Clear warning to everyone. It's overdue."

"It won't work," Leah said. "These people don't know each
other. What do they care if they have to start again?"

"They care," Gabriel told her. Even with his blue-black beard, he was one of the best looking men Lilith had ever seen. And he was still sleeping exclusively with Tate. Lilith liked him, but she was aware that he did not quite trust her. She could see that in his expression when she caught him watching her sometimes. Yet he was careful to keep her goodwill—keep his options open.

"They've made personal ties here," he said to Leah. "Think what they had before: War, chaos, family and friends dead. Then solitary. A jail cell and shit to eat. They care very much. So do you."

She turned to face him angrily, mouth already open, but the handsome face seemed to disarm her. She sighed and nodded sadly. For a moment she seemed close to tears.

"How many times can you have everyone taken from you and still have the will to start again?" Tate muttered.

As many times as it took, Lilith thought wearily. As many times as human fear, suspicion, and stubbornness made necessary. The Oankali were as patient as the waiting Earth.

She realized that Gabriel was staring at her.

"You're still worried about them, aren't you?" he asked.

She nodded.

"I think they believed you. All of them, not just Van Weerden and Jean."

"I know. They'll believe me for a little while. Then some of them will decide I'm lying to them or that I've been lied to."

"Are you sure you haven't?" Tate asked.

"I'm sure I have," Lilith said bitterly. "By omission, at least."

"But then—"

"This is what I *know*," Lilith said. "Our rescuers, our captors are extraterrestrials. We are aboard their ship. I've seen and felt enough—including weightlessness—to be convinced that it is a ship. We're in space. And we're in the hands of people who manipulate DNA as naturally as we manipulate pencils and paintbrushes. That's what I know. That's what I've told you all. And if any of you decide to behave as though it isn't true, we'll all be lucky if we're just put to sleep and split up."

She looked at the three faces and forced a weary smile. "End of speech," she said. "I'd better get something for Joseph."

"You should have gotten him out here," Tate said.

"Don't worry about it," Lilith told her.

"You could bring me a meal now and then," Gabriel said to her as Lilith left them.

"See what you've done!" Tate called after her.

Lilith found herself smiling an unforced smile as she took more food from the cabinets. It was inevitable that some of the people she Awakened would disbelieve her, dislike her, distrust her. At least there were others she could talk to, relax with.

There was hope if she could only keep the skeptics from self-destructing.

9

For a time, Joseph would not speak or take food from her hands. Once she understood this, she sat with him to wait. She had not Awakened him when she came back to the room, had sealed the room and slept beside him until his movements woke her. Now she sat with him, worried but feeling no real hostility from him. He did not seem to resent her presence.

He was sorting out his feelings, she thought. He was trying to understand what had happened.

She had put a few pieces of fruit on the bed between them. She had said, knowing he would not answer, "It was a neurosensory illusion. Nikanj stimulates nerves directly, and we remember or create experiences to suit the sensations. On a physical level, Nikanj feels what we feel. It can't read our thoughts. It can't get away with hurting us—unless it's willing to suffer the same pain." She hesitated. "It said it strengthened you a little. You'll have to be careful at first, and exercise. You won't get hurt easily. If something does happen to you you'll heal the way I do."

He had not spoken, had not looked at her, but she knew he had heard. There was nothing vacant about him.

She sat with him, waited, oddly comfortable, nibbling at the fruit now and then. After a time, she lay back, feet on the floor, body stretched across the bed. The movement attracted him.

He turned, stared at her as though he had forgotten she was there. "You should get up," he said. "The light's coming back. Morning."

"Talk to me," she said.

He rubbed his head. "It wasn't real? Not any of it?"

"We didn't touch each other."

He grabbed her hand and held it. "That thing...did it all."

"Neural stimulation."

"How?"

"They hook into our nervous systems somehow. They're more sensitive than we are. Anything we feel a little, they feel a lot—and they feel it almost before we're conscious of it. That helps them stop doing anything painful before we notice that they've begun."

"They've done it to you before?"

She nodded.

"With...other men?"

"Alone or with Nikanj's mates."

Abruptly, he got up and began to pace.

"They aren't human," she said.

"Then how can they...? Their nervous systems can't be like ours. How can they make us feel...what I felt?"

"By pushing the right electrochemical buttons. I don't claim to understand it. It's like a language that they have a special gift for. They know our bodies better than we do."

"Why do you let them...touch you?"

"To have changes made. The strength, the fast healing—"

He stopped in front of her, faced her. "Is that all?" he demanded.

She stared at him, seeing the accusation in his eyes, refusing to defend herself. "I liked it," she said softly. "Didn't you?"

"That thing will never touch me again if I have anything to say about it."

She did not challenge this.

"I've never felt anything like that in my *life*," he shouted.

She jumped, but said nothing.

"If a thing like that could be bottled, it would have outsold any illegal drug on the market."

"I'm going to Awaken ten people this morning," she said. "Will you help?"

"You're still going to do that?"

"Yes."

He breathed deeply. "Let's go then." But he did not move. He still stood watching her. "Is it . . . like a drug?" he asked.

"You mean am I addicted?"

"Yes."

"I don't think so. I was happy with you. I didn't want Nikanj here."

"I don't want him here again."

"Nikanj isn't male—and I doubt whether it really cares what either of us wants."

"Don't let him touch you! If you have a choice, keep away from him!"

The refusal to accept Nikanj's sex frightened her because it reminded her of Paul Titus. She did not want to see Paul Titus in Joseph.

"It isn't male, Joseph."

"What difference does that make!"

"What difference does any self-deception make? We need to know them for what they are, even if there are no human parallels—and believe me, there are none for the ooloi." She got up, knowing that she had not given him the promise he wanted, knowing that he would remember her silence. She unsealed the doorway and left the room.

10

Ten new people.

Everyone was kept busy trying to keep them out of trouble and give them some idea of their situation. The woman Peter was helping laughed in his face and told him he was crazy when he mentioned, as he said, "the possibility that our captors might somehow be extraterrestrials..."

Leah's charge, a small blond man, grabbed her, hung on, and might have raped her if he had been bigger or she smaller. She stopped him from doing any harm, but Gabriel had to help her get him off. She was surprisingly tolerant of the man's efforts. She seemed more amused than angry.

Nothing the new people did for the first few minutes was taken seriously or held against them. Leah's attacker was simply held until he stopped trying to get to her, until he grew quiet and began to look around at the many human faces, until he began to cry.

The man's name was Wray Ordway and a few days after his Awakening, he was sleeping with Leah with her full consent.

Two days after that, Peter Van Weerden and six followers

seized Lilith and held her while a seventh follower, Derrick Wolski, swept a dozen or so leftover biscuits out of one of the food cabinets and climbed into it before it could close.

When Lilith realized what Derrick was doing she stopped struggling. There was no need to hurt anyone. The Oankali would take care of Derrick.

"What does he think he's going to do?" she asked Curt. He had taken part in holding her, though, of course Celene had not. He still held one of her arms.

Watching him, she shook the others off. Now that Derrick was gone from sight, they did not try hard to hold her. She knew now that if she had been willing to hurt or kill them, they could not have held her. She was not stronger than all six combined, but she was stronger than any two. And faster than any of them. The knowledge was not as comforting as it should have been.

"What's he supposed to be doing?" she repeated.

Curt released the arm she had left in his hands. "Finding out what's really going on," he said. "There are people refilling those cabinets and we intend to find out who they are. We want to get a look at them before they're ready to be seen—before they're ready to convince us they're Martians."

She sighed. He had been told that the cabinets refilled automatically. Just one more thing he had decided not to believe. "They're not Martians," she said.

He crooked his mouth in something less than a smile. "I knew that. I never believed your fairy tales."

"They're from another solar system," she said. "I don't know which one. It doesn't matter. They left it so long ago, they don't even know whether it still exists."

He cursed her and turned away.

"What's going to happen?" another voice asked.

Lilith looked around, saw Celene, and sighed. Wherever Curt was, Celene was trembling nearby. Lilith had matched them as well as Nikanj had matched her with Joseph. "I don't know," she said. "The Oankali won't let him get hurt, but I don't know whether they'll put him back in here."

Joseph strode up to her, obviously concerned. Someone had apparently gone to his room and told him what was going on.

"It's all right," she said. "Derrick has gone out to look at the Oankali." She shrugged at his look of alarm. "I hope they send him back—or bring him back. These people are going to have to see for themselves."

"That could start a panic!" he whispered.

"I don't care. They'll recover. But if they keep doing stupid things like this, they'll eventually manage to hurt themselves."

Derrick was not sent back.

Eventually even Peter and Jean did not object when Lilith went to the wall and opened the cabinet to prove that Derrick had not asphyxiated inside. She had to open every cabinet in the general area of the one he had used because most of the others could not locate the individual cabinet on the broad, unmarked expanse of wall. Lilith had at first been surprised at her own ability to locate each one easily and exactly. Once she found them the first time she remembered their distance from floor and ceiling, from right and left walls. Some people, since they could not do this themselves, found the ability suspicious. Some people found everything about her suspicious.

"What happened to Derrick!" Jean Pelerin demanded.

"He did something stupid," Lilith told her. "And while he was doing it, you helped hold me so that I couldn't stop him."

Jean drew back a little, spoke louder. "What happened to him?"

"I don't know."

"Liar!" The volume increased again. "What did your friends do to him? Kill him?"

"What ever happened to him, you're partly to blame," Lilith said. "Handle your own guilt." She looked around at other equally guilty, equally accusing faces. Jean never made her complaints privately. She needed an audience.

Lilith turned and went to her room. She was about to seal herself in when Tate and Joseph joined her. A moment later, Gabriel followed them in. He sat on the corner of Lilith's table and faced her.

"You're losing," he said flatly.

"You're losing," she countered. "If I lose, everyone loses."

"That's why we're here."

"If you have an idea, I'll listen."

"Give them a better show. Get your friends to help you impress them."

"My friends?"

"Look, I don't care. You say they're extraterrestrials. Okay. They're extraterrestrials. What the hell are they going to gain if those assholes out there kill you?"

"I agreed. I was hoping they would send or bring Derrick back. They might still. But their timing is terrible."

"Joe says you can talk to them."

She turned to stare at Joseph in betrayal and surprise.

"Your enemies are gathering allies," he said. "Why should you be alone?"

She looked at Tate and the woman shrugged. "Those people out there are assholes," she said. "If they had a brain between them they'd shut up and open their eyes and ears until they had some idea what was really going on."

"That's all I hoped for," Lilith said. "I didn't expect it, but I hoped for it."

"Those are frightened people looking for someone to save them," Gabriel said. "They don't want reason or logic or your hopes or expectations. They want Moses or somebody to come and lead them into lives they can understand."

"Van Weerden can't do that," Lilith said.

"Of course he can't. But right now they think he can, and they're following. Next, he'll tell them the only way to get out of here is to knock you around until you tell all your secrets. He'll say you know the way out. And by the time it's clear that you don't, you'll be dead."

Would she? He had no idea how long it would take to torture her to death. Her and Joseph. She looked at him bleakly.

"Victor Dominic," Joseph said. "And Leah and that guy she's picked up and Beatrice Dwyer and—"

"Potential allies?" Lilith asked.

"Yes, and we'd better hurry. I saw Beatrice with one of the guys from the other side this morning."

"Loyalties can change according to who people are sleeping with," Lilith said.

"So what!" demanded Gabriel. "So you don't trust anybody? So you wind up in pieces on the floor?"

Lilith shook her head. "I know it has to be done. So stupid, isn't it. It's like 'Let's play Americans against the Russians. Again.'"

"Talk to your friends," Gabriel said. "Maybe that's not the show they had in mind. Maybe they'll help you rewrite the script."

She stared at him, frowning. "Do you really talk like that?"

"Whatever works," he said.

11

The Oankali did not choose to play the part of Lilith's friends. When she sealed herself into her room and spoke to them, they neither appeared nor answered her calls. And they continued to hold Derrick. Lilith thought he had probably been made to sleep again.

None of this surprised her. She would organize the humans into a coherent unit or she would serve as a scapegoat for whoever else organized them. Nikanj and its mates would save her life if they could—if it seemed her life was in immediate danger. But beyond that, she was on her own.

But she did have *powers.* Or that was the way people thought of the things she could do with the walls and the suspended animation plants. Peter Van Weerden had nothing. Some people believed he had caused Derrick's disappearance, perhaps his death. Fortunately Peter was not eloquent enough, not charismatic enough to shift blame for this to Lilith—though he tried.

What he did manage to do was portray Derrick as a hero, a

martyr who had acted for the group, who had at least *tried* to do something. What the hell was Lilith doing, he would demand. What was her group doing? Sitting on their hands, talking and talking, waiting for their captors to tell them what to do next.

People who favored action sided with Peter. People like Leah and Wray, Tate and Gabriel who were biding their time, waiting for more information or a real chance to escape sided with Lilith.

There were also people like Beatrice Dwyer who were afraid of any kind of action, but who had lost hope of ever controlling their own destinies. These sided with Lilith in the hope of peace and continued life. They wanted, Lilith thought, only to be let alone. That was all many people had wanted before the war. It was the one thing they could not have, then or now.

Nevertheless, Lilith recruited these, too, and when she Awakened ten more people, she used only her recruits to help them. Peter's people were reduced to heckling and jeering. The new people saw them first as troublemakers.

Perhaps that was why Peter decided to impress his followers by helping one of them get a woman.

The woman, Allison Zeigler, had not yet found a man she liked, but she had chosen Lilith's side over Peter's. She screamed Lilith's name when Peter and the new man, Gregory Sebastes, stopped arguing with her and decided to drag her off to Gregory's room.

Lilith, alone in her own room, frowned, not certain what she had heard. Another fight?

Wearily, she put down the stack of dossiers that she had been going through in search of a few more allies. She went out and saw the trouble at once.

Two men holding a struggling woman between them. The trio was prevented from reaching any of the bedrooms by Lilith's people who stood blocking the way. And Lilith's people were prevented from reaching the trio by several of Peter's people.

A standoff—potentially deadly.

"What the hell is she saving herself for?" Jean was demanding. "It's her duty to get together with someone. There aren't that many of us left."

"It's my duty to find out where I am and how to get free," Allison shouted. "Maybe you want to give whoever's holding us prisoner a human baby to fool around with, but I don't!"

"We pair off!" Curt bellowed, drowning her out. "One man, one woman. Nobody has the right to hold you. It just causes trouble."

"Trouble for who!" someone demanded.

"Who the shit are you to tell us our rights!" called someone else.

"What is she to you!" Gregory used his free hand to knock someone away from Allison. "Get your own damn woman!"

At that moment, Allison hit him. He cursed and hit her. She screamed, twisted her body violently. Blood streamed from her nose.

Lilith reached the crowd. "Stop," she called. "Let her go!" But her voice was lost in the many.

"*Goddammit, stop!*" She shouted in a voice that surprised even her.

People near her froze, staring at her, but the group around Allison was too involved to notice her until she reached it.

This was too familiar, too much like what Paul Titus had said and done.

She stepped up to the knot of people surrounding Allison, too furious to worry about their blocking her. Two of them caught her arms. She threw them aside without ever seeing their faces. For once she did not care what happened to them. Cavemen. *Fools!*

She grabbed Peter's free arm as he tried to hit her. She held the arm, squeezed it, twisted it.

Peter screamed and fell to his knees, his grip on Allison released, forgotten. For a moment, Lilith stared at him. He was garbage. Human garbage. How had she made the mistake of Awakening him? And what could she do with him now?

She threw him aside, not caring that he hit a nearby wall.

The other man, Gregory Sebastes, held his ground. Curt stood beside him, challenging Lilith. They had seen what she had done to Peter, but they did not seem to believe it. They let her walk up to them.

She hit Curt hard in the stomach, doubling him, toppling him.

Gregory let go of Allison and lunged at Lilith.

She hit him, catching him in midair, snapping his head back, collapsing him to the floor unconscious.

Abruptly, all was still except for Curt's gasping and Peter's groaning—"My arm! Oh, god, my arm!"

Lilith looked at each of Peter's people, daring them to attack, almost wanting them to attack. But now five of them were injured, and Lilith was untouched. Even her own people stood back from her.

"There'll be no rape here," she said evenly. She raised her voice. "Nobody here is property. Nobody here has the right to the use of anybody else's body. There'll be no back-to-the-Stone-Age, cave-man bullshit!" She let her voice drop to normal. "We stay human. We treat each other like people, and we get through this like people. Anyone who wants to be something less will have his chance in the forest. There'll be plenty of room for him to run away and play at being an ape."

She turned and walked back toward her room. Her body trembled with residual anger and frustration. She did not want the others to see her tremble. She had never come closer to losing control, killing people.

Joseph spoke her name softly. She swung around, ready to fight, then made herself relax as she recognized his voice. She stood looking at him, longing to go to him, but restraining herself. What did he think of what she had done?

"I know those guys don't deserve it," he said, "but some of them need help. Peter's arm is broken. The others...Can you get the Oankali to help them?"

Alarmed, she looked back at the carnage she had created. She drew a deep breath, managed to still her trembling. Then she spoke quietly in Oankali.

"Whoever is on watch, come in and check these people. Some of them may be badly hurt."

"Not so badly," a disembodied voice answered in Oankali. "The ones on the floor will heal without help. I'm in contact with them through the floor."

"What about the one with the broken arm?"

"We'll take care of him. Shall we keep him?"

"I'd love to have you keep him. But no, leave him with us. You're already suspected of being murderers."

"Derrick is asleep again."

"I thought so. What shall we do with Peter?"

"Nothing. Let him think for a while about his behavior."

"Ahajas?"

"Yes?"

Lilith drew another deep breath. "I'm surprised to realize how good it is to hear your voice."

There was no answer. Nothing more to be said.

"What did he say?" Joseph wanted to know.

"She. She said no one was seriously hurt. She said the Oankali would take care of Peter after he's had time to think about his behavior."

"What do we do with him until then?"

"Nothing."

"I thought they wouldn't talk to you," Gabriel said, his voice filled with unconcealed suspicion. He and Tate and a few others had come over to her. They stood back cautiously.

"They talk when they want to," she said. "This is an emergency so they decided to talk."

"You knew that one, didn't you?"

She looked at Gabriel. "Yes, I knew her."

"I thought so. Your tone and the way you looked when you talked to her ... You relaxed more, seemed almost wistful."

"She knows I never wanted this job."

"Was she a friend?"

"As much as it's possible to be friends with someone of a totally different species." She gave a humorless laugh. "It's hard enough for human beings to be friends with each other."

Yet she did think of Ahajas as a friend—Ahajas, Dichaan, Nikanj ... But what was she to them? A tool? A pleasurable perversion? An accepted member of the household? Accepted as what? Round and round. It would have been easier not to care. Down on Earth, it would not matter. The Oankali used her relentlessly for their own purposes, and she worried about what they thought of her.

"How can you be this strong?" Tate demanded. "How can you do all this?"

Lilith rubbed a hand over her face wearily. "The same way I can open walls," she said. "The Oankali changed me a little. I'm strong. I move fast. I heal fast. And all that is supposed to help me get as many of you as possible through this experience and back on Earth." She looked around. "Where's Allison?"

"Here." The woman stepped forward. She had already cleaned most of the blood from her face and now seemed to be trying to look as though nothing had happened. That was Allison. She would not be seen at anything less than her best for a moment longer than necessary.

Lilith nodded. "Well, I can see you're all right."

"Yes. Thank you." Allison hesitated. "Look, I really am grateful to you no matter what the truth turns out to be, but ..."

"But?"

Allison looked down, then seemed to force herself to face Lilith again. "There isn't any nice way of saying this, but I've got to ask. Are you really human?"

Lilith stared at her, tried to raise indignation, but managed only weariness. How many times would she have to answer that question? And why did she bother? Would her words ease anyone's suspicions?

"This would be so goddamn much easier if I weren't human," she said. "Think about it. If I weren't human, why the hell would I care whether you got raped?"

She turned once more toward her room, then stopped, turned back, remembering. "I'm Awakening ten more people tomorrow. The final ten."

12

There was a shuffling of people. Some avoided Lilith because they were afraid of her—afraid she was not human, or not human enough. Others came to her because they believed that she would win. They did not know what that would mean, but they thought it would be better to be with her than to have her as an enemy.

Her core group, Joseph, Tate and Gabriel, Leah and Wray did not change. Peter's core group shifted. Victor was added. He was a strong personality and he had been Awake longer than most people. That encouraged a few of the newer people to follow him.

Peter himself was replaced by Curt. Peter's broken arm kept him quiet, sullen, and usually alone in his room. Curt was brighter and more physically impressive anyway. He would probably have led the group from the first if he had moved a little faster.

Peter's arm remained broken, swollen, painful and useless for two days. On the night of the second day, he was healed. He slept late, missed breakfast, but when he awoke, his arm was no longer broken—and he was a badly frightened man. He could not simply pass off two days of debilitating pain as illusion or trickery. The bones of his arm had been broken, and badly broken. Everyone who looked at it had seen the displacement, the swelling, the discoloration. Everyone had seen that he could not use his hand.

Now everyone saw a whole arm, undistorted, normal, and a hand that worked easily and well. Peter's own people looked askance at him.

Following lunch on the day of his healing, Lilith told the people carefully censored stories of her life among the Oankali. Peter did not stay to listen.

"You need to hear these things more than the others do," she told him later. "The Oankali will be a shock even if you're prepared. They fixed your arm while you were asleep because they didn't want you terrified and fighting them while they tried to help you."

"Tell them how grateful I am," he muttered.

"They want sanity, not gratitude," she said. "They want—and I want—you to be bright enough to survive."

He stared at her with contempt so great that it made his face almost unrecognizable.

She shook her head, spoke softly. "I hurt you because you were trying to hurt another person. No one else has hurt you at all. The Oankali have saved your life. Eventually, they'll send you back to Earth to make a new life for yourself." She paused. "A little thought, Pete. A little sanity."

She got up to leave him. He said nothing to her, only watched her with hatred and contempt. "Now there are forty-three of us," she said. "The Oankali could show themselves anytime. Don't do anything that will make them keep you here alone."

She left him, hoping he would begin to think. Hoping, but not believing.

Five days after Peter's healing, the evening meal was drugged.

Lilith was not warned. She ate with the others, sitting off to one side with Joseph. She was aware as she ate of growing relaxation, a particular kind of comfort that made her think of—

She sat up straight. What she felt now she had felt before only when she was with Nikanj, when it had established a neural link with her.

And the sweet fog of anticipation dissipated. Her body seemed to shrug it off and she was alert again. Nearby, other people still spoke to one another, laughing a little more than they had before. Laughter had never quite disappeared from the group, though at times it had been rare. There had been more fighting, more bed-hopping and less laughter for the past few days.

Now men and women had begun to hold hands, to sit closer to one another. They slipped arms around one another and sat together probably feeling better than they had since they had been Awakened. It was unlikely that any of them could shake off the feeling the way Lilith had. No ooloi had modified them.

She looked around to see whether the Oankali were coming in yet. There was no sign of them. She turned to Joseph who was sitting next to her frowning.

"Joe?"

He looked at her. The frown smoothed away and he reached for her.

She let him draw her closer, then spoke into his ear. "The Oankali are about to come in. We've been drugged."

He shook off the drug. "I thought..." He rubbed his face. "I thought something was wrong." He breathed deeply, then looked around. "There," he said softly.

She followed the direction of his gaze and saw that the wall between the food cabinets was rippling, opening. In at least eight places, Oankali were coming in.

"Oh no," Joseph said, stiffening, looking away. "Why didn't you leave me comfortably drugged?"

"Sorry," she said, and rested her head on his arm. He had had only one brief experience with one Oankali. Whatever happened might be almost as hard on him as it was on the others. "You're modified," she said. "I don't think the drug could have held you once things got interesting."

More Oankali came through the openings. Lilith counted twenty-eight altogether. Would that be enough to handle forty-three terrified humans when the drug wore off?

People seemed to react to the nonhuman presence in slow motion. Tate and Gabriel stood up together, leaning on each other, staring at the Oankali. An ooloi approached them and they drew back. They were not terrified as they could have been, but they were frightened.

The ooloi spoke to them and Lilith realized it was Kahguyaht.

She stood up, staring at the trio. She could not distinguish individual words in what Kahguyaht was saying, but its tone was not one she would have associated with Kahguyaht. The tone was quiet, calming, oddly compelling. It was a tone Lilith had learned to associate with Nikanj.

Somewhere else in the room, a scuffle broke out. Curt, in spite of the drug, had attacked the ooloi that approached him. All the Oankali present were ooloi.

Peter tried to go to Curt's aid, but behind him, Jean screamed, and he turned back to help her.

Beatrice fled from her ooloi. She managed to run several steps before it caught her. It wrapped one sensory arm around her and she collapsed unconscious.

Around the room, other people collapsed—all the fighters, all the runners. No form of panic was tolerated.

Tate and Gabriel were still awake. Leah was awake, but Wray was unconscious. An ooloi seemed to be calming her, probably assuring her that Wray was all right.

Jean was still awake in spite of her momentary panic, but Peter was down.

Celene was awake and frozen in place. An ooloi touched her, then jerked away as though in pain. Celene had fainted.

Victor Dominic and Hilary Ballard were awake and together, holding one another, though they had shown no interest in one another until now.

Allison screamed and threw food at her ooloi, then turned and ran. Her ooloi caught her, but kept her conscious, probably because she did not struggle. She went rigid, but seemed to listen as her ooloi spoke soothingly.

Elsewhere in the room, small groups of people, supporting one another, confronted the ooloi without panic. The drug had quieted them just enough. The room was a scene of quiet, strangely gentle chaos.

Lilith watched Kahguyaht with Tate and Gabriel. The ooloi was sitting down now, facing them, talking to them, even giving them time to stare at the way its joints bent and the way its sensory tentacles followed movement. When it moved, it moved very slowly. When it spoke, Lilith could hear none of the hectoring contempt or amused tolerance that she was used to.

"You know that one?" Joseph asked.

"Yes. It's one of Nikanj's parents. I never got along with it."

Across the room, Kahguyaht's head tentacles swept in her direction for a moment and she knew it had heard. She considered saying more, giving it an earful—figuratively.

But before she could begin, Nikanj arrived. It stood before Joseph and looked at him critically. "You're doing very well," it said. "How do you feel?"

"I'm all right."

"You will be." It glanced at Tate and Gabriel. "Your friends won't be, I think. Not both of them, anyway."

"What? Why not?"

Nikanj rustled its tentacles. "Kahguyaht will try. I warned it, and it admits I have a talent for humans, but it wants them badly. The woman will survive, but the man may not."

"Why!" Lilith demanded.

"He may choose not to. But Kahguyaht is skillful. Those two humans are the calmest in the room apart from you two." It focused for a moment on Joseph's hands, on the fact that he had gouged one with the nails of the other and that the gouged hand was dripping blood onto the floor.

Nikanj shifted its attention, even turning its body away from Joseph. Its instinct was to help, to heal a wound, stop pain. Yet it knew enough to let Joseph go on hurting himself for now.

"What are you doing, foretelling the future?" Joseph asked. His voice was a harsh whisper. "Gabe will kill himself?"

"Indirectly, he might. I hope not. I can't foretell anything. Maybe Kahguyaht will save him. He's worth saving. But his past behavior says he will be hard to work with." It reached out and took Joseph's hands, apparently unable to stand the gouging any longer.

"You were only given a weak, ooloi-neutral drug in your food," it told him. "I can help you with something better."

Joseph tried to pull away, but it ignored his effort. It examined the hand he had injured, then further tranquilized him, all the while talking to him quietly.

"You know I won't hurt you. You're not afraid of being hurt or of pain. And your fear of my strangeness will pass eventually. No, be still. Let your body go limp. Let it relax. If your body is relaxed, it will be easier for you to handle your fear. That's it. Lean back against this wall. I can help you maintain this state without blurring your intellect. You see?"

Joseph turned his head to look at Nikanj, then turned away, his movements slow, almost languid, belying the emotion behind them. Nikanj moved to sit next to him and maintain its hold on him. "Your fear is less than it was," it said. "And even what you feel now will pass quickly."

Lilith watched Nikanj work, knowing that it would drug Joseph only lightly—perhaps stimulate the release of his own endorphins and leave him feeling relaxed and slightly high. Nikanj's words, spoken with quiet assurance, only reinforced new feelings of security and well-being.

Joseph sighed. "I don't understand why the sight of you should scare me so," Joseph said. He did not sound frightened. "You don't look that threatening. Just...very different."

"Different is threatening to most species," Nikanj answered. "Different is dangerous. It might kill you. That was true to your animal ancestors and your nearest animal relatives. And it's true for you." Nikanj smoothed its head tentacles. "It's safer for your people to overcome the feeling on an individual basis than as members of a large group. That's why we've handled this the way we have." It looked around at individuals and pairs of humans, each with an ooloi.

Nikanj focused on Lilith. "It would have been easier for you to be handled this way—with drugs, with an adult ooloi."

"Why wasn't I?"

"You were being prepared for me, Lilith. Adults believed you would be best paired with me during my subadult stage. Jdahya believed he could bring you to me without drugs, and he was right."

Lilith shuddered. "I wouldn't want to go through anything like that again."

"You won't. Look at your friend Tate."

Lilith turned and saw that Tate had extended a hand to Kahguyaht. Gabriel grabbed it and hauled it back, arguing.

Tate said only a few words while Gabriel said many, but after a while, he let her go. Kahguyaht had not moved or spoken. It waited. It let Tate look at it again, perhaps build up her courage again. When she extended her hand again, it seized the hand in a coil of sensory arm in a move that seemed impossibly swift, yet gentle, nonthreatening. The arm moved like a striking cobra, yet there was that strange gentleness. Tate did not even seem startled.

"How can it move that way?" Lilith murmured.

"Kahguyaht was afraid she would not have the courage to finish the gesture," Nikanj said. "It was right, I think."

"I drew back any number of times."

"Jdahya had to make you do all the work yourself. He couldn't help."

"What will happen now?" Joseph asked.

"We'll stay with you for several days. When you're used to us, we'll take you to the training floor we've created—the forest." It focused on Lilith. "For a little while, you won't have any duties. I could take you and your mate outside for a while, show him more of the ship."

Lilith looked around the room. There were no more struggles, no manifest terror. People who could not control themselves were unconscious. Others were totally focused on their ooloi and suffering through confused combinations of fear and drug-induced well-being.

"I'm the only human who has any idea what's going on," she said. "Some of them might want to talk to me."

Silence.

"Yeah. What about it, Joe? Want to look around outside?"

He frowned. "What just didn't get said?"

She sighed. "The humans here aren't going to want us near them for a while. In fact, you may not want them near you. It's a reaction to the ooloi drugs. So we can stay here and be ignored or we can go outside."

Nikanj coiled the end of one sensory arm around her wrist, prompting her to consider a third possibility. She said nothing, but the eagerness that suddenly blossomed in her was so intense, it was suspicious.

"Let go!" she said.

It released her, but was now completely focused on her. It had felt her body's leap of response to its wordless suggestion—or to its chemical suggestion.

"Did you do that?" she demanded. "Did you . . . inject something."

"Nothing." It wrapped its free sensory arm around her neck. "Oh, but I will 'inject something.' We can go out later." It stood up, bringing them both up with it.

"What?" Joseph said as he was hauled to his feet. "What's happening?"

No one answered him, but he did not resist being guided into Lilith's bedroom. As Lilith sealed the doorway, he asked again, "What's going on?"

Nikanj slid its sensory arm from Lilith's neck. "Wait," it told her. Then it focused on Joseph, releasing him, but not moving away. "The second time will be the hardest for you. I left you no choice the first time. You could not have understood what there was to choose. Now you have some small idea. And you have a choice."

He understood now. "No!" he said sharply. "Not again."

Silence.

"I'd rather have the real thing!"

"With Lilith?"

"Of course." He looked as though he would say something more, but he glanced at Lilith and fell silent.

"Rather with any human than with me," Nikanj supplied softly.

Joseph only stared at it.

"And yet I pleased you. I pleased you very much."

"Illusion!"

"Interpretation. Electrochemical stimulation of certain nerves, certain parts of your brain . . . What happened was real. Your body knows how real it was. Your interpretations were illusion. The sensations were entirely real. You can have them again—or you can have others."

"No!"

"And all that you have, you can share with Lilith."

Silence.

"All that she feels, she'll share with you." It reached out and caught his hand in a coil of sensory arm. "I won't hurt you. And I offer a oneness that your people strive for, dream of, but can't truly attain alone."

He pulled his arm free. "You said I could choose. I've made my choice!"

"You have, yes." It opened his jacket with its many-fingered true hands and stripped the garment from him. When he would have backed away, it held him. It managed to lie down on the bed with him without seeming to force him down. "You see. Your body has made a different choice."

He struggled violently for several seconds, then stopped. "Why are you doing this?" he demanded.

"Close your eyes."

"What?"

"Lie here with me for a while and close your eyes."

"What are you going to do?"

"Nothing. Close your eyes."

"I don't believe you."

"You're not afraid of me. Close your eyes."

Silence.

After a long while, he closed his eyes and the two of them lay together. Joseph held his body rigid at first, but slowly, as nothing happened, he began to relax. Sometime later his breathing evened and he seemed to be asleep.

Lilith sat on the table, waiting, watching. She was patient and interested. This might be her only chance ever to watch close up as an ooloi seduced someone. She thought it should have bothered her that the "someone" in this case was Joseph. She knew more than she wanted to about the wildly conflicting feelings he was subject to now.

Yet, in this matter, she trusted Nikanj completely. It was enjoying itself with Joseph. It would not spoil its enjoyment by hurting him or rushing him. In a perverse way, Joseph too was probably enjoying himself, though he could not have said so.

Lilith was dozing when Nikanj stroked Joseph's shoulders, rousing him. His voice roused her.

"What are you doing?" he demanded.

"Waking you."

"I wasn't asleep!"

Silence.

"My god," he said after a while. "I did fall asleep, didn't I? You must have drugged me."

"No."

He rubbed his eyes, but made no effort to get up.

"Why didn't you . . . just do it?"

"I told you. This time you can choose."

"I've chosen! You ignored me."

"Your body said one thing. Your words said another." It moved a sensory arm to the back of his neck, looping one coil loosely around his neck. "This is the position," it said. "I'll stop now if you like."

There was a moment of silence, then Joseph gave a long sigh. "I can't give you—or myself—permission," he said. "No matter what I feel, I can't."

Nikanj's head and body became mirror smooth. The change was so dramatic that Joseph jumped and drew back. "Does that . . . amuse you somehow?" he asked bitterly.

"It pleases me. It's what I expected."

"So . . . what happens now?"

"You are very strong-willed. You can hurt yourself as badly as you think necessary to achieve a goal or hold to a conviction."

"Let go of me."

It smoothed its tentacles again. "Be grateful, Joe. I'm not going to let go of you."

Lilith saw Joseph's body stiffen, struggle, then relax, and she knew Nikanj had read him correctly. He neither struggled nor argued as Nikanj positioned him more comfortably against its body. Lilith saw that he had closed his eyes again, his face peaceful. Now he was ready to accept what he had wanted from the beginning.

Silently, Lilith got up, stripped off her jacket, and went to the bed. She stood over it, looking down. For a moment, she saw Nikanj as she had once seen Jdahya—as a totally alien being, grotesque, repellant beyond mere ugliness with its night crawler body tentacles, its snake head tentacles, and its tendency to keep both moving, signaling attention and emotion.

She froze where she stood and had all she could to keep from turning and running away.

The moment passed, left her almost gasping. She jumped when Nikanj touched her with the tip of a sensory arm. She stared at it for a moment longer wondering how she had lost her horror of such a being.

Then she lay down, perversely eager for what it could give her. She positioned herself against it, and was not content until she felt the deceptively light touch of the sensory hand and felt the ooloi body tremble against her.

13

Humans were kept drugged for days—drugged, and guarded, each individual or pair by an ooloi.

"Imprinting is the best word for what they're doing," Nikanj told Joseph. "Imprinting, chemical and social."

"What you're doing to me!" Joseph accused.

"What I'm doing to you, what I've done to Lilith. It has to be done. No one will be returned to Earth without it."

"How long will they be drugged?"

"Some are not heavily drugged now. Tate Marah isn't. Gabriel Rinaldi is." It focused on Joseph. "You aren't. You know."

Joseph looked away. "No one should be."

"In the end, no one will be. We dull your natural fear of strangers and of difference. We keep you from injuring or killing us or yourselves. We teach you more pleasant things to do."

"That's not enough!"

"It's a beginning."

14

Peter's ooloi proved that ooloi were not infallible. Drugged, Peter was a different man. For perhaps the first time since his Awakening, he was at peace, not fighting even with himself, not trying to prove anything, joking with Jean and their ooloi about his arm and the fighting.

Lilith, hearing this later, wondered what there was to laugh at in that incident. But the ooloi-produced drugs could be potent. Under their influence, Peter might have laughed at anything. Under their influence, he accepted union and pleasure. When that influence was allowed to wane and Peter began to think, he apparently decided he had been humiliated and enslaved. The drug seemed to him to be not a less painful way of getting used to frightening nonhumans, but a way of turning him against himself, causing him to demean himself in alien perversions. His humanity was profaned. His manhood was taken away.

Peter's ooloi should have noticed that at some point what Peter said and the expression he assumed ceased to agree with what his body told it. Perhaps it did not know enough about human beings to handle someone like Peter. It was older than Nikanj—more a contemporary of Kahguyaht. But it was not as perceptive as either of them—and perhaps not as bright.

Sealed in Peter's room, alone with Peter, it allowed itself to be attacked, pounded by Peter's bare fists. Unfortunately for Peter, he hit a sensitive spot with his first hammering blow, and triggered the ooloi's defensive reflexes. It gave him a lethal sting before it could regain control of itself and he collapsed in convulsions. His own contracting muscles broke several of his bones, then he went into shock.

The ooloi tried to help him once it had recovered from the worst of its own pain, but it was too late. He was dead. The ooloi sat down beside his body, its head and body tentacles drawn into hard lumps. It did not move or speak. Its cool flesh grew even cooler, and it seemed to be as dead as the human it was apparently mourning.

There were no Oankali on watch above. Peter might have been saved if there had been. But the great room was full of ooloi. Where was the need to keep watch?

By the time one of these ooloi noticed Jean sitting alone and forlorn outside the sealed room, it was too late. There was nothing to do but take Peter's body out and send for the ooloi's mates. The ooloi remained catatonic.

Jean, still lightly drugged, frightened, and alone, retreated from the people clustering around the room. She stood apart and watched as the body was carried out. Lilith noticed her, approached her, knowing she couldn't help, but hoping at least to give comfort.

"No!" Jean said, backing toward a wall. "Get away!"

Lilith sighed. Jean was going through a prolonged period of ooloi-induced reclusiveness. All of the humans who had been kept heavily drugged were this way—unable to tolerate the near-ness of anyone except their human mate and the ooloi who had drugged them. Neither Lilith nor Joseph had experienced this extreme reaction. Lilith had hardly noticed any reaction at all beyond an increased aversion to Kahguyaht back when Nikanj matured and bound her to it. More recently, Joseph had reacted by simply staying close to Lilith and Nikanj for a couple of days. Then his reaction passed. Jean's was far from passing. What would happen to her now?

Lilith looked around for Nikanj. She spotted it in a cluster of ooloi, went to it and laid a hand on its shoulder.

It focused on her without turning or breaking the various sen-sory tentacle and sensory arm contacts it had with the others. She spoke to the point of a thin cone of head tentacles.

"Can't you help Jean?"

"Help is coming for her."

"Look at her! She's going to break before it gets here."

The cone focused on Jean. She had wedged herself into a cor-ner. Now she stood crying silently and looking around in con-fusion. She was a tall, strongly built woman. Now, though, she looked like a large child.

Nikanj detached itself from the other ooloi, apparently end-ing whatever communication was going on. The other ooloi relaxed away from one another. They went to their various human charges who stood waiting for them in widely separated ones and twos. The moment the news of the death had gone around, every human except Lilith and Jean had been drugged heavily. Nikanj had refused to drug Lilith. It trusted her to control her own behavior and the other ooloi trusted it. As for Jean, there was no one present who could drug her without harming her.

Nikanj closed to within about ten feet of Jean. It stopped there and waited until she saw it.

She trembled, but did not try to cringe farther into her corner.

"I won't come closer," Nikanj said softly. "Others will come to help you. You aren't alone."

"But...But I am alone," she whispered. "They're dead. I saw them."

"One is dead," Nikanj corrected, keeping its voice low.

She hid her face in her hands and shook her head from side to side.

"Peter is dead," Nikanj told her, "but Tehjaht is only...injured. And you have siblings coming to help."

"What?"

"They'll help you."

She sat down on the floor, head down, voice muffled when she spoke. "I've never had any brothers or sisters. Not even before the war."

"Tehjaht has mates. They'll take care of you."

"No. They'll blame me...because Tehjaht is hurt."

"They'll help you." Very softly. "They'll help both you and Tehjaht. *They will help.*"

She frowned, looking more childlike than ever as she tried to understand. Then her face changed. Curt, heavily drugged, edged along the wall toward her. He kept himself comfortably far from Nikanj, but moved a little too close to Jean. She cringed back from him.

Curt shook his head, took a step backward. "Jeanie?" he called, his heavy voice sounding too loud, sounding drunk.

Jean jumped, but said nothing.

Curt faced Nikanj. "She's one of ours! We should be the ones to take care of her!"

"It isn't possible," Nikanj said.

"It should be possible! It should be! Why isn't it?"

"Her bonding with her ooloi is too strong, too heavily reinforced—as yours is with your ooloi. Later when the bond is more relaxed, you'll be able to go near her again. Later. Not now."

"Goddammit, she needs us now!"

"No."

Curt's ooloi came up to him, took him by the arm. Curt would have pulled away, but suddenly his strength seemed to leave him. He stumbled, fell to his knees. Nearby, Lilith looked away. Curt was as unlikely to forgive any humbling as Peter had been. And he would not always be drugged. He would remember.

Curt's ooloi helped Curt to his feet and led him away to the room he now shared with it and with Celene. As he left, the wall opened at the far end of the room and a male and female Oankali came in.

Nikanj gestured to the pair and they came toward it. They held on to one another, walking as though wounded, as though holding one another up. They were two when they should have been three, missing an essential part.

The male and female made their way to Nikanj, and past it to Jean. Frightened, Jean stiffened. Then she frowned as though something had been said, and she had not quite heard.

Lilith watched sadly, knowing that the first signals Jean received were olfactory. The male and female smelled good, smelled like family, all brought together by the same ooloi. When they took her hands, they felt right. There was a real chemical affinity.

Jean seemed still to be afraid of the two strangers, but she was also relieved. They were what Nikanj had said they would be. People who could help. Family.

She let them lead her into the room where Tehjaht sat frozen. No words had been spoken. Strangers of a different species had been accepted as family. A human friend and ally had been rejected.

Lilith stood staring after Jean, hardly aware of Joseph's coming to stand beside her. He was drugged, but the drug had only made him reckless.

"Peter was right," he said angrily.

She frowned. "Peter? Right to try to kill? Right to die?"

"He died human! And he almost managed to take one of them with him!"

She looked at him. "So what? What's changed? On Earth we can change things. Not here."

"Will we want to by then? What will we be, I wonder? Not human. Not anymore."

PART IV

The Training Floor

1

The training room was brown and green and blue. Brown, muddy ground was visible through thin, scattered leaf litter. Brown, muddy water flowed past the land, glittering in the light of what seemed to be the sun. The water was too laden with sediment to appear blue, though above it, the ceiling—the sky—was a deep, intense blue. There was no smoke, no smog, only a few clouds—remains of a recent rain.

Across the wide river, there was the illusion of a line of trees on the opposite bank. A line of green. Away from the river, the predominant color was green. Above was the very real green canopy—trees of all sizes, many burdened with a profusion of other life: bromeliads, orchids, ferns, mosses, lichens, lianas, parasitic vines, plus a generous complement of insect life and a few frogs, lizards, and snakes.

One of the first things Lilith had learned during her own earlier training period was not to lean against the trees.

There were few flowers, and those mainly bromeliads and orchids, high in the trees. On the ground, a colorful stationary object was likely to be a leaf or some kind of fungus. Green was everywhere. The undergrowth was thin enough to walk through without difficulty except near the river where in some places a machete was essential—and not yet permitted.

"Tools will come later," Nikanj told Lilith. "Let the humans get used to being here now. Let them explore and see for themselves that they are in a forest on an island. Let them begin to feel what it's like to live here." It hesitated. "Let them settle more firmly into their places with their ooloi. They can tolerate one another now. Let them learn that it isn't shameful to be together with one another and with us."

It had gone with Lilith to the riverbank at a place where a great piece of earth had been undercut and had fallen into the river, taking several trees and much undergrowth with it. There was no trouble here in reaching the water, though there was a sharp drop of about ten feet. At the edge of the drop was one of the giants of the island—a huge tree with buttresses that swept well over Lilith's head and, like walls, separated the surrounding land into individual rooms. In spite of the great variety of life that the tree supported, Lilith stood between a pair of buttresses, two-thirds enclosed by the tree. She felt enveloped in a solidly Earthly thing. A thing that would soon be undercut as its neighbors had been, that would soon fall into the river and die.

"They'll cut the trees down, you know," she said softly. "They'll make boats or rafts. They think they're on Earth."

"Some of them believe otherwise," Nikanj told her. "They believe because you do."

"That won't stop the boat building."

"No. We won't try to stop it. Let them row their boats to the walls and back. There's no way out for them except the way we offer: to learn to feed and shelter themselves in this environment—to become self-sustaining. When they've done that, we'll take them to Earth and let them go."

It knew they would run, she thought. It must know. Yet it

talked about mixed settlements, human and Oankali—trade-partner settlements within which ooloi would control the fertility and "mix" the children of both groups.

She looked up at the sloping, wedge-shaped buttresses. Semienclosed as she was, she could not see Nikanj or the river. There was only brown and green forest—the illusion of wilderness and isolation.

Nikanj left her the illusion for a while. It said nothing, made no sound. Her feet tired and she looked around for something to sit on. She did not want to go back to the others any sooner than she had to. They could tolerate one another again now; the most difficult phase of their bonding was over. There was very little drugging still going on. Curt and Gabriel were still drugged along with a few others. Lilith worried about these. Oddly, she also admired them for being able to resist conditioning. Were they strong, then? Or simply unable to adapt?

"Lilith?" Nikanj said softly.

She did not answer.

"Let's go back."

She had found a dry, thick liana root to sit on. It hung like a swing, dropping down from the canopy, then curving upward again to lock itself into the branches of a nearby smaller tree before dropping to the ground and digging in. The root was thicker than some trees and the few insects on it looked harmless. It was an uncomfortable seat—twisted and hard—but Lilith was not yet ready to leave it.

"What will you do with the humans who can't adapt?" she asked.

"If they aren't violent, we'll take them to Earth with the rest of you." Nikanj came around the buttress, destroying her sense of solitude and home. Nothing that looked and moved as Nikanj did could come from home. She got up wearily and walked with it.

"Have the ants bitten you?" it asked.

She shook her head. It did not like her to conceal small injuries.

It considered her health very much its business, and looked after her insect bites—especially her mosquito bites—at the end of each day. She thought it would have been easier to have left the mosquitoes out of this small simulation of Earth. But Oankali did not think that way. A simulation of a tropical forest of Earth had to be complete with snakes, centipedes, mosquitoes and other things Lilith would have preferred to live without. Why should the Oankali worry, she thought cynically. Nothing bit them.

"There are so few of you," Nikanj said as they walked. "No one wants to give up on any of you."

She had to think back to realize what it was talking about.

"Some of us thought we should hold off bonding with you until you were brought here," it told her. "Here it would have been easier for you to band together, become a family."

Lilith glanced at it uneasily, but said nothing. Families had children. Was Nikanj saying children should be conceived and born here?

"But most of us couldn't wait," it continued. It wrapped a sensory arm around her neck loosely. "It might be better for both our peoples if we were not so strongly drawn to you."

2

Tools, when they were finally handed out, were water-proof tarpaulins, machetes, axes, shovels, hoes, metal pots, rope, hammocks, baskets, and mats. Lilith spoke privately with each of the most dangerous humans before they were given their tools.

One more try, she thought wearily.

"I don't care what you think of me," she told Curt. "You're the kind of man the human race is going to need down on Earth. That's why I woke you. I want you to live to get down there." She hesitated. "Don't go Peter's way, Curt."

He stared at her. Only recently free of the drug, only recently capable of violence, he stared.

"Make him sleep again!" Lilith told Nikanj. "Let him forget! Don't give him a machete and wait for him to use it on someone."

"Yahjahyi thinks he'll be all right," Nikanj said. Yahjahyi was Curt's ooloi.

"Does it?" Lilith said. "What did Peter's ooloi think?"

"It never told anyone what it thought. As a result, no one

realized it was in trouble. Incredible behavior. I said it would be better if we weren't so drawn to you."

She shook her head. "If Yahjahyi thinks Curt is all right, it's deluding itself."

"We've observed Curt and Yahjahyi," Nikanj said. "Curt will go through a dangerous time now, but Yahjahyi is ready. Even Celene is ready."

"Celene!" Lilith said with contempt.

"You did a good job matching them. Much better than with Peter and Jean."

"I didn't match Peter and Jean. Their own temperaments did—like fire and gasoline."

"...yes. Anyway, Celene is not ready to lose another mate. She'll hold on to him. And Curt, since he sees her as much more vulnerable than she is, will have good reason not to risk himself, not to chance leaving her alone. They'll be all right."

"They won't," Gabriel told her later. He too was free of the drug, finally, but he was handling it better. Kahguyaht, who had been so eager to push Lilith, coerce her, ridicule her, seemed to be infinitely patient with Tate and Gabriel.

"Look at things from Curt's point of view," Gabriel said. "He's not in control even of what his own body does and feels. He's taken like a woman and...No, don't explain!" He held up his hand to stop her from interrupting. "He knows the ooloi aren't male. He knows all the sex that goes on is in his head. It doesn't matter. It doesn't fucking matter! Someone else is pushing all his buttons. He can't let them get away with that."

Honestly frightened, Lilith asked, "How have you...made your peace with it?"

"Who says I have?"

She stared at him. "Gabe, we can't lose you, too."

He smiled. Beautiful, perfect, white teeth. They made her think of some predator. "I don't take the next step," he said, "until I see where I'm standing now. You know I still don't believe this isn't Earth."

"I know."

"A tropical forest in a space ship. Who'd believe that?"

"But the Oankali. You can see that they're not of Earth."

"Sure. But they're here now on what sure looks, sounds, and smells like Earth."

"It isn't."

"So you say. Sooner or later I'll find out for myself."

"Kahguyaht could show you things that would make you sure now. They might even convince Curt."

"Nothing will convince Curt. Nothing will reach him."

"You think he'll do what Peter did?"

"Much more efficiently."

"Oh god. Did you know they put Jean back into suspended animation? She won't even remember Peter when she wakes up."

"I heard. That will make it easier on her when they put her with another guy, I guess."

"Is that what you would want for Tate?"

He shrugged, turned, and walked away.

3

Lilith taught all the humans to make thatch shingles and place them in overlapping rows on rafters so that they would not leak. She showed them the best trees to cut for flooring and frame. They all worked several days to construct a large thatch-roofed cabin on stilts, well above the river's high-water mark. The cabin was a twin to the one they had all squeezed into so far—the one Lilith and the ooloi had constructed when the ooloi brought them all through the miles of corridors to the training room.

The ooloi left this second construction strictly to the humans. They watched or sat talking among themselves or disappeared on errands of their own. But when the work was finished they brought in a small feast to celebrate.

"We won't provide food for much longer," one of them told the group. "You'll learn to live on what grows here and to cultivate gardens."

No one was surprised. They had already been cutting hands of green bananas from existing trees and hanging them from beams or from the porch railing. As the bananas ripened, the humans discovered they had to compete with the insects for them.

A few people had also been cutting pineapples and picking papayas and breadfruits from existing trees. Most people did not like the breadfruit until Lilith showed them the seeded form of the fruit, the breadnut. When they roasted the seeds as she instructed and ate them, they realized they had been eating them all along back in the great room.

They had pulled sweet cassava from the ground and dug up the yams Lilith had planted during her own training.

Now it was time for them to begin planting their own crops.

And, perhaps, now it was time for the Oankali to begin to see what they would harvest in their human crop.

Two men and a woman took their allotted tools and vanished into the forest. They did not really know enough yet to be on their own, but they were gone. Their ooloi did not go after them.

The group of ooloi put their head tentacles and sensory arms together for a moment and seemed to come to a very fast agreement: None of them would pay any attention to the three missing people.

"No one has escaped," Nikanj told Joseph and Lilith when they asked what would be done. "The missing people are still on the island. They're being watched."

"Watched through all these trees?" Joseph demanded.

"The ship is keeping track of them. If they're hurt, they'll be taken care of."

Other humans left the settlement. As the days passed, some of their ooloi seemed acutely uncomfortable. They kept to themselves, sat rock still, their head and body tentacles drawn into thick, dark lumps that looked, as Leah said, like grotesque tumors. These ooloi could be shouted at, rained on, tripped over. They never moved. When their head tentacles ceased to follow the movements of those around them, their mates arrived to tend them.

Male and female Oankali came out of the forest and took charge of their particular ooloi. Lilith never saw any of them called, but she saw one pair arrive.

She had gone alone to a place on the river where there was a heavily laden breadnut tree. She had climbed the tree, not only to get the fruit, but to enjoy the solitude and the beauty of the tree. She had never been much of a climber even as a child, but during her training, she had developed climbing skill and confidence—and a love of being so close to something so much of Earth.

From the tree, she saw two Oankali come out of the water. They did not seem to swim in toward land, but simply stood up near shore and walked in. Both focused on her for a moment, then headed inland toward the settlement.

She had watched them in utter silence, but they had known she was there. One more male and female, come to rescue a sick, abandoned ooloi.

Would it give the humans a feeling of power to know that they could make their ooloi feel sick and abandoned? Ooloi did not endure well when bereft of all those who carried their particular scent, their particular chemical marker. They lived. Metabolisms slowed, they retreated deep within themselves until called back by their families or, less satisfactorily, by another ooloi behaving as a kind of physician. So why didn't they go to their mates when their humans left? Why did they stay and get sick?

Lilith walked back to the settlement, a long crude basket filled with breadnuts on her back. She found the male and female ministering to their ooloi holding it between them and entangling its head and body tentacles with their own. Wherever the three touched, tentacles joined them. It was an intimate, vulnerable position, and other ooloi lounged nearby, guarding without seeming to guard. There were also a few humans watching. Lilith looked around the settlement, wondering how many of the humans not present would not come back from their day of wandering or food gathering. Did those who left come together on some other part of the island? Had they built a shelter? Were they building a boat? A wild thought struck her: What if they were right? What if they somehow were on Earth? What if it were possible to row a boat to freedom? What if, in spite of all she had seen and felt, this was some kind of hoax? How would it be perpetrated? *Why* would it be perpetrated? Why would the Oankali go to so much trouble?

No. She did not understand why the Oankali had done some of what they had done, but she believed the basics. The ship. The Earth, waiting to be recolonized by its people. The Oankali's price for saving the few remaining fragments of humanity.

But more people were leaving the settlement. Where were they? What if—The thought would not let her alone no matter what facts she felt she knew. *What if the others were right?*

Where had the doubt come from?

That evening as she brought in a load of firewood, Tate blocked her path.

"Curt and Celene are gone," she said quietly. "Celene let it slip to me that they were leaving."

"I'm surprised it took them so long."

"I'm surprised Curt didn't brain an Oankali before he left."

Nodding in agreement, Lilith stepped around her and put down her load of wood.

Tate followed and again planted herself in Lilith's path.

"What?" Lilith asked.

"We're going too. Tonight." She kept her voice very low—though no doubt more than one Oankali heard her.

"Where?"

"We don't know. Either we'll find the others or we won't. We'll find something—or make something."

"Just the two of you?"

"Four of us. Maybe more."

Lilith frowned, not knowing how to feel. She and Tate had become friends. Wherever Tate was going, she would not escape.

If she did not injure herself or anyone else, she would probably be back.

"Listen," Tate said, "I'm not just telling you for the hell of it. We want you to go with us."

Lilith steered her away from the center of the camp. The Oankali would hear no matter what they did, but there was no need to involve other humans.

"Gabe has already talked to Joe," Tate said. "We want—"

"Gabe what!"

"Shut up! You want to tell everyone? Joe said he'd go. Now what about you?"

Lilith stared at her hostilely. "What about me?"

"I need to know now. Gabe wants to leave soon."

"If I leave with you, we'll leave after breakfast tomorrow morning."

Tate, being Tate, said nothing. She smiled.

"I didn't say I was going. All I mean is that there's no reason to sneak away in the night and step on a coral snake or something. It's pitch black out there at night."

"Gabe thinks we'll have more time before they discover we're gone."

"Where's his mind—and yours? Leave tonight and they'll notice you're gone by tomorrow morning—if you don't wake everyone on your way out by tripping over something or someone. Leave tomorrow morning and they won't notice you're gone until tomorrow night at dinner." She shook her head. "Not that they'll care. They haven't so far. But if you want to slip away, at least do it in a way that will give you a chance to find shelter before nightfall—or in case it rains."

"When it rains," Tate said. "It always rains sooner or later. We thought…maybe once we were clear of this place, we'd cross the river, head north, keep heading north until we found a dryer, cooler climate."

"If we are on Earth, Tate, considering what was done to Earth and especially to the northern hemisphere, south would be a better direction."

Tate shrugged. "You don't get a vote unless you come with us."

"I'll talk to Joe."

"But—"

"And you ought to get Gabe to help you with your acting. I haven't said a thing you and Gabe hadn't already thought of. Neither of you is stupid. And you, at least, are no good at bullshitting people."

Characteristically, Tate laughed. "I used to be." She sobered. "Okay, yeah. We've pretty much worked out the best way of doing it—tomorrow morning and south and with someone who probably knows how to stay alive in this country better than anyone but the Oankali."

There was a silence.

"We really are on an island, you know," Lilith said.

"No, I don't *know*," Tate answered. "But I'm willing to take your word for it. We'll have to cross the river."

"And in spite of what we see on what seems to be the other side, I believe we'll find a wall over there."

"In spite of the sun, the moon and the stars? In spite of the rain and the trees that have obviously been here for hundreds of years?"

Lilith sighed. "Yes."

"All because the Oankali said so."

"And because of what I saw and felt before I Awoke you."

"What the Oankali let you see and made you feel. You wouldn't believe some of the stuff Kahguyaht has made me feel."

"Wouldn't I?"

"I mean, you can't trust what they do to your senses!"

"I knew Nikanj when it was too young to do anything to my senses without my being aware of it."

Tate looked away, stared toward the river where the glint of water could still be seen. The sun—artificial or real—had not quite vanished and the river looked browner than ever. "Look," she said, "I don't mean anything by this, but I have to say it. You and Nikanj..." She let her voice die, abruptly looked at Lilith as though demanding a response. "Well?"

"Well, what?"

"You're closer to him—to it—than we are to Kahguyaht. You..."

Lilith stared at her silently.

"Hell, all I mean is, if you won't go with us, don't try to stop us."

"Has anyone tried to stop anyone from leaving?"

"Just don't say anything. That's all."

"Maybe you are stupid," Lilith said softly.

Tate looked away again and shrugged. "I promised Gabe I'd get you to promise."

"Why?"

"He thinks if you give your word, you'll keep it."

"Otherwise, I'll run and tell, right?"

"I'm beginning not to care what you do."

Lilith shrugged, turned and started back toward camp. It seemed to take Tate several seconds to see that she meant it. Then she ran after Lilith, pulled her back away from the camp.

"All right, I'm sorry you're insulted," Tate rasped. "Now are you going or aren't you?"

"You know the breadnut tree up the bank—the big one?"

"Yes?"

"If we're going, we'll meet you there after breakfast tomorrow."

"We won't wait long."

"Okay."

Lilith turned and walked back to camp. How many Oankali had heard the exchange? One? A few? All of them? No matter. Nikanj would know in minutes. So it would have time to send for Ahajas and Dichaan. It would not have to sit and go catatonic like the others.

In fact, she still wondered why the others had not done it.

Surely they had known that their chosen humans were leaving. Kahguyaht would know. What would it do?

Something occurred to her suddenly—a memory of tribal people sending their sons out to live for a while alone in the forest or desert or whatever as a test of manhood.

Boys of a certain age who had been taught how to live in the environment were sent out to prove what they had learned.

Was that it? Train the humans in the basics, then let them go out on their own when they were ready?

Then why the catatonic ooloi?

"Lilith?"

She jumped, then stopped and let Joseph catch up with her. They walked together to the fire where people were sharing baked yams and Brazil nuts from a tree someone had stumbled upon.

"Did you talk to Tate?" he asked.

She nodded.

"What did you tell her?"

"That I'd talk to you."

Silence.

"What do you want to do?" she asked.

"Go."

She stopped, turned to look at him, but his face told her nothing.

"Would you leave me?" she whispered.

"Why would you stay? To be with Nikanj?"

"Would you leave me?"

"*Why would you stay?*" The whispered words had the impact of a shout.

"Because this is a ship. Because there's nowhere to run."

He looked up at the bright half moon and at the first scattering of stars. "I've got to see for myself," he said softly. "This *feels* like home. Even though I've never been in a tropical forest before in my life, but this smells and tastes and looks like home."

"...I know."

"I've got to see!"

"Yes."

"Don't make me leave you."

She seized his hand as though it were an animal about to escape.

"Come with us!" he whispered.

She closed her eyes, shutting out the forest and the sky, the people talking quietly around the fire, the Oankali, several physically joined in silent conversation. How many of the Oankali had heard what she and Joseph were saying? None of them behaved as though they had heard.

"All right," she said softly. "I'll go."

4

Joseph and Lilith found no one waiting at the breadnut tree after breakfast the next morning. Lilith had seen Gabriel leave camp, carrying a large basket, his ax, and his machete as though intending to chop wood. People did that as they saw need just as Lilith took her own machete, ax, and baskets and went to gather forest foods when she saw need. She took people with her when she wanted to teach and went alone when she wanted to think.

This morning only Joseph was with her. Tate had left camp before breakfast. Lilith suspected that she might have gone to one of the gardens Lilith and Nikanj's family had planted. There she could dig cassava or yams or cut papayas, bananas, or pineapple. It would not help much. They would soon have to live on what they found in the forest.

Lilith carried roasted breadnuts both because she liked them and because they were a good source of protein. She also carried yams, beans, and cassava. At the bottom of her basket she carried extra clothing, a hammock of light, strong Oankali cloth, and a few sticks of dry tinder.

"We won't wait much longer," Joseph said. "They should be here. Maybe they've come and gone."

"More likely they'll be here as soon as they decide we weren't followed. They'll want to be sure I haven't sold them out, told the Oankali."

Joseph looked at her, frowned. "Tate and Gabe?"

"Yes."

"I don't think so."

She shrugged.

"Gabe said you should get out for your own good. He said he'd heard people beginning to talk against you again—now that they can think for themselves again."

"I'll be going toward the dangerous ones, Joe, not away from them. So will you."

He stared at the river for a while, then put his arm around her. "Do you want to go back?"

"Yes. But we won't."

He did not argue. She resented his silence, but accepted it. He wanted to go that badly. His feeling that he was on Earth was that strong.

Sometime later, Gabriel led Tate, Leah, Wray, and Allison to the breadnut tree. He stopped, stared at Lilith for a moment. She was certain he had heard all she had said.

"Let's go," she said.

They headed upriver by mutual consent since no one really wanted to head back toward camp. They stayed near the river to avoid getting lost. This meant occasionally hacking their way through undergrowth and aerial roots, but no one seemed to mind.

In the humidity, everyone perspired freely. Then it began to rain. Beyond walking more carefully in the mud, no one paid any attention. The mosquitoes bothered them less. Lilith slapped at a persistent one. There would be no Nikanj tonight to heal her insect bites, no gentle, multiple touches of sensory tentacles and sensory hands. Was she the only one who would miss them?

The rain ceased eventually. The group walked on until the sun was directly overhead. Then they sat on the wet trunk of a fallen tree, ignoring fungi and brushing away insects. They ate bread-nuts and the ripest of the bananas Tate had brought. They drank from the river, having long ago learned to ignore the sediment. It couldn't be seen in the handfuls of water that they drank, and it was harmless.

There was strangely little conversation. Lilith went aside to relieve herself and when she stepped clear of the tree that had concealed her, every eye was on her. Then abruptly everyone found something else to notice—one another, a tree, a piece of food, their fingernails.

"Oh god," Lilith muttered. And more loudly: "Let's talk, people." She stood before the fallen tree that they either sat or leaned on. "What is it?" she asked. "Are you waiting for me to desert you and go back to the Oankali? Or maybe you think I have some magic way of signaling them from here? What is it you suspect me of?"

Silence.

"What is it, Gabe?"

He met her gaze levelly. "Nothing." He spread his hands. "We're nervous. We don't know what's going to happen. We're scared. You shouldn't have to take the brunt of our feelings, but...but you're the different one. Nobody knows how different."

"She's here!" Joseph said, moving to stand beside her. "That should tell you how much like us she is. Whatever we risk, she risks it too."

Allison slid down off the log. "What is it we risk?" she demanded. She spoke directly to Lilith. "What will happen to us?"

"I don't know. I've guessed, but my guesses aren't worth much."

"Tell us!"

Lilith looked at the others, saw them all waiting. "I think these are our final tests," she said. "People leave camp when they feel ready. They live as best they can. If they can sustain themselves here, they can sustain themselves on Earth. That's why people have been allowed to walk away. That's why no one chases them."

"We don't know that no one chases them," Gabriel said.

"No one is chasing us."

"We don't even know that."

"When will you let yourself know it?"

He said nothing. He stared upriver with an air of impatience.

"Why did you want me on this trip, Gabe? Why did you personally want me here?"

"I didn't. I just—"

"Liar."

He frowned, glared at her. "I just thought you deserved a chance to get away from the Oankali—if you wanted it."

"You thought I might be useful! You thought you'd eat better and be better able to survive out here. You didn't think you were doing me a favor, you thought you were doing yourself one. It could work out that way." She looked around at the others. "But it won't. Not if everyone's sitting around waiting for me to play Judas." She sighed. "Let's go."

"Wait," Allison said as people were getting up. "You still think we're on a ship, don't you?" she asked Lilith.

Lilith nodded. "We are on a ship."

"Does anyone else here think so?" Allison demanded.

Silence.

"I don't know where we are," Leah said. "I don't see how all this could be part of a ship, but whatever it is, wherever it is, we're going to explore it and figure it out. We'll know soon."

"But she already knows," Allison insisted. "Lilith *knows* this is a ship no matter what the truth is. So what's she doing here?"

Lilith opened her mouth to answer but Joseph spoke first. "She's here because I wanted her here. I want to explore this place as badly as you all do. And I want her with me."

Lilith wished she had come from behind her tree and pretended not to notice all the eyes and all the silence. All the suspicion.

"Is that it?" Gabriel asked. "You came because Joe asked you to?"

"Yes," she said softly.

"Otherwise you would have stayed with the Oankali?"

"I would have stayed at camp. After all, I know I can live out here. If these are final tests, I've already passed mine."

"And what kind of grade did the Oankali give you?" It was probably the most honest question he had ever asked her—filled with hostility, suspicion, and contempt.

"It was a pass-fail course, Gabe. A live-die course." She turned and began walking upriver, breaking trail. After a while, she heard them following.

5

Upriver was the oldest part of the island, the part with the greatest number of huge old trees, many with broad buttresses. This land had once been connected to the mainland—had become first a peninsula, then an island as the river changed course and cut through the connecting neck of land. Or that was what was supposed to have happened. That was the Oankali illusion. Or was it an illusion?

Lilith found her moments of doubt coming more often as she walked. She had not been along this bank of the river. Like the Oankali, she had not worried about getting lost. She and Nikanj had walked through the interior several times, and she had found it easier to look up at the green canopy and believe herself within a vast room.

But the river seemed so large. As they followed the bank, the far bank changed, seemed nearer, seemed more heavily forested here, more deeply eroded there, ranged from low bluffs to flat bank that slipped into the river, blending almost seamlessly with its reflection. She could pick out individual trees—treetops any-way. Those that towered above the canopy.

"We should stop for the night," she said when the sun told her it was late afternoon. "We should make camp here and tomorrow, we should start to build a boat."

"Have you been here before?" Joseph asked her.

"No. But I've been near here. The opposite bank is as close to us as it gets in this area. Let's see what we can do about shelter. It's going to rain again."

"Wait a minute," Gabriel said.

She looked at him and knew what was coming. She had taken charge out of habit. Now she would hear about it.

"I didn't invite you along to tell us what to do," he said. "We're not in the prison room now. We don't take orders from you."

"You brought me along because I had knowledge you didn't have. What do you want to do? Keep walking until it's too late to put up a shelter? Sleep in the mud tonight? Find a wider section of river to cross?"

"I want to find the others—if they're still free."

Lilith hesitated for a moment in surprise. "And if they're together." She sighed. "Is that what the rest of you want?"

"I want to get as far from the Oankali as I can," Tate said. "I want to forget what it feels like when they touch me."

Lilith pointed. "If that's land over there instead of some kind of illusion, then that's your goal. Your first goal anyway."

"We find the others first!" Gabriel insisted.

Lilith looked at him with interest. He was in the open now. Probably in his mind he was in some kind of struggle with her. He wanted to lead and she did not—yet she had to. He could easily get someone killed.

"If we build a shelter now," she said, "I'll find the others tomorrow if they're anywhere nearby." She held up her hand to stop the obvious objection. "One or all of you can come with me and watch if you want to. It's just that I can't get lost. If I leave you and you don't move, I'll be able to find you again. If we all travel together, I can bring you back to this spot. After all, it's just possible that some or all of the others have already crossed the river. They've had time."

People were nodding.

"Where do we camp?" Allison asked.

"It's early," Leah protested.

"Not to me it isn't," Wray said. "Between the mosquitoes and my feet, I'm glad to stop."

"The mosquitoes will be bad tonight," Lilith told him. "Sleeping with an ooloi was better than any mosquito repellant. Tonight, they'll probably eat us alive."

"I can stand it," Tate said.

Had she hated Kahguyaht so much? Lilith wondered. Or was she only beginning to miss it and trying to defend herself against her own feelings?

"We can clear here," she said aloud. "Don't cut those two saplings. Wait a minute." She looked to see if either young tree were home to colonies of stinging ants. "Yes, these are all right. Find two more of this size or a little bigger and cut them. And cut aerial roots. Thin ones to use as rope. Be careful. If anything stings or bites you out here...We're on our own. You could die. And don't go out of sight of this area. It's easier to get lost than you think."

"But you're so good you can't get lost," Gabriel said.

"Good has nothing to do with it. I have an eidetic memory and I've had more time to get used to the forest." She had never told them why she had an eidetic memory. Every Oankali change she had told them about had diminished her credibility with them.

"Too good to be true," Gabriel said softly.

They chose the highest ground they could find and built a shelter. They believed they would be using it for a few days, at least. The shelter was wall-less—no more than a frame with a roof. They could hang hammocks from it or spread mats beneath it on mattresses of leaves and branches. It was just large enough to keep everyone out of the rain. They roofed it with the tarpaulins some of them had brought. Then they used branches to sweep the ground beneath clean of leaves, twigs and fungi.

Wray managed to get a fire going with a bow Leah had brought along, but he swore he would never do it again. "Too much work," he said.

Leah had brought corn from the garden. It was dark when they roasted it along with some of Lilith's yams. They ate these along with the last of the breadnuts. The meal was filling, though not satisfying.

"Tomorrow we can fish," Lilith told them.

"Without even a safety pin, a string, and a stick?" Wray said.

Lilith smiled. "Worse than that. The Oankali wouldn't teach me how to kill anything, so the only fish I caught were the ones stranded in some of the little streams. I cut a slender, straight sapling pole, sharpened one end, hardened it in the fire, and taught myself to spear fish. I actually did it—speared several of them."

"Ever try it with bow and arrow?" Wray asked.

"Yes. I was better with the spear."

"I'll try it," he said. "Or maybe I can even put together a jungle version of a safety pin and string. Tomorrow, while the rest of you look for the others, I'll start learning to fish."

"*We'll* fish," Leah said.

He smiled and took her hand—then let it go in almost the same motion. His smile faded and he stared into the fire. Leah looked away into the darkness of the forest.

Lilith watched them, frowning. What was going on? Was it just trouble between them—or was it something else?

It began to rain suddenly, and they sat dry and united by the darkness and the noise outside. The rain poured down and the insects took shelter with them, biting them and sometimes flying into the fire which had been built up again for light and comfort once the cooking was done.

Lilith tied her hammock to two crossbeams and lay down. Joseph hung his hammock near her—too near for a third person to lie between them. But he did not touch her. There was no privacy. She did not expect to make love. But she was bothered by the care he took not to touch her. She reached out and touched his face to make him turn toward her.

Instead, he drew away. Worse, if he had not drawn away, she would have. His flesh felt wrong somehow, oddly repellant. It had not been this way when he came to her before Nikanj moved in between them. Joseph's touch had been more than welcome. He had been water after a very long drought. But then Nikanj had come to stay. It had created for them the powerful threefold unity that was one of the most alien features of Oankali life. Had that unity now become a necessary feature of their human lives? If it had, what could they do? Would the effect wear off?

An ooloi needed a male and female pair to be able to play its part in reproduction, but it neither needed nor wanted two-way contact between that male and female. Oankali males and females never touched each other sexually. That worked fine for them. It could not possibly work for human beings.

She reached out and took Joseph's hand. He tried to jerk away reflexively, then he seemed to realize something was wrong. He held her hand for a long, increasingly uncomfortable moment. Finally it was she who drew away, shuddering with revulsion and relief.

6

The next morning just after dawn, Curt and his people found the shelter.

Lilith started awake, knowing that something was not right. She sat up awkwardly in the hammock and put her feet on the ground. Near Joseph, she saw Victor and Gregory. She turned toward them, relieved. Now there would be no need to look for the others. They could all get busy building the boat or raft they would need to cross the river. Everyone would find out for certain whether the other side was forest or illusion.

She looked around to see who else had arrived. That was when she saw Curt.

An instant later, Curt hit her across the side of the head with the flat of his machete.

She dropped to the ground, stunned. Nearby, she heard Joseph shout her name. There was the sound of more blows.

She heard Gabriel swearing, heard Allison scream.

She tried desperately to get up, and someone hit her again. This time she lost consciousness.

Lilith awoke to pain and solitude. She was alone in the small shelter she had helped build.

She got up, ignoring her aching head as best she could. It would stop soon.

Where was everyone?

Where was Joseph? He would not have deserted her even if the others did.

Had he been taken away by force? If so, why? Had he been injured and left as she had been?

She stepped out of the shelter and looked around. There was no one. Nothing.

She looked for some sign of where they had gone. She knew nothing in particular about tracking, but the muddy ground did show marks of human feet. She followed them away from the camp. Eventually, she lost them.

She stared ahead, trying to guess which way they had gone and wondering what she would do if she found them. At this point, all she really wanted to do was see that Joseph was all right. If he had seen Curt hit her, he would surely have tried to intervene.

She remembered now what Nikanj had said about Joseph having enemies. Curt had never liked him. Nothing had happened between the two of them in the great room or at the settlement. But what if something had happened now?

She must go back to the settlement and get help from the Oankali. She must get nonhumans to help her against her own people in a place that might or might not be on Earth.

Why couldn't they have left her Joseph? They had taken her machete, her ax, her baskets—everything except her hammock and her extra clothing. They could at least have left Joseph to see that she was all right. He would have stayed to do that if they had let him.

She walked back to the shelter, collected her clothing and hammock, drank water from a small, clear stream that fed into the river, and started back toward the settlement.

If only Nikanj were still there. Perhaps it could spy on the human camp without the humans' knowing, without fighting. Then if Joseph were there, he could be freed...if he wanted to be. Would he want it? Or would he choose to stay with the others who were trying to do the thing she had always wanted them all to do? *Learn and run.* Learn to live in this country, then lose themselves in it, go beyond the reach of the Oankali. Learn to touch one another as human beings again.

If they were on Earth as they believed, they might have a chance. If they were aboard a ship, nothing they did would matter.

If they were aboard a ship, Joseph would definitely be restored to her. But if they were on Earth...

She walked quickly, taking advantage of the path cleared the day before.

There was a sound behind her, and she turned quickly. Several ooloi emerged from the water and waded onto the bank to thrash their way through the thick bank undergrowth.

She turned and went back to them, recognizing Nikanj and Kahguyaht among them.

"Do you know where they've gone?" she asked Nikanj.

"We know," it said. It settled a sensory arm around her neck.

She put her hand to the arm, securing it where it was, welcoming it in spite of herself. "Is Joe all right?"

It did not answer, and that frightened her. It released her and led her through the trees, moving quickly. The other ooloi followed, all of them silent, all clearly knowing where they were going and probably knowing what they would find there.

Lilith no longer wanted to know.

She kept their fast pace easily, staying close to Nikanj. She almost slammed into it when it stopped without warning near a fallen tree.

The tree had been a giant. Even on its side, it was high and hard to climb, rotten and covered with fungi. Nikanj leaped onto it and off the other side with an agility Lilith could not match.

"Wait," it said as she began to climb the trunk. "Stay there." Then it focused on Kahguyaht. "Go on," it urged. "There could be more trouble while you wait here with me."

Neither Kahguyaht nor any of the other ooloi moved. Lilith noticed Curt's ooloi among them, and Allison's and—

"Come over now, Lilith."

She climbed over the trunk, jumped down on the other side. And there was Joseph.

He had been attacked with an ax.

She stared, speechless, then rushed to him. He had been hit more than once—blows to the head and neck. His head had been all but severed from his body. He was already cold.

The hatred that someone must have felt for him... "Curt?" she demanded of Nikanj. "Was it Curt?"

"It was us," Nikanj said very softly.

After a time, she managed to turn from the grisly corpse and face Nikanj. "What?"

"Us," Nikanj repeated. "We wanted to keep him safe, you and I. He was slightly injured and unconscious when they took him away. He had fought for you. But his injuries healed. Curt saw the flesh healing. He believed Joe wasn't human."

Why didn't you help him!" she screamed. She had begun to cry. She turned again to see the terrible wounds and did not understand how she could even look at Joseph's body so mutilated, dead. She had had no last words from him, no memory of fighting alongside him, no chance to protect him. Her last memory was of him flinching away from her too-human touch.

"I'm more different than he was," she whispered. "Why didn't Curt kill me?"

"I don't believe he meant to kill anyone," Nikanj said. "He was angry and afraid and in pain. Joseph had injured him when he hit you. Then he saw Joseph healing, saw the flesh mending itself before his eyes. He screamed. I've never heard a human scream that way. Then he... used his ax."

"Why didn't you help?" she demanded. "If you could see and hear everything, why—"

"We don't have an entrance near enough to this place."

She made a sound of anger and despair.

"And there was no sign that Curt meant to kill. He blames you for almost everything, yet he didn't kill you. What happened here was...totally unplanned."

She had stopped listening. Nikanj's words were incomprehensible to her. Joseph was dead—hacked to death by Curt. It was all some kind of mistake. Insanity!

She sat on the ground beside the corpse, first trying to understand, then doing nothing at all; not thinking, no longer crying. She sat. Insects crawled over her and Nikanj brushed them off. She did not notice.

After a time, Nikanj lifted her to her feet, managing her weight easily. She meant to push it away, make it let her alone. It had not helped Joseph. She did not need anything from it now. Yet she only twisted in its grasp.

It let her pull free and she stumbled back to Joseph. Curt had walked away and left him as though he were a dead animal. He should be buried.

Nikanj came to her again, seemed to read her thoughts. "Shall we pick him up on our way back and have him sent to Earth?" it asked. "He can end as part of his homeworld."

Bury him on Earth? Let his flesh be part of the new beginning there? "Yes," she whispered.

It touched her experimentally with a sensory arm. She glared at it, wanting desperately to be let alone.

"No!" it said softly. "No, I let you alone once, the two of you, thinking you could look after one another. I won't let you alone now."

She drew a deep breath, accepted the familiar loop of sensory arm around her neck. "Don't drug me," she said. "Leave me... leave me what I feel for him, at least."

"I want to share, not mute or distort."

"Share? Share my feelings now?"

"Yes."

"*Why?*"

"Lilith..." It began to walk and she walked beside it automatically. The other ooloi moved silently ahead of them. "Lilith, he was mine too. You brought him to me."

"You brought him to me."

"I would not have touched him if you had rejected him."

"I wish I had. He'd be alive."

Nikanj said nothing.

"Let me share what you feel," she said.

It touched her face in a startlingly human gesture. "Move the sixteenth finger of your left strength hand," it said softly. One more case of Oankali omniscience: *We understand your feelings, eat your food, manipulate your genes. But we're too complex for you to understand.*

"Approximate!" she demanded. "Trade! You're always talking about trading. Give me something of yourself!"

The other ooloi focused back toward them and Nikanj's head and body tentacles drew themselves into lumps of some negative emotion. Embarrassment? Anger? She did not care. Why should it feel comfortable about parasitizing her feelings for Joseph—her feelings for anything? It had helped set up a human experiment. One of the humans had been lost. What did it feel? Guilty for not having been more careful with valuable subjects? Or were they even valuable?

Nikanj pressed the back of her neck with a sensory hand—warning pressure. It would give her something then. They stopped walking by mutual consent and faced one another.

It gave her...a new color. A totally alien, unique, nameless thing, half seen, half felt or...tasted. A blaze of something frightening, yet overwhelmingly, compelling.

Extinguished.

A half known mystery beautiful and complex. A deep, impossibly sensuous promise.

Broken.

Gone.

Dead.

The forest came back around her slowly and she realized she was still standing with Nikanj, facing it, her back to the waiting ooloi.

"That's all I can give you," Nikanj said. "That's what I feel. I don't even know whether there are words in any human language to speak of it."

"Probably not," she whispered. After a moment, she let herself hug it. There was some comfort even in cool, gray flesh. Grief was grief, she thought. It was pain and loss and despair—an abrupt end where there should have been a continuing.

She walked more willingly with Nikanj now, and the other ooloi no longer isolated them in front or behind.

7

Curt's camp boasted a bigger shelter, not as well made. The roof was a jumble of palm leaves—not thatch, but branches crisscrossed and covering one another. No doubt it leaked. There were walls, but no floor. There was an indoor fire, hot and smoky. That was the way the people looked. Hot, smoky, dirty, angry.

They gathered outside the shelter with axes, machetes, and clubs, and faced the cluster of ooloi. Lilith found herself standing with aliens, facing hostile, dangerous humans.

She drew back. "I can't fight them," she said to Nikanj. "Curt, yes, but not the others."

"We'll have to fight if they attack," Nikanj said. "But you stay out of it. We'll be drugging them heavily—fighting to subdue without killing in spite of their weapons. Dangerous."

"No closer!" Curt called.

The Oankali stopped.

"This is a human place!" Curt continued. "It's off limits to you and your animals." He stared at Lilith, held his ax ready.

She stared back, afraid of the ax, but wanting him. Wanting to kill him. Wanting to take the ax from him and beat him to death with her own hands. Let him die here and rot in this alien place where he had left Joseph.

"Do nothing," Nikanj whispered to her. "He has lost all hope of Earth. He's lost Celene. She'll be sent to Earth without him. And he's lost mental and emotional freedom. Leave him to us."

She could not understand it at first—literally could not comprehend the words it spoke. There was nothing in her world but a dead Joseph and an obscenely alive Curt.

Nikanj held her until it too had to be acknowledged as part of her world. When it saw that she looked at it, struggled against it instead of simply struggling toward Curt, it repeated its words until she heard them, until they penetrated, until she was still. It never made any attempt to drug her, and it never let her go.

Off to one side, Kahguyaht was speaking to Tate. Tate stood well back from it, holding a machete and staying close to Gabriel who held an ax. It was Gabriel who had convinced her to abandon Lilith. It had to be. And what had convinced Leah? Practicality? A fear of being abandoned alone, left as much an outcast as Lilith?

Lilith found Leah and stared at her, wondering. Lilith looked away. Then her attention was drawn back to Tate.

"Go away," Tate was pleading in a voice that did not sound like her. "We don't want you! I don't want you! Let us alone!" She sounded as though she would cry. In fact, tears streamed down her face.

"I have never lied to you," Kahguyaht told her. "If you manage to use your machete on anyone, you'll lose Earth. You'll never see your homeworld again. Even this place will be denied to you." It stepped toward her. "Don't do this Tate. We're giving you the thing you want most: Freedom and a return home."

"We've got that here," Gabriel said.

Curt came to join him. "We don't need anything else from you!" he shouted.

The others behind him agreed loudly.

"You would starve here," Kahguyaht said. "Even in the short time you've been here, you've had trouble finding food. There isn't enough, and you don't yet know how to use what there is." Kahguyaht raised its voice, spoke to all of them. "You were allowed to leave us when you wished so that you could practice the skills you'd learned and learn more from each other and from Lilith. We had to know how you would behave after leaving us. We knew you might be injured, but we didn't think you would kill one another."

"We didn't kill a human being," Curt shouted. "We killed one of your animals!"

"We?" Kahguyaht said mildly. "And who helped you kill him?"

Curt did not answer.

"You beat him," Kahguyaht continued, "and when he was unconscious, you killed him with your ax. You did it alone, and in doing it, you've exiled yourself permanently from your Earth." It spoke to the others. "Will you join him? Will you be taken from this training room and placed with Toaht families to live the rest of your lives aboard the ship?"

The faces of some of the others began to change—doubts beginning or growing.

Allison's ooloi went to her, became the first to touch the human it had come to retrieve. It spoke very quietly. Lilith could not hear what it said, but after a moment, Allison sighed and offered it her machete.

It declined the knife with a wave of one sensory arm while settling the other arm around her neck. It drew her back behind the line of Oankali where Lilith stood with Nikanj. Lilith stared at her, wondering how Allison could turn against her. Had it only been fear? Curt could frighten just about anyone if he worked at it. And this was Curt with an ax—an ax he had already used on one man...

Allison met her gaze, looked away, then faced her again. "I'm sorry," she whispered. "We thought we could avoid bloodshed by going along with them, doing what they said. We thought . . . I'm sorry."

Lilith turned away, tears blurring her vision again. Somehow, she had been able to put Joseph's death aside for a few minutes. Allison's words brought it back.

Kahguyaht stretched out a sensory arm to Tate but Gabriel snatched her away.

"We don't want you here!" he grated. He thrust Tate behind him.

Curt shouted—a wordless scream of rage, a call to attack. He lunged at Kahguyaht and several of his people joined his attack, lunging at the other ooloi with their weapons.

Nikanj thrust Lilith toward Allison and plunged into the fighting. Allison's ooloi paused only long enough to say, "Keep her out of this!" in rapid Oankali. Then it, too, joined the fight.

Things happened almost too quickly to follow. Tate and the few other humans who seemed to want nothing more than to get clear found themselves caught in the middle. Wray and Leah, half supporting one another, stumbled out of the fighting between a pair of ooloi who seemed about to be slashed by three machete-wielding humans. Lilith realized suddenly that Leah was bleeding, and she ran to help get her away from the danger.

The humans shouted. The ooloi did not make a sound. Lilith saw Gabriel swing at Nikanj, narrowly missing it, saw him raise his ax again for what was clearly intended to be a death blow. Then Kahguyaht drugged him from behind.

Gabriel made a small gasp of sound—as though there were not enough strength in him to force out a scream. He collapsed.

Tate screamed, grabbed him, and tried to drag him clear of the fighting. She had dropped her machete, was clearly no threat.

Curt had not dropped his ax. It gave him a long, deadly reach. He swung it like a hatchet, controlling it easily in spite of its weight, and no ooloi risked being hit by it.

Elsewhere a man did manage to swing his ax through part of an ooloi's chest, leaving a gaping wound. When the ooloi fell, the man closed in for the kill, aided by a woman with a machete.

A second ooloi stung them both from behind. As they fell, the injured ooloi got up. In spite of the cut it had taken, it walked over to where Lilith's group waited. It sat down heavily on the ground.

Lilith looked at Allison, Wray, and Leah. They stared at the ooloi, but made no move toward it. Lilith went to it, noticing that it focused on her sharply in spite of its wound. She suspected the wound would not have stopped it from stinging her to unconsciousness or death if it felt threatened.

"Is there anything I can do to help?" she asked. Its wound was just about where its heart would have been if it had been human. It was oozing thick clear fluid and blood so bright red that it seemed false. Movie blood. Poster-paint blood. Such a terrible wound should have been awash in bodily fluids, but the ooloi seemed to be losing very little.

"I'll heal," it said in its disconcertingly calm voice. "This isn't serious." It paused. "I never believed they would try to kill us. I never knew how hard it would be not to kill them."

"You should have known," Lilith said. "You've had plenty of time to study us. What did you think would happen when you told us you were going to extinguish us as a species by tampering genetically with our children?"

The ooloi focused on her again. "If you had used a weapon, you could probably have killed at least one of us. These others couldn't, but you could."

"I don't want to kill you. I want to get away from you. You know that."

"I know you think that."

It turned its attention from her and began doing something to its wound with its sensory arms.

"Lilith!" Allison called.

Lilith looked back at her, then looked where she was pointing.

Nikanj was down, writhing on the ground as no ooloi had so far. Kahguyaht abruptly stopped fencing with Curt, lunged under his ax, hit him, and drugged him. Curt was the last human to go down. Tate was still conscious, still holding Gabriel, who was unconscious from Kahguyaht's sting. Some distance away, Victor was conscious, weaponless, making his way to the injured ooloi near Lilith—Victor's ooloi, she realized.

Lilith did not care how the two would meet. They could both take care of themselves. She ran toward Nikanj, avoiding the sensory arms of another ooloi who might have stung her.

Kahguyaht was already kneeling beside Nikanj, speaking to it low-voiced. It fell silent as she knelt on Nikanj's opposite side. She saw Nikanj's wound at once. Its left sensory arm had been hacked almost off. The arm seemed to be hanging by little more than a length of tough gray skin. Clear fluid and blood spurted from the wound.

"My god!" Lilith said. "Can it . . . can it heal?"

"Perhaps," Kahguyaht answered in its insanely calm voice. She hated their voices. "But you must help it."

"Yes, of course, I'll help. What shall I do?"

"Lie beside it. Hold it and hold the sensory arm in place so that it can reattach—if it will."

"Reattach?"

"Get your clothing off. It may be too weak to burrow through clothing."

Lilith stripped, refusing to think how she would look to the humans still conscious. They would be certain now that she was a traitor. Stripping naked on the battlefield to lie down with the enemy. Even the few who had accepted her might turn on her now. But she had just lost Joseph. She could not lose Nikanj too. She could not simply watch it die.

She lay down beside it and it strained toward her silently. She looked up for more instructions from Kahguyaht, but Kahguyaht had gone away to examine Gabriel. Nothing important going on for it here. Only its child, horribly wounded.

Nikanj penetrated her body with every head and body tentacle that could reach her, and for once it felt the way she had always imagined it should. It hurt! It was like abruptly being used as a pincushion. She gasped, but managed not to pull away. The pain was endurable, was probably nothing to what Nikanj was feeling—however it experienced pain.

She reached twice for the nearly severed sensory arm before she could make herself touch it. It was covered with slimy bodily fluids and white, blue-gray, and red-gray tissues hung from it.

She grasped it as best she could and pressed it to the stump it had been hacked from.

But surely more was necessary than this. Surely the heavy, complex, muscular organ could not reattach itself with no aid but the pressure of a human hand.

"Breathe deeply," Nikanj said, hoarsely. "Keep breathing deeply. Use both hands to hold my arm."

"You're plugged into my left arm," she gasped.

Nikanj made a harsh, ugly sound. "I have no control. I'll have to let you go completely, then begin again. If I can."

Several seconds later, tens of dozens of "needles" were withdrawn from Lilith's body. She rearranged Nikanj as gently as she could so that its head was on her shoulder and she could reach the nearly severed limb with both hands. She could support it and hold it where it belonged. She could rest one of her own arms on the ground and the other across Nikanj's body. This was a position she could hold for a while as long as no one disturbed her.

"All right," she said, bracing for the pincushion effect again.

Nikanj did nothing.

"Nikanj!" she whispered, frightened.

It stirred, then penetrated her flesh so abruptly in so many places—and so painfully—that she cried out. But she managed not to move beyond an initial reflexive jerk.

"Breathe deeply," it said. "I ... I'll try not to hurt you anymore."

"It's not that bad. I just don't see how this can help you."

"Your body can help me. Keep breathing deeply."

It said nothing more, made no sound of its own pain. She lay with it, eyes closed most of the time, and let the time pass, let herself lose track of it. From time to time, hands touched her. The first time she felt them, she looked to see what they were doing and realized that they were Oankali hands, brushing insects from her body.

Much later when she had lost track of time she was surprised to open her eyes to darkness; she felt someone lift her head and slip something under it.

Someone had covered her body with cloth. Spare clothing? And someone had wedged cloth under the parts of her body that seemed to need easing.

She heard talking, listened for human voices, and could not distinguish any. Parts of her body went numb, then underwent their own painful reawakening with no effort on her part. Her arms ached, then were eased, though she never changed position. Someone put water to her lips and she drank between gasps.

She could hear her own breathing. No one had to remind her to breathe deeply. Her body demanded it. She had begun breathing through her mouth. Whoever was looking after her noticed this and gave her water more often. Small amounts to wet her mouth. The water made her wonder what would happen if she had to go to the bathroom, but the problem never occurred.

Bits of food were put into her mouth. She did not know what it was, could not taste it, but it seemed to strengthen her.

At some point she recognized Ahajas, Nikanj's female mate as the owner of the hands that gave her food and water. She was confused at first and wondered whether she had been moved out of the forest and back to the quarters the family shared. But when it was light, she could still see the forest canopy—real trees burdened with epiphytes and lianas. A rounded termite nest the size of a basketball hung from a branch just above her. Nothing like that existed in the orderly, self-manicured Oankali living areas.

She drifted away again. Later she realized she was not always conscious. Yet she never felt as though she had slept. And she never let go of Nikanj. She could not let go of it. It had frozen her hands, her muscles into position as a kind of living cast to hold it while it healed.

At times her heart beat fast, thundering in her ears as though she had been running hard.

Dichaan took over the task of giving her food and water and protecting her from insects. He kept flattening his head and body tentacles when he looked at Nikanj's wound. Lilith managed to look at it to see what was pleasing him.

There first seemed nothing to be pleased about. The wound oozed fluids that turned black and stank. Lilith was afraid that some kind of infection had set in, but she could do nothing. At least none of the local insects seemed attracted to it—and none of the local microorganisms, probably. More likely Nikanj had brought whatever caused its infection into the training room with it.

The infection seemed to heal eventually, though clear fluid continued to leak from the wound. Not until it stopped completely did Nikanj let her go.

She began to rouse slowly, began to realize that she had not been fully conscious for a long time. It was as though she were Awakening again from suspended animation, this time without pain. Muscles that should have screamed when she moved after lying still for so long made no protest at all.

She moved slowly, straightening her arms, stretching her legs, arching her back against the ground. But something was missing.

She looked around, suddenly alarmed, and found Nikanj sitting beside her, focusing on her.

"You're all right," it said in its normal neutral voice. "You'll feel a little unsteady at first, but you're all right."

She looked at its left sensory arm. The healing was not yet complete. There was still visible what looked like a bad cut—as though someone had slashed at the arm and managed only a flesh wound.

"Are you all right?" she asked.

It moved the arm easily, normally, used it to stroke her face in an acquired human gesture.

She smiled, sat up, steadied herself for a moment, then stood up and looked around. There were no humans in sight, no Oankali except Nikanj, Ahajas, and Dichaan. Dichaan handed her a jacket and a pair of pants, both clean. Cleaner than she was. She took the clothing, and put it on reluctantly. She was not as dirty as she thought she should have been, but she still wanted to wash.

"Where are the others?" she asked. "Is everyone all right?"

"The humans are back at the settlement," Dichaan said. "They'll be sent to Earth soon. They've been shown the walls here. They know they're still aboard the ship."

"You should have shown them the walls on their first day here."

"We will do that next time. That was one of the things we had to learn from this group."

"Better yet, prove to them they're in a ship as soon as they're Awakened," she said. "Illusion doesn't comfort them for long. It just confuses them, helps them make dangerous mistakes. I had begun to wonder myself where we really were."

Silence. Stubborn silence.

She looked at Nikanj's still-healing sensory arm. "Listen to me," she said. "Let me help you learn about us, or there'll be more injuries, more deaths."

"Will you walk through the forest," Nikanj asked, "or shall we go the shorter way beneath the training room?"

She sighed. She was Cassandra, warning and predicting to people who went deaf whenever she began to warn and predict. "Let's walk through the forest," she said.

It stood still, keenly focused on her.

"What?" she asked.

It looped its injured sensory arm around her neck. "No one has ever done what we did here. No one has ever healed a wound as serious as mine so quickly or so completely."

"There was no reason for you to die or be maimed," she said. "I couldn't help Joseph. I'm glad I could help you—even though I don't have any idea how I did it."

Nikanj focused on Ahajas and Dichaan. "Joseph's body?" it said softly.

"Frozen," Dichaan said. "Waiting to be sent to Earth."

Nikanj rubbed the back of her neck with the cool, hard tip of its sensory arm. "I thought I had protected him enough," it said. "It should have been enough."

"Is Curt still with the others?"

"He's asleep."

"Suspended animation?"

"Yes."

"And he'll stay here? He'll never get to Earth?"

"Never."

She nodded. "That isn't enough, but it's better than nothing."

"He has a talent like yours," Ahajas said. "The ooloi will use him to study and explore the talent."

"Talent...?"

"You can't control it," Nikanj said, "but we can. Your body knows how to cause some of its cells to revert to an embryonic stage. It can awaken genes that most humans never use after birth. We have comparable genes that go dormant after metamorphosis. Your body showed mine how to awaken them, how to stimulate growth of cells that would not normally regenerate. The lesson was complex and painful, but very much worth learning."

"You mean..." She frowned. "You mean my family problem with cancer, don't you?"

"It isn't a problem anymore," Nikanj said, smoothing its body tentacles. "It's a gift. It has given me my life back."

"Would you have died?"

Silence.

After a while, Ahajas said, "It would have left us. It would have become Toaht or Akjai and left Earth."

"Why?" Lilith asked.

"Without your gift, it could not have regained full use of the sensory arm. It could not have conceived children." Ahajas hesitated. "When we heard what had happened, we thought we had lost it. It had been with us for so little time. We felt... Perhaps we felt what you did when your mate died. There seemed to be nothing at all ahead for us until Ooan Nikanj told us that you were helping it, and that it would recover completely."

"Kahguyaht behaved as though nothing unusual were happening," Lilith said.

"It was frightened for me," Nikanj said. "It knows you dislike it. It thought any instructions from it beyond the essential would anger or delay you. It was badly frightened."

Lilith laughed bitterly. "It's a good actor."

Nikanj rustled its tentacles. It took its sensory arm from Lilith's neck and led the group toward the settlement.

Lilith followed automatically, her thoughts shifting from Nikanj to Joseph to Curt. Curt whose body was to be used to teach the ooloi more about cancer. She could not make herself ask whether he would be conscious and aware during these experiments. She hoped he would be.

8

It was nearly dark when they reached the settlement. People were gathered around fires, talking, eating. Nikanj and its mates were welcomed by the Oankali in a kind of gleeful silence—a confusion of sensory arms and tentacles, a relating of experience by direct neural stimulation. They could give each other whole experiences, then discuss the experience in nonverbal conversation. They had a whole language of sensory images and accepted signals that took the place of words.

Lilith watched them enviously. They didn't lie often to humans because their sensory language had left them with no habit of lying—only of withholding information, refusing contact.

Humans, on the other hand, lied easily and often. They could not trust one another. They could not trust one of their own who seemed too close to aliens, who stripped off her clothing and lay down on the ground to help her jailer.

There was silence at the fire where Lilith chose to sit. Allison, Leah and Wray, Gabriel and Tate. Tate gave her a baked yam and, to her surprise, baked fish. She looked at Wray.

Wray shrugged. "I caught it with my hands. Crazy thing to do. It was half as big as I am. But it swam right up to me just begging to be caught. The Oankali claimed I could have been caught myself by some of the things swimming in the river—electric eels, piranha, caiman... They brought all the worst things from Earth. Nothing bothered me, though."

"Victor found a couple of turtles," Allison said. "Nobody knew how to cook them so they cut the meat up and roasted it."

"How was it?" Lilith asked.

"They ate it." Allison smiled. "And while they were cooking it and eating it, the Oankali kept away from them."

Wray grinned broadly. "You don't see any of them around this fire either, do you?"

"I'm not sure," Gabriel answered.

Silence.

Lilith sighed. "Okay, Gabe, what have you got? Questions, accusations or condemnations?"

"Maybe all three."

"Well?"

"You didn't fight. You chose to stand with the Oankali!"

"Against you?"

Angry silence.

"Where were you standing when Curt hacked Joseph to death?"

Tate laid her hand on Lilith's arm. "Curt just went crazy," she said. She spoke very softly. "No one thought he would do anything like that."

"He did it," Lilith said. "And you all watched."

They picked at their food silently for a while, no longer enjoying the fish, sharing it with people from other fires who came offering Brazil nuts, pieces of fruit or baked cassava.

"Why did you take your clothes off?" Wray demanded suddenly. "Why did you lie down on the ground with an ooloi in the middle of the fighting?"

"The fighting was over," Lilith said. "You know that. And the ooloi I lay down with was Nikanj. Curt had all but severed one of its sensory arms. I think you know that, too. I let it use my body to heal itself."

"But why should you want to help it?" Gabriel whispered harshly. "Why didn't you just let it die?" Every Oankali in the area must have heard him.

"What good would that do?" she demanded. "I've known Nikanj since it was a child. Why should I let it die, then be stuck with some stranger? How would that help me or you or anyone here?"

He drew back from her. "You've always got an answer. And it never quite rings true."

She went over in her mind the things she could have said to him about his own tendency not to ring true. Ignoring them all, she asked, "What is it, Gabe? What do you believe I can do or could have done to set you free on Earth one minute sooner?"

He did not answer, but he remained stubbornly angry. He was helpless and in a situation he found intolerable. Someone must be to blame.

Lilith saw Tate reach out to him, take his hand. For a few seconds they clung to the tips of one another's fingers, reminding Lilith of nothing so much as a very squeamish person suddenly given a snake to hold. They managed to let one another go without seeming to recoil in revulsion, but everyone knew what they felt. Everyone had seen. That was something else Lilith had to answer for, no doubt.

"What about *that*!" Tate demanded bitterly. She shook the hand Gabriel had touched as though to shake it clean of something. "What do we do about that?"

Lilith let her shoulders slump. "I don't know. It was the same for Joseph and me. I never got around to asking Nikanj what it had done to us. I suggest you ask Kahguyaht."

Gabriel shook his head. "I don't want to see him . . . *it*, let alone ask it anything."

"Really?" asked Allison. Her voice was so full of honest questioning that Gabriel only glared at her.

"No," Lilith said. "Not really. He wishes he hated Kahguyaht. He tries to hate it. But in the fighting, it was Nikanj he tried to kill. And here, now, it's me he blames and distrusts. Hell, the Oankali set me up to be the focus of blame and distrust, but I don't hate Nikanj. Maybe I can't. We're all a little bit co-opted, at least as far as our individual ooloi are concerned."

Gabriel stood up. He loomed over Lilith, glaring down. The camp had gone quiet, everyone watching him.

"I don't give a shit what you feel!" he said. "You're talking about your feelings, not mine. Strip and screw your Nikanj right here for everyone to see, why don't you. We know you're their whore! Everybody here knows!"

She looked at him, abruptly tired, fed up. "And what are you when you spend your nights with Kahguyaht?"

She believed for a moment that he would attack her. And, for a moment, she wanted him to.

Instead, he turned and stalked away toward the shelters. Tate glared at Lilith for a moment, then went after him.

Kahguyaht left the Oankali fire and came over to Lilith. "You could have avoided that," it said softly.

She did not look up at it. "I'm tired," she said. "I resign."

"What?"

"I quit! No more scapegoating for you; no more being seen as a Judas goat by my own people. I don't deserve any of this."

It stood over her for a moment longer, then went after Gabriel and Tate. Lilith looked after it, shook her head, and laughed bitterly. She thought of Joseph, seemed to feel him beside her, hear him telling her to be careful, asking her what was the point in turning both peoples against her.

There was no point. She was just tired. And Joseph was not there.

9

People avoided Lilith. She suspected they saw her either as a traitor or as a ticking bomb.

She was content to be let alone. Ahajas and Dichaan asked her if she wanted to go home with them when they left, but she declined the offer. She wanted to stay in an Earthlike setting until she went to Earth. She wanted to stay with human beings even though for a time, she did not love them.

She chopped wood for the fire, gathered wild fruits for meals or casual eating, even caught fish by trying a method she remembered reading about. She spent hours binding together strong grass stems and slivers of split cane, fashioning them into a long, loose cone that small fish could swim into, but not out of. She fished the small streams that flowed into the river and eventually provided most of the fish the group ate. She experimented with smoking it and had surprisingly good results. No one refused the fish because she had caught it. On the other hand, no one asked how she made her fish traps—so she did not tell them. She did no more teaching unless people came to her and asked questions.

This was more punishing to her than to the Oankali since she had discovered that she liked teaching. But she found more gratification in teaching one willing student than a dozen resentful ones.

Eventually people did begin to come to her. A few people. Allison, Wray and Leah, Victor . . . She shared her knowledge of fish traps with Wray finally. Tate avoided her—perhaps to please Gabriel, perhaps because she had adopted Gabriel's way of thinking. Tate had been a friend. Lilith missed her, but somehow could not manage any bitterness against her. There was no other close friend to take Tate's place. Even the people who came to her with questions did not trust her. There was only Nikanj.

Nikanj never tried to make her change her behavior. She had the feeling it would not object to anything she did unless she began hurting people. She lay with it and its mates at night and it pleasured her as it had before she met Joseph. She did not want this at first, but she came to appreciate it.

Then she realized she was able to touch a man again and find pleasure in it.

"Are you so eager to match me with someone else?" she asked Nikanj. That day she had handed Victor an armload of cassava cuttings for planting and she had been surprised, briefly pleased at the feel of his hand, as warm as her own.

"You're free to find another mate," Nikanj told her. "We'll be Awakening other humans soon. I wanted you to be free to choose whether or not to mate."

"You said we would be put down on Earth soon."

"You stopped teaching here. People are learning more slowly. But I think they'll be ready soon." Before she could question it further, other ooloi called it away to swim with them. That probably meant it was leaving the training room for a while. Ooloi liked to use the underwater exits whenever they could. Whenever they were not guiding humans.

Lilith looked around the camp, saw nothing that she wanted to do that day. She wrapped smoked fish and baked cassava in a banana leaf and put it into one of her baskets with a few ripe bananas. She would wander. Later, she would probably come back with something useful.

It was late when she headed back, her basket filled with bean pods that provided an almost candy-sweet pulp and palm fruit that she had been able to cut from a small tree with her machete. The bean pods—inga, they were called—would be a treat for everyone. Lilith did not like this particular kind of palm fruit as much, but others did.

She walked quickly, not wanting to be caught in the forest after dark. She thought she could probably find her way home in the dark, but she did not want to have to. The Oankali had made this jungle too real. Only they were invulnerable to the things whose bite or sting or sharp spines were deadly.

It was almost too dark to see under the canopy when she arrived back at the settlement.

Yet at the settlement, there was only one fire. This was a time for cooking and talking and working on baskets, nets, and other small things that could be done mindlessly while people enjoyed one another's company. But there was only one fire—and only one person near it.

As she reached the fire, the person stood up, and she saw that it was Nikanj. There was no sign of anyone else.

Lilith dropped her basket and ran the last few steps into camp. "Where are they?" she demanded. "Why didn't someone come to find me?"

"Your friend Tate says she's sorry for the way she behaved," Nikanj told her. "She wanted to talk to you, says she would have done it within the next few days. As it happened, she didn't have a few more days here."

"Where is she?"

"Kahguyaht has enhanced her memory as I have yours. It thinks that will help her survive on Earth and help the other humans."

"But…" She stepped closer to it, shaking her head. "But what about me? I did all you asked. I didn't hurt anyone. *Why am I still here!*"

"To save your life." It took her hand. "I was called away today to hear the threats that had been made against you. I had already heard most of them. Lilith, you would have wound up like Joseph."

She shook her head. No one had threatened her directly. Most people were afraid of her.

"You would have died," Nikanj repeated. "Because they can't kill us, they would have killed you."

She cursed it, refusing to believe, yet on another level, believing, knowing. She blamed it and hated it and wept.

"You could have waited!" she said finally. "You could have called me back before they left."

"I'm sorry," it said.

"Why didn't you call me? *Why?*"

It knotted its head and body tentacles in distress. "You could have reacted very badly. With your strength, you could have injured or killed someone. You could have earned a place alongside Curt." It relaxed the knots and let its tentacles hang limp. "Joseph is gone. I didn't want to risk losing you too."

And she could not go on hating it. Its words reminded her too much of her own thoughts when she lay down to help it in spite of what other humans might think of her. She went to one of the cut logs that served as benches around the fire and sat down.

"How long do I have to stay here?" she whispered. "Do they ever let the Judas goat go?"

It sat beside her awkwardly, wanting to fold itself onto the log, but not finding enough room to balance there.

"Your people will escape us as soon as they reach Earth," it told her. "You know that. You encouraged them to do it—and of course, we expected it. We'll tell them to take what they want of their equipment and go. Otherwise they might run away with less than they need to live. And we'll tell them they're welcome to come back to us. All of them. Any of them. Whenever they like."

Lilith sighed. "Heaven help anyone who tries."

"You think it would be a mistake to tell them?"

"Why bother asking me what I think?"

"I want to know."

She stared into the fire, got up and pulled a small log onto it. She would not do this again soon. She would not see fire or collect inga and palm fruit or catch a fish...

"Lilith?"

"Do you want them to come back?"

"They will come back eventually. They must."

"Unless they kill one another."

Silence.

"Why must they come back?" she asked.

It turned its face away.

"They can't even touch one another, the men and the women. Is that it?"

"That will pass when they've been away from us for a while. But it won't matter."

"Why not?"

"They need us now. They won't have children without us. Human sperm and egg will not unite without us."

She thought about that for a moment, then shook her head. "And what kind of children would they have with you?"

"You haven't answered," it said.

"What?"

"Shall we tell them they can come back to us?"

"No. And don't be too obvious about helping them get away either. Let them decide for themselves what they'll do. Otherwise people who decide later to come back will seem to be obeying you, betraying their humanity for you. That could get them killed. You won't get many back, anyway. Some will think the human species deserves at least a clean death."

"Is it an unclean thing that we want, Lilith?"

"Yes!"

"Is it an unclean thing that I have made you pregnant?"

She did not understand the words at first. It was as though it had begun speaking a language she did not know.

"You...what?"

"I have made you pregnant with Joseph's child. I wouldn't have done it so soon, but I wanted to use his seed, not a print. I could not make you closely enough related to a child mixed from a print. And there's a limit to how long I can keep sperm alive."

She was staring at it, speechless. It was speaking as casually as though discussing the weather. She got up, would have backed away from it, but it caught her by both wrists.

She made a violent effort to break away, realized at once that she could not break its grip. "You said—" She ran out of breath and had to start again. "You said you wouldn't do this. You said—"

"I said not until you were ready."

"I'm not ready! I'll never be ready!"

"You're ready now to have Joseph's child. Joseph's daughter."

"...daughter?"

"I mixed a girl to be a companion for you. You've been very lonely."

"Thanks to you."

"Yes. But a daughter will be a companion for a long time."

"It won't be a daughter." She pulled again at her arms, but it would not let her go. "It will be a thing—not human." She stared down at her own body in horror. "It's inside me, and it isn't human!"

Nikanj drew her closer, looped a sensory arm around her throat. She thought it would inject something into her and make her lose consciousness. She waited almost eager for the darkness.

But Nikanj only drew her down to the log bench again. "You'll have a daughter," it said. "And you are ready to be her mother. You could never have said so. Just as Joseph could never have invited me into his bed—no matter how much he wanted me there. Nothing about you but your words reject this child."

"But it won't be human," she whispered. "It will be a thing. A monster."

"You shouldn't begin to lie to yourself. It's a deadly habit. The child will be yours and Joseph's. Ahajas' and Dichaan's. And because I've mixed it, shaped it, seen that it will be beautiful and without deadly conflicts, it will be mine. It will be my first child, Lilith. First to be born, at least. Ahajas is also pregnant."

"Ahajas?" When had it found the time? It had been everywhere.

"Yes. You and Joseph are parents to her child as well." It used its free sensory arm to turn her head to face it. "The child that comes from your body will look like you and Joseph."

"I don't believe you!"

"The differences will be hidden until metamorphosis."

"Oh god. That too."

"The child born to you and the child born to Ahajas will be siblings."

"The others won't come back for this," she said. "I wouldn't have come back for it."

"Our children will be better than either of us," it continued. "We will moderate your hierarchical problems and you will lessen our physical limitations. Our children won't destroy themselves in a war, and if they need to regrow a limb or to change themselves in some other way they'll be able to do it. And there will be other benefits."

"But they won't be human," Lilith said. "That's what matters. You can't understand, but that *is* what matters."

Its tentacles knotted. "The child inside you matters." It released her arms, and her hands clutched uselessly at one another.

"This will destroy us," she whispered. "My god, no wonder you wouldn't let me leave with the others."

"You'll leave when I do—you, Ahajas, Dichaan, and our children. We have work to do here before we leave." It stood up. "We'll go home now. Ahajas and Dichaan are waiting for us."

Home? she thought bitterly. When had she last had a true home? When could she hope to have one. "Let me stay here," she said. It would refuse. She knew it would. "This is as close to Earth as it seems you'll let me come."

"You can come back here with the next group of humans. Come home now."

She considered resisting, making it drug her and carry her back. But that seemed a pointless gesture. At least she would get another chance with a human group. A chance to teach them . . . but not a chance to be one of them. Never that. Never?

Another chance to say, "*Learn and run!*"

She would have more information for them this time. And they would have long, healthy lives ahead of them. Perhaps they could find an answer to what the Oankali had done to them. And perhaps the Oankali were not perfect. A few fertile people might slip through and find one another. Perhaps. *Learn and run!* If she were lost, others did not have to be. Humanity did not have to be.

She let Nikanj lead her into the dark forest and to one of the concealed dry exits.

About the Author

I'm a fifty-three-year-old writer who can remember being a ten-year-old writer and who expects someday to be an eighty-year-old writer. I'm also comfortably asocial—a hermit in the middle of a large city, a pessimist if I'm not careful, a feminist, a Black, a former Baptist, an oil-and-water combination of ambition, laziness, insecurity, certainty, and drive.

I've had eleven novels published so far: *Patternmaster, Mind of My Mind, Survivor, Kindred, Wild Seed, Clay's Ark, Dawn, Adulthood Rites, Imago, Parable of the Sower,* and *Parable of the Talents,* as well as a collection of my shorter work, entitled *Bloodchild. Bloodchild* includes short stories published in anthologies and magazines. One, "Speech Sounds," won a Hugo Award as best short story of 1984. The title story, "Bloodchild," won both the 1985 Hugo and the 1984 Nebula awards as best novelette.

—Octavia E. Butler

In 1995 Octavia E. Butler was awarded a MacArthur Grant. In what is popularly called the genius program, the John D. and Catherine T. MacArthur Foundation rewards creative people who push the boundaries of their fields.

In 2000 Parable of the Talents received the Nebula Award for Best Novel, and Ms. Butler was given the PEN Center West Lifetime Achievement Award.

Octavia Butler passed away on February 24, 2006.

Reading Group Guide

Discussion Questions

1. The Oankali identify intelligence and hierarchy as the human race's fatal combination of characteristics. Do you agree? What do you think are humans' most advantageous and dangerous qualities?

2. What are some political and social hierarchies in our world? Why do they exist, and how could they weaken us?

3. What do you think are the flaws of the Oankali's species?

4. Jdahya says to Lilith that "intelligence does enable you to deny facts you dislike" (page 42). What do you think he means by this?

5. Why do you think the Oankali are reluctant to allow Lilith writing tools or books?

6. Throughout the book, what distinctions are drawn between humans and animals?

7. In what ways, explicit and subtle, does Jdahya encourage Lilith to mentally and emotionally adapt to the Oankali and the genetic trade they have planned?

8. Lilith repeatedly must learn to accept ideas—like human-alien breeding—that she at first finds strange or repellent. Can you think of an idea you rejected at first but then grew to accept or believe in? What changed your mind?

9. Kahguyaht says that at first, "I believed that because of the way human genetics were expressed in culture, a human male should be chosen to parent the first group" (page 124). Why do you think the Oankali chose Lilith to Awaken and

lead the first group of humans to return to Earth? Do you think her identity as a Black woman affects the way the group responds to her leadership?

10. Lilith tells the rest of the humans that she will not allow rape within their group, but then she lets Nikanj have a sexual relationship with Joseph even though he says he cannot give it permission to do so. Discuss the role of consent, in both sexual and other contexts, throughout the novel.

11. What parallels do you notice between the Oankali's treatment of the humans and colonizing countries and cultures in our own world?

12. Paul and Joseph both have trouble acknowledging that the *ooloi* are a third sex, which Lilith considers "a kind of deliberate, persistent ignorance" (page 99). Why do you think the two men react this way? Can you think of similar instances of deliberate ignorance within our own society?

13. Discuss the intersection of sex and gender within the novel.

14. The Oankali give Lilith increased strength, a natural resistance to cancer, the ability to pass through doors and raise furniture on the ship, and an eidetic memory. What special abilities would you most like to possess?

Lilith's first true human-alien child will either create a new future for the human race or doom it to self-destruction, in this brilliant sequel to Octavia Butler's *Dawn*.

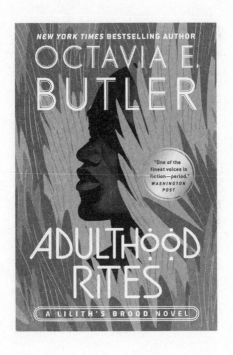

NEW EDITION AVAILABLE AUGUST 2021

Please turn the page for an excerpt.

1

He remembered much of his stay in the womb.

While there, he began to be aware of sounds and tastes. They meant nothing to him, but he remembered them. When they recurred, he noticed.

When something touched him, he knew it to be a new thing—a new experience. The touch was first startling, then comforting. It penetrated his flesh painlessly and calmed him. When it withdrew, he felt bereft, alone for the first time. When it returned, he was pleased—another new sensation. When he had experienced a few of these withdrawals and returns, he learned anticipation.

He did not learn pain until it was time for him to be born.

He could feel and taste changes happening around him—the slow turning of his body, then later the sudden headfirst thrust, the compression first of his head, then gradually along the length of his body. He hurt in a dull, distant way.

Yet he was not afraid. The changes were right. It was time for them. His body was ready. He was propelled along in regular pulses and comforted from time to time by the touch of his familiar companion.

There was light!

Vision was first a blaze of shock and pain. He could not escape the light. It grew brighter and more painful, reached its maximum as the compression ended. No part of his body was free from the sharp, raw brilliance. Later, he would recall it as heat, as burning.

It cooled abruptly.

Something muted the light. He could still see, but seeing was no longer painful. His body was rubbed gently as he lay submerged in something soft and comforting. He did not like the rubbing. It made the light seem to jerk and vanish, then leap back to visibility. But it was the familiar presence that touched him, held him. It stayed with him and helped him endure the rubbing without fear.

He was wrapped in something that touched him everywhere except his face. He did not like the heavy feel of it, but it shut out the light and did not hurt him.

Something touched the side of his face, and he turned, mouth open, to take it. His body knew what to do. He sucked and was rewarded by food and by the taste of flesh as familiar as his own. For a time, he assumed it was his own. It had always been with him.

He could hear voices, could even distinguish individual sounds, though he understood none of them. They captured his attention, his curiosity. He would remember these, too, when he was older and able to understand them. But he liked the soft voices even without knowing what they were.

"He's beautiful," one voice said. "He looks completely Human."

"Some of his features are only cosmetic, Lilith. Even now his senses are more dispersed over his body than yours are. He is . . . less Human than your daughters."

"I'd guessed he would be. I know your people still worry about Human-born males."

"They were an unsolved problem. I believe we've solved it now."

"His senses are all right, though?"

"Of course."

"That's all I can expect, I guess." A sigh. "Shall I thank you for making him look this way—for making him seem Human so I can love him? . . . for a while."

"You've never thanked me before."

". . . no."

"And I think you go on loving them even when they change."

"They can't help what they are . . . what they become. You're sure everything else is all right, too? All the mismatched bits of him fit together as best they can?"

"Nothing in him is mismatched. He's very healthy. He'll have a long life and be strong enough to endure what he must endure."

2

He was Akin.

Things touched him when this sound was made. He was given comfort or food, or he was held and taught. Body to body understanding was given to him. He came to perceive himself as himself—individual, defined, separate from all the touches and smells, all the tastes, sights, and sounds that came to him. He was Akin.

Yet he came to know that he was also part of the people who touched him—that within them, he could find fragments of himself. He was himself, and he was those others.

He learned quickly to distinguish between them by taste and touch. It took longer for him to know them by sight or smell, but taste and touch were almost a single sensation for him. Both had been familiar to him for so long.

He had heard differences in voices since his birth. Now he began to attach identities to those differences. When, within days of his birth, he had learned his own name and could say it aloud, the others taught him their names. These they repeated when they could see that they had his attention. They let him watch their mouths shape the words. He came to understand quickly that each of them could be called by one or both of two groups of sounds.

Nikanj Ooan, Lilith Mother, Ahajas Ty, Dichaan Ishliin, and the one who never came to him even though Nikanj Ooan had taught him that one's touch and taste and smell. Lilith Mother had shown him a print image of that one, and he had scanned it with all his senses: Joseph Father.

He called for Joseph Father and, instead, Nikanj Ooan came and taught him that Joseph Father was dead. Dead. Ended. Gone away and not coming back. Yet he had been part of Akin, and Akin must know him as he knew all his living parents.

Akin was two months old when he began to put together simple sentences. He could not get enough of being held and taught.

"He's quicker than most of my girls," Lilith commented as she held him against her and let him drink. It could have been difficult to learn from her smooth, unhelpful skin except that it was as familiar as his own—and superficially like his own. Nikanj Ooan taught him to use his tongue—his least Human visible organ—to study Lilith when she fed him. Over many feedings, he tasted her flesh as well as her milk. She was a rush of flavors and textures—sweet milk, salty skin smooth in some places, rough in others. He concentrated on one of the smooth places, focused all his attention on probing it, perceiving it deeply, minutely. He perceived the many cells of her skin, living and dead. Her skin taught him what it meant to be dead. Its dead outer layer contrasted sharply with what he could perceive of the living flesh beneath. His tongue was as long and sensitive and malleable as the sensory tentacles of Ahajas and Dichaan. He sent a filament of it into the living tissue of her nipple. He had hurt her the first time he tried this, and the pain had been channeled back to him through his tongue. The pain had been so sharp and startling that he withdrew, screaming and weeping. He refused to be comforted until Nikanj showed him how to probe without causing pain.

"That," Lilith had commented, "was a lot like being stabbed with a hot, blunt needle."

"He won't do it again," Nikanj had promised.

Akin had not done it again. And he had learned an important lesson: He would share any pain he caused. Best, then, to be careful and not cause pain. He would not know for months how unusual it was for an infant to recognize the pain of another person and recognize himself as the cause of that pain.

Now he perceived, through the tendril of flesh he had extended into Lilith, expanses of living cells. He focused on a few cells, on a single cell, on the parts of that cell, on its nucleus, on chromosomes within the nucleus, on genes along the chromosomes. He investigated the DNA that made up the genes, the nucleotides of the DNA. There was something beyond the nucleotides that he could not perceive—a world of smaller particles that he could not cross into. He did not understand why he could not make this final crossing—if it were the final one. It frustrated him that anything was beyond his perception. He knew of it only through shadowy ungraspable feelings. When he was older he came to think of it as a horizon, always receding when he approached it.

He shifted his attention from the frustration of what he could not perceive to the fascination of what he could. Lilith's flesh was much more exciting than the flesh of Nikanj, Ahajas, and Dichaan. There was something wrong with hers—something he did not understand. It was both frightening and seductive. It told him Lilith was dangerous, though she was also essential. Nikanj was interesting but not dangerous. Ahajas and Dichaan were so alike he had to struggle to perceive differences between them. In some ways Joseph had been like Lilith. Deadly and compelling. But he had not been as much like Lilith as Ahajas was like Dichaan. In fact, though he had clearly been Human and native to this place, this *Earth,* like Lilith, he had not been Lilith's relative. Ahajas and Dichaan were brother and sister, like most Oankali male and female mates. Joseph was unrelated, like Nikanj—but although

Nikanj was Oankali, it was also ooloi, not male or female. Ooloi were supposed to be unrelated to their male and female mates so that they could focus their attention on their mates' genetic differences and construct children without making dangerous mistakes of overfamiliarity and overconfidence.

"Be careful," he heard Nikanj say. "He's studying you again."

"I know," Lilith answered. "Sometimes I wish he'd just nurse like Human babies."

Lilith rubbed Akin's back, and the flickering of light between and around her fingers broke his concentration. He withdrew his flesh from hers, then released her nipple and looked at her. She closed clothing over her breast but went on holding him on her lap. He was always glad when people held him and talked to each other, allowing him to listen. He had already learned more words from them than he had yet had occasion to use. He collected words and gradually assembled them into questions. When his questions were answered, he remembered everything he was told. His picture of the world grew.

"At least he isn't any stronger or faster in physical development than other babies," Lilith said. "Except for his teeth."

"There have been babies born with teeth before," Nikanj said. "Physically, he'll look his Human age until his metamorphosis. He'll have to think his way out of any problems his precocity causes."

"That won't do him much good with some Humans. They'll resent him for not being completely Human and for looking more Human than their kids. They'll hate him for looking much younger than he sounds. They'll hate him because they haven't been allowed to have sons. Your people have made Human-looking male babies a very valuable commodity."

"We'll allow more of them now. Everyone feels more secure about mixing them. Before now, too many ooloi could not perceive the necessary mixture. They could have made mistakes and their mistakes could be monsters."

"Most Humans think that's what they've been doing."

"Do you still?"

Silence.

"Be content, Lilith. One group of us believed it would be best to dispense with Human-born males altogether. We could construct female children for Human females and male children for Oankali females. We've done that until now."

"And cheated everyone. Ahajas wants daughters, and I want sons. Other people feel the same way."

"I know. And we control children in ways we should not to make them mature as Oankali-born males and Human-born females. We control inclinations that should be left to individual children. Even the group that suggested we go on this way knows we shouldn't. But they were afraid. A male who's Human enough to be born to a Human female could be a danger to us all. We must try though. We'll learn from Akin."

Akin felt himself held closer to Lilith. "Why is he such an experiment?" she demanded. "And why should Human-born men be such a problem? I know most prewar men don't like you. They feel you're displacing them and forcing them to do something perverted. From their point of view, they're right. But you could teach the next generation to love you, no matter who their mothers are. All you'd have to do is start early. Indoctrinate them before they're old enough to develop other opinions."

"But..." Nikanj hesitated. "But if we had to work that blindly, that clumsily, we couldn't have trade. We would have to take your children from you soon after they were born. We wouldn't dare trust you to raise them. You would be kept only for breeding—like nonsentient animals."

Silence. A sigh. "You say such god-awful things in such a gentle voice. No, hush, I know it's the only voice you've got. Nika, will Akin survive the Human males who will hate him?"

"They won't hate him."

"They will! He isn't Human. Un-Human women are offensive to them, but they don't usually try to hurt them, and they do sleep with them—like a racist sleeping with racially different women. But Akin...They'll see him as a threat. Hell, he *is* a threat. He's one of their replacements."

"Lilith, they will not hate him." Akin felt himself lifted from Lilith's arms and held close to Nikanj's body. He gasped at the lovely shock of contact with Nikanj's sensory tentacles, many of which held him while others burrowed painlessly into his flesh. It was so easy to connect with Nikanj and to learn. "They will see him as beautiful and like themselves," Nikanj said. "By the time he's old enough for his body to reveal what he actually is, he'll be an adult and able to hold his own."

"Able to fight?"

"Only to save his life. He'll tend to avoid fighting. He'll be like Oankali-born males now—a solitary wanderer when he's not mated."

"He won't settle down with anyone?"

"No. Most Human males aren't particularly monogamous. No construct males will be."

"But—"

"Families will change, Lilith—are changing. A complete construct family will be a female, an ooloi, and children. Males will come and go as they wish and as they find welcome."

"But they'll have no homes."

"A home like this would be a prison to them. They'll have what they want, what they need."

"The ability to be fathers to their kids?"

Nikanj paused. "They might choose to keep contact with their children. They won't live with them permanently—and no construct, male or female, young or old, will feel that as a deprivation. It will be normal to them, and purposeful, since there will always be many more females and ooloi than males." It rustled its head and body tentacles. "Trade means change. Bodies change. Ways of living must change. Did you think your children would only *look* different?"

3

Akin spent some part of the day with each of his parents. Lilith fed him and taught him. The others only taught him, but he went to them all eagerly. Ahajas usually held him after Lilith.

Ahajas was tall and broad. She carried him without seeming to notice his weight. He had never felt weariness in her. And he knew she enjoyed carrying him. He could feel pleasure the moment she sank filaments of her sensory tentacles into him. She was the first person to be able to reach him this way with more than simple emotions. She was the first to give him multisensory images and signaling pressures and to help him understand that she was speaking to him without words. As he grew, he realized that Nikanj and Dichaan also did this. Nikanj had done it even before he was born, but he had not understood. Ahajas had reached him and taught him quickly. Through the images she created for him, he learned about the child growing within her. She gave him images of it and even managed to give it images of him.

It had several presences: all its parents except Lilith. And it had him. Sibling.

He knew he would be male when he grew up. He understood male, and female, and ooloi. And he knew that because he would be male, the unborn child who would begin its life seeming much less Human than he did would eventually become female. There was a balance, a naturalness to this that pleased him. He should have a sister to grow up with—a sister but not an ooloi sibling. Why? He wondered whether the child inside Ahajas would become ooloi, but Ahajas and Nikanj both assured him it would not. And they would not tell him how they knew. So this sibling should become a sister. It would take years to develop sexually, but he already thought of it as "she."

Dichaan usually took him once Ahajas had returned him to Lilith and Lilith had fed him. Dichaan taught him about strangers.

First there were his older siblings, some born to Ahajas and becoming more Human, and some born to Lilith and becoming more Oankali. There were also children of older siblings, and finally, frighteningly, unrelated people. Akin could not understand why some of the unrelated ones were more like Lilith than Joseph had been. And none of them were like Joseph.

Dichaan read Akin's unspoken confusion.

"The differences you perceive between Humans—between groups of Humans—are the result of isolation and inbreeding, mutation, and adaptation to different Earth environments," he said, illustrating each concept with quick multiple images. "Joseph and Lilith were born in very different parts of this world—born to long separated peoples. Do you understand?"

"Where are Joseph's kind?" Akin asked aloud.

"Now there are villages of them to the southwest. They're called Chinese."

"I want to see them."

"You will. You can travel to them when you're older." He ignored

Akin's rush of frustration. "And someday I'll take you to the ship. You'll be able to see Oankali differences, too." He gave Akin an image of the ship—a vast sphere made up of huge, still-growing, many-sided plates like the shell of a turtle. In fact, it was the outer shell of a living being. "There," Dichaan said, "you'll see Oankali who will never come to Earth or trade with Humans. For now, they tend the ship in ways that require a different physical form." He gave Akin an image, and Akin thought it resembled a huge caterpillar.

Akin projected silent questioning.

"Speak aloud," Dichaan told him.

"Is it a child?" Akin asked, thinking of the changes caterpillars underwent.

"No. It's adult. It's larger than I am."

"Can it talk?"

"In images, in tactile, bioelectric, and bioluminescent signals, in pheromones, and in gestures. It can gesture with ten limbs at once. But its throat and mouth parts won't produce speech. And it is deaf. It must live in places where there is a great deal of noise. My parents' parents had that shape."

This seemed terrible to Akin—Oankali forced to live in an ugly form that did not even allow them to hear or speak.

"What they are is as natural to them as what you are is to you," Dichaan told him. "And they are much closer to the ship than we can be. They're companions to it, knowing its body better than you know your own. When I was a little older than you are now, I wanted to be one of them. They let me taste a little of their relationship with the ship."

"Show me."

"Not yet. It's a very powerful thing. I'll show you when you're a little older."

Everything was to happen when he was older. He must wait! He must always wait! In frustration, Akin had stopped speaking.

He could not help hearing and remembering all that Dichaan told him, but he would not speak to Dichaan again for days.

Yet it was Dichaan who began leaving him in the care of his older sisters, letting him begin to investigate them—while they thoroughly investigated him. His favorite among them was Margit. She was six years old—too small to carry him long, but he was content to ride on her back or sit on her lap for as long as she could handle him comfortably. She did not have sensory tentacles like his Oankali-born sisters, but she had clusters of sensitive nodules that would probably be tentacles when she grew up. She could match some of these to the smooth, invisible sensory patches on his skin, and the two of them could exchange images and emotions as well as words. She could teach him.

"You should be careful," she said as she took him to shelter in their family house, away from a hard afternoon rain. "Your eyes don't track a lot of the time. Can you see with them?"

He thought about this. "I can," he said, "but I don't always. Sometimes it's easier to see things from other parts of my body."

"When you're older, you'll be expected to turn your face and body toward people when you talk to them. Even now, you should look at Humans with your eyes. If you don't, they yell at you or repeat things because they're not sure they have your attention. Or they start to ignore you because they think you're ignoring them."

"No one's done that to me."

"They will. Just wait until you get past the stage when they try to talk stupid to you."

"Baby talk, you mean?"

"Human talk!"

Silence.

"Don't worry," she said after a while. "It's them I'm mad at, not you."

"Why?"

"They blame me for not looking like them. They can't help doing it, and I can't help resenting it. I don't know which is worse—the ones who cringe if I touch them or the ones who pretend it's all right while they cringe inside."

"What does Lilith feel?" Akin asked only because he already knew the answer.

"For her, I might as well look the way you do. I remember when I was about your age, she would wonder how I would find a mate, but Nikanj told her there would be plenty of males like me by the time I grew up. She never said anything after that. She tells me to stick with the constructs. I do, mostly."

"Humans like me," he said. "I guess because I look like them."

"Just remember to look at them with your eyes when they talk to you or you talk to them. And be careful about tasting them. You won't be able to get away with that for much longer. Besides, your tongue doesn't look Human."

"Humans say it shouldn't be gray, but they don't realize how different it really is."

"Don't let them guess. They can be dangerous, Akin. Don't show them everything you can do. But...hang around them when you can. Study their behavior. Maybe you can collect things about them that we can't. It would be wrong if anything that they are is lost."

"Your legs are going to sleep," Akin observed. "You're tired. You should take me to Lilith."

"In a little while."

She did not want to give him up, he realized. He did not mind. She was, Humans said, gray and warty—more different than most Human-born children. And she could hear as well as any construct. She caught every whisper whether she wanted to or not, and if she were near Humans, they soon began to talk about her. "If she looks this bad now, what will she look like after metamorphosis?" they would begin. Then they would speculate or pity her or condemn her or laugh at her. Better a few more minutes of peace alone with him.

Her full Human name was Margita Iyapo Domonkos Kaal-nikanjlo. Margit. She had all four of his living parents in common with him. Her Human father, though, was Vidor Domonkos, not the dead Joseph. Vidor—some people called him Victor—had moved to a village several miles upriver when he and Lilith tired of one another. He came back two or three times a year to see Margit. He did not like the way she looked, yet he loved her. She had seen that he did, and Akin was certain she had read his emotion correctly. He had never met Vidor himself. He had been too young for contact with strangers during the man's last visit.

"Will you tell Vidor to let me touch him when he comes to see you again?" Akin asked.

"Father? Why?"

"I want to find you in him."

She laughed. "He and I have a lot in common. He doesn't like having anyone explore him, though. Says he doesn't need anything burrowing through his skin." She hesitated. "He means that. He only let me do it once. Just talk to him if you meet him, Akin. In some ways he can be just as dangerous as any other Human."

"Your father?"

"Akin...All of them! Haven't you explored any of them? Can't you feel it?" She gave him a complex image. He understood it only because he had explored a few Humans himself. Humans were a compelling, seductive, deadly contradiction. He felt drawn to them, yet warned against them. To touch a Human deeply—to taste one—was to feel this.

"I know," he said. "But I don't understand."

"Talk to Ooan. It knows and understands. Talk to Mother, too. She knows more than she likes to admit."

"She's Human. You don't think she's dangerous, too, do you?"

"Not to us." She stood up with him. "You're getting heavier. I'll be glad when you learn to walk."

"Me, too. How old were you when you walked?"

"Just over a year. You're almost there."

"Nine months."

"Yes. It's too bad you couldn't learn walking as easily as you learned talking." She returned him to Lilith, who fed him and promised to take him into the forest with her.

Lilith gave him bits of solid food now, but he still took great comfort in nursing. It frightened him to realize that someday she would not let him nurse. He did not want to grow that old.